To Laura,

Enjoy the Journey!

Jaspa's Journey:

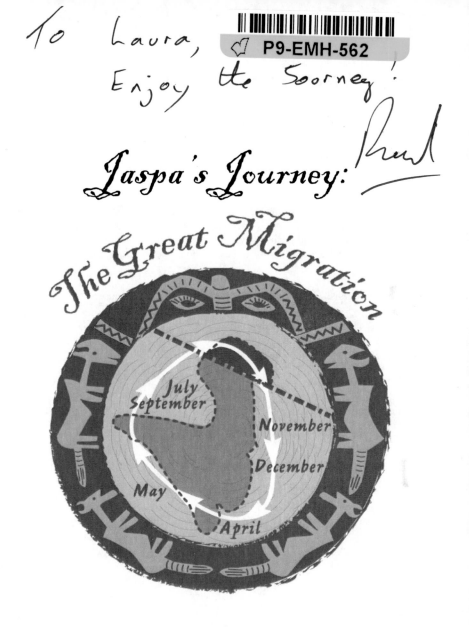

The Great Migration

July
September

November

December

May

April

Rich Meyrick

DREAMCATCHER PUBLISHING
SAINT JOHN • NEW BRUNSWICK • CANADA

Copyright © 2009 Rich Meyrick

DreamCatcher Publishing acknowledges the support of the Province of New Brunswick.

Library and Archives Canada Cataloguing in Publication

Title: Jaspa's Journey: The Great Migration / Meyrick, Rich, 1969-

ISBN 978-0-9810721-0-4

1. Serengeti Plain (Tanzania)--Juvenile fiction.

PS8626.E974J38 2009   jC813'.6   C2009-901130-1

Printed and Bound in Canada using recycled paper.

Typesetter: Michel Plourde

Cover and Logo Design: Cynthia Perry

Website: www.jaspasjourney.com

55 Canterbury St, Suite 8
Saint John, NB Canada
E2L 2C6
Tel: 506-632-4008
Fax: 506-632-4009
dreamcatcherpub@nb.aibn.com
www.dreamcatcherpublishing.ca

For Audrey
Stop, drop and roll

And for Pe'ul
Without whom Jaspa would never have left home

"Travel is fatal to prejudice, bigotry, and narrow-mindedness, and many of our people need it solely on these accounts. Broad, wholesome, charitable views of men and things cannot be acquired by vegetating in one corner of the earth all one's lifetime."

~Mark Twain

Acknowledgements

Jaspa's Journey would not have been possible without the help and support of my family and friends. I would especially like to voice my appreciation to the following people (in no particular order) for helping make The Great Migration a more enjoyable, exciting and believable story: Mick, Mike, Barbara, Lisa, Nicole, Neil, Penny, the whole Meyrick family. My agent and publisher, Elizabeth Margaris, deserves a special mention for seeing the potential in Jaspa and turning dreams into reality. Thanks also to Cynthia Perry for the wonderful artwork she produced for the book, Elizabeth Ruth for her advice and encouragement, and Chris Glasby for introducing Jaspa to her class. Last, but definitely not least, I'd like to thank my wife, Sue, for her endless support and input, and for her unshakable belief in both Jaspa and me.

Characters (in order of appearance)

Ben McRae	human; 11 year old boy from Edinburgh, Scotland; Seer
Sam McRae	human; Ben's little sister
Mr & Mrs McRae	humans; Ben and Sam's parents
Gravee	Dogses; Ben's friend from Edinburgh, Scotland
Jaspa	Giraffeses
Bisckits	Giraffeses; Jaspa's younger brother
Mackee	Giraffeses; Jaspa's uncle; Portia's father
Cookees	Giraffeses; Jaspa's father
Sofee	Giraffeses (deceased); Jaspa's mother; Mackee's sister
Portia	Giraffeses; Jaspa's cousin
Frankee	Giraffeses; Jaspa's friend
Tabora	Gnuses; Jaspa's guide; Nomad Talekeeper and Taleteller
Oripot	Elephantses; Tabora's friend; Gatekeeper of Elephantu
Hembe	Elephantses; Oripot's wife
Nagare	Gnuses
Nippee	Crocodileses
Ngorika	Vultureses; Jaspa's friend
Hook	vulture; Ngorika's companion
Moringe Babu	human; worker at Kilimanjaro International Airport; Seer

Gravee's Glossary

One of the main characters in Jaspa's Journey is called Gravee (pronounced Gravy). He's Scottish, and has an accent some people find a little difficult to understand at first. To help the non-Scottish, here's a list of some of Gravee's more unusual words and pronunciations.

aboot	about	lugs	ears
an'	and	mah	my
arenae	aren't	mair	more
auld	old	mebbe	maybe
aye	yes	mingin'	smelly
bampot	idiot, crazy person	nae	no, not
bairn	child	noo	now
bin	been	och!	oh!
bonnie	beautiful	o' coorse	of course
braw	really good, fine	oft	often
cannae	can't	oor	our
dae	do	oot	out
doot	doubt	ower	over
Dae ye ken?	Do you understand?	piece	sandwich
		prob'ly	probably
dinnae	don't	puir	poor
galoot	clumsy person, idiot	reek	smell
		reit	right, correct
gonnae	going to	roond	round
greetin'	crying	Scooby	clue
greit	great, big	stonkin'	really big
hame	home	tae	to
heid	head	thin'	thing
huv	have	wee'	small, little
huvnae	haven't	wi'	with
intae	into	wisnae	wasn't
isnae	isn't	wudnae	wouldn't
ken	know	ye	you
laddie	boy	yer	your or you're
lang	long	yerself	yourself
lassie	girl		

And one final piece of advice... If you're still having trouble understanding Gravee, try reading what he says out loud... No honestly, try it... It really does help!

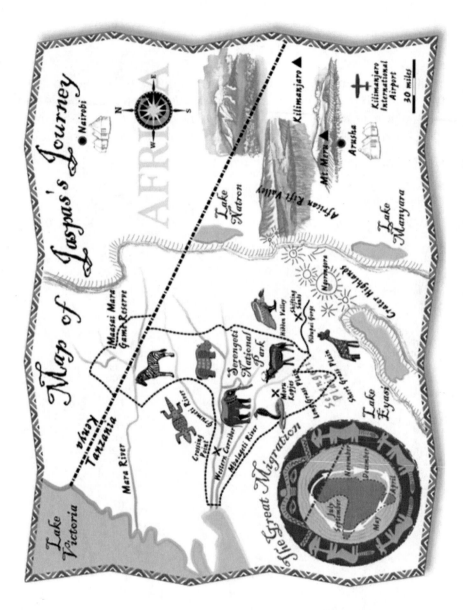

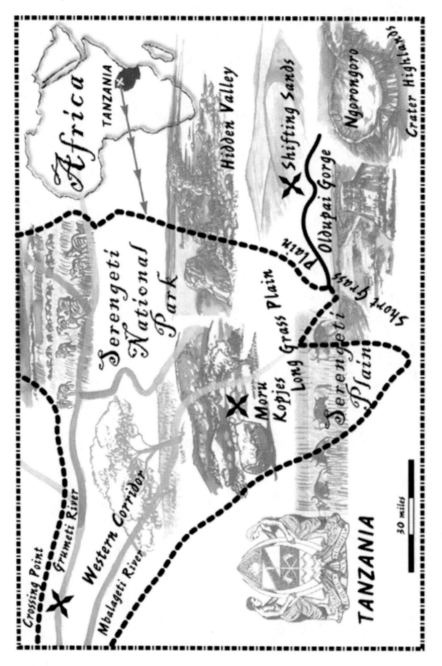

Author's Note

Something to bear in mind as you're reading this book: with only one or two small exceptions, everywhere that Jaspa goes and everything he sees is real. Really real. If you're lucky enough you could go there too, and follow in Jaspa's footsteps.

Part 1

The Schooling

1. On Safari

The gleaming white Land Cruiser skids to a halt, all four wheels kicking up clouds of dust, stones and bits of grass into the heavy afternoon air.

Ben McRae has been standing up in his seat, unenthusiastically looking out of the raised roof hatch. Caught off-guard by the unexpected braking, he's unceremoniously thrown back into the seat. On the way down he bangs his right elbow painfully on the vehicle's door.

Andwele, their local guide, points out the reason for the sudden stop. Barely 30 feet away is a pride of lions, sheltering from the scorching heat of the blistering African sun in the blissful shade provided by the spreading branches of an acacia tree.

Like anyone could have missed that! Ben thinks irritably, cupping his throbbing elbow in his left hand, willing the pain to stop. He's been feeling wretched for the last few days, and the smack to his elbow certainly isn't improving his humour.

Ben is an average-looking 11 year old boy. He's neither skinny nor chubby, neither short nor tall for his age. His eyes are brown, as are the freckles that appear on his cheeks if he spends too much time in the sun. Ben has dark hair that, like his dad's, has a tendency to get a little out of control if it gets too long. Even though he's regularly marched down to the barber's to get it cut, there's still a rebellious little tuft above Ben's right eye that refuses to lie down.

The vehicle's other occupants – Ben's parents, his little sister,

Sam, and four Canadian tourists – are naturally captivated by the dozing cats. All of them greedily drink in the scene, along with Andwele's knowledgeable commentary.

"The lioness closest to the large rock is called Jenny," the guide informs them. "She actually had her ninth birthday only last week and is the mother of...."

Surprisingly though, Ben isn't listening to Jenny's family history. Nor is he looking at the lions any more. He even momentarily forgets the awful burden that's been plaguing his every waking thought, and all of his dreams, for the last 72 hours.

As he had sat there rubbing his sore, bruised elbow, something else had caught his eye.

Something none of the others have spotted.

Something **far** more interesting than mere lions!

***

Eight days ago, the McRae family had flown into northern Tanzania, East Africa. As their plane approached Kilimanjaro International Airport, Ben had stared wide-eyed at the towering mass of the biggest mountain he'd ever seen. The mountain that lends the airport its name. The mountain that boasts the highest point in all of Africa. The colossal volcano, Kilimanjaro.

As they'd descended towards the runway, Ben had gazed spellbound at the mountain's precipitous, seemingly never-ending slopes. Most of all, the young boy had been amazed to see the sunlight glinting off the snow crowning Kilimanjaro's central summit.

Rising majestically to the northeast of the airport, Kilimanjaro's mighty presence dominates the entire landscape. Standing 19,340 feet above sea level, and almost three miles above the surrounding plain, the tallest of its three peaks is so high it's permanently surrounded by icefields, despite being less than 250 miles south of the equator.

No wonder it's called the Shining Mountain, Ben had thought. He read somewhere that's what Kilimanjaro means in the native language of Swahili.

No sooner had they landed, than Ben and his family were hustled into a taxi and driven to another, smaller airfield roughly 30 miles away, on the far side of the city of Arusha. Once there, they'd been bundled into another aircraft, a single-engined propeller plane this time, for the hour-long hop to the Seronera Lodge, nestled in the heart of the world-famous Serengeti National Park.

***

Unfortunately, because of their jobs, the children's parents have both been forced to spend an increasing amount of time away from home in recent years. In an effort to make up for this, the family take holidays together as often as possible. Clearly, Ben and Sam wish their mum and dad didn't have to go away so often, but these fun-filled, frequently exotic, vacations ensure the McRaes remain a close-knit bunch. Moreover, as a result of these regular trips, Ben already considers himself to be quite the seasoned traveller and explorer, despite his young age.

Ben had quickly learned that he got a lot more out of their holidays if he knew a bit about their destination beforehand. So, in the weeks leading up to their African safari, he'd spent hours and hours leafing through books and browsing the Internet for anything he could find on the Serengeti.

One of the first things he'd discovered was that Africa had once been called the *Dark Continent,* because so little was known about it. This had seemed about right to Ben. After all, the first time **he'd** heard of the Serengeti was when his mum announced they were going to visit it! Gradually, however, he'd come to realise that although the word *Serengeti* might be unfamiliar to him, the place that bears this strange, mysterious, magical name was far from it.

Ben had thought back to all the TV programmes he and his sister had ever seen on African wildlife. In his mind's eye he'd imagined endless grasslands covered with teeming herds of wildebeest, zebra and gazelle. He'd recalled lethargic hippopotamuses wallowing in muddy waterholes and elegant giraffes feeding daintily on the leaves of lofty acacia trees. He'd pictured proud lions, snarling hyenas and sleek cheetahs, each hunting in their own distinctive style. And the more Ben had learnt, the more he'd become aware that most of his impressions of Africa were actually visions of the Serengeti.

***

One particularly damp and dreary Sunday afternoon, about three weeks before they were due to travel, Ben had lain on his front on the floor of their Edinburgh living room, reading aloud to his little sister from a large book, which he'd borrowed from the local library.

"The Serengeti is renowned throughout the world as a place of exceptional natural beauty and scientific importance," he'd recited. *"Although it mostly lies within the borders of the East African country of Tanzania, part of it spills out northwards into neighbouring Kenya."*

Sam has a slightly slimmer face than her big brother, who is at least a head taller than she is, although the sun still brings out the freckles they both inherited from their mum. She has shoulder-length, straight, blondish hair, which she normally wears in a ponytail for practical reasons. Well, have you ever tried getting paint or glue out of **your** hair?

Now, whilst Sam had more-or-less grasped what Ben had read, she'd have willingly admitted – to anyone other than her brother, of course – that she hadn't understood **all** the big words. After all, she **is** only six and, in any case, is more of a picture-person. Perhaps unsurprisingly then, she'd suggested, "Can we have a look on a map? I like maps."

Ben had thought this was a great idea. In fact, he'd wished he'd come up with it, although he'd been careful not to let his sister know this! The children had raced each other down the hall to the study, almost knocking their mum over in their enthusiasm to be the first there.

The walls of the McRaes' study are lined with bookcase after bookcase, each one reaching from floor to ceiling and crammed full of books of all shapes and sizes. The biggest books are on the bottom shelf, immediately to the right of the door.

Kneeling down, Ben had dragged out a huge atlas from its place between a brick-sized dictionary and a mammoth volume on climate change belonging to their dad. Grunting with the effort, he'd picked up the atlas and carried it over to the desk, dropping it next to the computer keyboard with a thud.

Flipping through the pages of the enormous book, the children had quickly found the section on Africa. The opening two pages presented a pair of overview maps, covering the entire continent. The first was entitled *Africa: physical,* and showed the major mountain ranges, river basins and plains, with differences in height indicated by various shades of green, yellow and brown. It also showed the continent's most important rivers and largest lakes, as well as the seas, oceans and landmasses that surround Africa's distinctive outline.

What it **didn't** show was where either Tanzania or the Serengeti were.

Fortunately, the second map had proved somewhat more helpful to the children. Labelled *Africa: political,* it showed all the counties of Africa, each one highlighted in a colour that stood out clearly from its neighbours.

Within a few seconds, Ben had spotted Tanzania, coloured yellow, about half way down Africa's east coast, with Kenya, tinted pink, immediately north of it.

"But where's the Serengeti?" Sam had asked.

Sure enough, although the map clearly illustrated where Tanzania and Kenya were, it provided no details on the internal geography of the two countries beyond a few dots marking their main cities and the odd blue squiggle of a major river. It certainly didn't show the Serengeti.

"Hold on," Ben had said, as he began scanning through the following pages of the atlas.

Each double spread covered a different part of Africa, shaded with the same colours used in the original physical overview map, except in much greater detail. Hills and mountains and valleys, rivers and marshes and deserts, all were picked out and carefully labelled. Marching between them, like little black ants, were the strange names of countless human settlements. Over the top of everything else were strong, no-nonsense red lines that sliced the continent up into its constituent countries.

Finally, Ben had come to a pair of pages bearing the title *East Africa.* For several moments, the confusion of black lettering had swum before his eyes. Then the name *Tanzania,* printed in firm capitals, had jumped out at him from the middle of the page, followed almost immediately by *Kenya,* towards the top right-hand corner.

Ben had followed the red border between the two countries with his finger, beginning at the Indian Ocean on the right of the page and slowly tracking it northwest and inland. His finger crossed the green and yellow of the flat, low-lying coastal plain before heading into higher, brown-toned lands further inland. It skirted north of the purple-grey mass of Kilimanjaro and continued past the flat blue of Lake Natron.

Then, just as he he'd begun to suspect he'd gone too far, Ben had spotted it. Nested in the northernmost corner of Tanzania, between Kenya and the bay-scattered shores of the impossibly large Lake Victoria.

The Serengeti Plain.

Ben had shivered with excitement and anticipation, knowing that soon it would be so much more than just a name in an atlas.

Sam had immediately set about tracing the map.

***

Ben's Internet searches had been equally fruitful. From one website he'd learnt that the Serengeti had been discovered less than a hundred years ago, in 1913, by an American called Stewart Edward White. This had baffled Ben, since he was pretty sure the native tribes he'd also read about, like the Datoga and the Maasai, had probably already known the Serengeti existed. After all, they'd lived there **long** before Mr White visited.

In fact, Ben had been fairly certain that, if Mr White had bothered to ask them, the Datoga and Maasai would have told him that their homeland didn't need discovering, thank you very much. Then again, it seemed to him that people from *history* had often wasted their time *discovering* things and places that local people had known about for centuries!

Anyway, Ben had gone on to learn that ever since Mr White's *discovery,* people had flocked to the Serengeti to go *On Safari!*

One author had written, *"Each year more and more people arrive to witness the wondrous landscape, and especially the amazing animals, with their own eyes."*

The realisation that **he'd** soon be one of those people had given Ben goosebumps all over.

***

Sadly, however, not everything Ben had discovered was so cheerful. One particular day, he'd been reading an Internet article on safaris out loud for Sam's benefit.

Sam had been drawing a picture of a lion at the time. It was green.

"In their early days," Ben had read, *"Most safaris were organised to give 'Big Game' hunters the chance to shoot the Serengeti's exotic wildlife. Many of the animals that fell prey to this grisly hobby, or at least parts of them, still adorn walls throughout Europe and North America."*

"NO!" Sam had screamed, bursting into tears and running to her mother.

"I don't want to go on safari any more!" the little girl had sobbed. "It's cruel!"

After a big hug, however, and an even bigger bowl of chocolate ice cream, Mrs McRae had finally managed to calm Sam down enough to listen to the rest of the article.

"Fortunately," Ben had continued, *"Things have changed a lot since then. These days, people come for the pleasure of simply seeing these incredible animals in their natural habitats. Today, the only trophies taken are photographs."*

This had made Sam feel **much** better, and she'd decided that maybe she did still want to go, after all.

***

Since arriving in Africa over a week ago, the McRae family have travelled the length and breadth of the Serengeti at a breakneck pace characterised by early mornings and late nights.

Mostly, they've pounded around the dusty plains in off-road vehicles similar to the one they're currently riding in. However, one particularly memorable afternoon was spent floating serenely above the Earth in a hot air balloon. They'd drifted along on with the wind, the indescribable peace broken only by the insistent bellowing and grunting of the great herds below them... Oh! And the occasional, deafening roar of the balloon's four massive propane burners!

As they've trekked the Serengeti's wild and unspoilt expanses, the McRaes have observed all manner of animals that they'd previously only seen on TV, in books or at the zoo. Lions, elephants, zebra, wildebeest, hippos, giraffes and so much more. They've seen them all. And often unbelievably close up.

Normally, Ben would shrug off his tiredness as a small price to pay for all the amazing things he's seen and done since arriving in Africa. Unfortunately, something happened three days ago that turned Ben's world on its head.

For three days the seconds have ticked by in a blur of anguish and heartache. For three long days Ben has been concealing a secret from his mum and dad, and even his sister. A black, soul-crushing secret that threatens to swallow him whole.

Because three days ago, although his parents are unaware, and his sister doesn't realise, Ben's best friend Gravee... disappeared.

***

During the last three days, Ben has fought to keep his fears trapped inside, to hide his distress from his parents and to save his sister from feeling the same gripping helplessness he does. Yet the thing he spots as he falls back into Land Cruiser temporarily distracts him from his worry and sadness.

You see, there are things other than lions and wildebeest and elephants that call the Serengeti home. Creatures that aren't included on any of the countless safari tours. Animals that don't appear in any books or on any websites. Beings that not even the Datoga or Maasai know about.

But Ben knows about them.

Because Ben, although he appears unremarkably average at first glance, has a rare ability.

The ability to *See* these mysterious individuals.

And he's *Seeing* one right now.

***

2. The Ses

In stark contrast to the flurry of excitement in the vehicle around him, Ben sits absolutely motionless. Spellbound. Hardly daring to even breathe.

None of the Land Cruiser's other occupants have spotted the tiny figure sitting on the fallen, rotting acacia branch. Not even Sam.

This doesn't surprise Ben one little bit. After all, a family of lions, even one lazily dozing away the Serengeti afternoon, has an amazing power to capture and focus most people's attention!

Besides, the fallen branch is probably... what?... about 150 feet away? And even from this distance Ben can tell that the individual sitting on it would comfortably fit into the palm of his hand.

"It's probably *blending*, too," he mutters to himself.

Ben's eyes drink in every detail of the little creature. It sits upright, with two legs dangling off the branch. The way its forelimbs rest on its lap leaves Ben in no doubt these are arms and not just front legs. Its face, whilst long, is round and friendly. Between slightly drooping ears are two stubby little horns and a thick black mane, which runs down the back of its head and short neck. If the little figure was to stand up right now, Ben would also see it has a shortish yellow tail. Its coat is covered in a series of rich brown patches separated by a network of lighter, almost yellow bands, much like the characteristic markings of one of the Serengeti's most recognisable residents.

*It just **has** to be a Giraffeses,* Ben concludes.

The probable-Giraffeses looks a little dumpy in comparison to regular giraffes, but that comes as no great shock to Ben. He's aware that *Ses* often have only a passing resemblance to their more familiar, animal relatives.

He knows this because Gravee explained it to him. In fact, Gravee's told him all about the *Ses*.

And Gravee should know...

He **is** one!

Or, if Ben's darkest dreads prove true, perhaps that should be **was** one...

***

Six months earlier...

The evening sunshine streamed in through two large, wood-framed windows, casting a criss-cross shadow across the floor and up the poster-covered wall. Outside the windows, the sun sank over Moray Place and the rest of Edinburgh's pleasant and stylish New Town district.

Two hundred and fifty years earlier, Edinburgh had been neither pleasant nor stylish. What it had been was overcrowded, dirty, dangerous and, by all accounts, not a particularly nice place to live. By 1766, living conditions in the Scottish capital had become so appalling that a radical way to combat them was dreamt up... Hold a competition to design a whole new town!

Proving that reality is sometime stranger than fiction, this idea was actually accepted. Over the next century Edinburgh's New Town, as it is still known today, grew up to the north of the traditional heart of the city, a triumph of wide, organised streets, spacious, inviting gardens and large, elegant buildings.

Unaware of how his street and house came to be, Ben sat on the floor of his second storey bedroom distractedly playing with a toy car. Close by, Gravee perched up on Ben's desk, posing for Sam who was making a model of him out of papier-mâché.

Without warning, Ben suddenly fired his car across the room and leaned back against his bed. Looking up at his tiny friend on the desk, he asked, "Can you tell us more about the *Ses*?"

Gravee scratched his white furry chin. "Ummmm," he murmured, giving himself time to think. "Well, ye ken what the Irish call *The Little People*, o' course?"

Ben looked blank, although this had nothing to do with Gravee's fairly broad Scottish accent. Having been brought up in Edinburgh himself, Ben had no trouble understanding Gravee. **Most** of the time, anyway.

On the other hand, the only *little people* he'd ever heard of were pygmies and Ben was pretty sure they didn't come from Ireland.

"Err?" he replied apologetically.

Gravee sighed and tried again, "What aboot leprechauns?"

The young boy's face remained a picture of puzzlement.

"Sidhe? Brownies? Red Caps?"

Still bewildered, Ben simply shook his head.

"I've got a red cap," Sam put in helpfully. "It's a Michael Shookamaka one."

Now it was Gravee's turn to look bemused, as Ben turned to give his sister a hard, disapproving stare. After a few seconds Gravee gave up trying to understand Sam's latest contribution to the conversation and returned his attention to the matter at hand.

"Och bairns!" he moaned. "Dinnae they teach ye anythin' useful in school?"

Taking a deep breath, Gravee tried again, "Have ye never heard o' gnomes? Pixies? Elves? Oh, come on, ye must o' heard o' **elves**?!"

"Oh!" said Ben, finally understanding. "You mean fairies and things?"

"At last!" Gravee cried triumphantly. "Aye, laddie! I mean fairies, reit enough!"

In case you weren't aware, Leprechauns are indeed a kind of Irish fairy famous for storing their gold at the end of rainbows. Sidhe (pronounced 'Shee') is the Gaelic name for another type of fairy that lives in Ireland, as well as in the Highlands of Scotland. Brownies and Red Caps also come from Scotland, but whereas Brownies are good-natured household elves, Red Caps are far more sinister, living in the ruins of old castles, their caps supposedly coloured by the blood of their victims! And all these years you thought Brownies were either young Girl Guides or cakes!

"Well, what about them?" Ben asked.

"All in peoples' heids!"

Completely taken aback by Gravee's abrupt answer, Ben could only stutter, "I'm sorry?"

"He said, they're *all in peoples' heads,*" declared his sister. "He means they're pretend," she translated.

Sam did that sometimes. Just when you thought she wasn't paying attention, or that something was too complicated for her to understand, she'd say something that made you realise you couldn't be more wrong. You had to be **very** careful what you said and did when Sam was around.

"That's reit!" cried Gravee, jumping up and pointing at Sam. "The wee lassie's got it!

"Fairies, elves, gnomes... Call 'em whatever ye want. The important thin' is that none o' them are real," he explained. "Folk made 'em all up. They dinnae exist!"

"You mean they're all make-believe?" Ben asked.

"Aye! Every last one," Gravee answered, rolling his eyes in exasperation. "Did I nae jist say that?

"But what about the Tooth Fairy?" asked Sam with a puzzled frown.

"Er..." said Gravee, suddenly looking cornered.

"And how does Father Christmas make all those presents without elves to help him?"

"Och, well, I dinnae ken aboot them, lassie," replied Gravee evasively, clearly feeling uncomfortable. "I'm talkin' aboot all th' **other** fairies an' elves an' such. None o' **them** are real.

"But th' *Ses,* noo..." he added proudly, composing himself once more, "Well, that's another thin' entirely."

***

Ben had lain awake quite late that night, staring at the ceiling, thinking over what Gravee had told them about the Ses.

Apparently, humans all over the world had been making up stories about fairies and pixies and the like for thousands of years. Nonetheless, whatever they were called or wherever they were supposed to live, regardless of whether they were judged to be good or evil, these little creatures all had one thing in common: They all looked, more-or-less, like tiny people.

Except humans aren't as unique as they sometimes like to think they are and, despite the stories, there are no *Little People* running around all over the place.

At least, no little human-like people!

At that point Gravee had paused, clearly pondering something. Then he'd admitted that, on second thoughts, perhaps humans were unique, after all. Though not in the way they believed they were. Indeed, as far as Gravee was aware, humans were quite possibly the only beings *not* to have such, for want of a better term, miniature relatives.

It turns out that most other types animals do.

And collectively they call themselves the *Ses* (pronounced with a short 'e', so it rhymes with 'fez', not 'sees').

Gravee had warned them, however, that it wasn't fair to think of the *Ses* simply as mini versions of *normal* animals.

To begin with, although *Ses* are generally small by human standards, even those of the same type can vary a lot in size. The smallest Whaleses, for instance, are only an inch or so long, but the biggest reach almost two feet in length. Nor do *Ses* always mirror the relative sizes of their better-known cousins. So although elephants, say, are generally bigger than sheep, Elephantses aren't necessarily bigger than Sheepses. Moreover, exceptionally small animals can occasionally have *Ses* counterparts that are **bigger** than they are. Shrewses, for example, are frequently larger than shrews.

Most importantly, Gravee had told them, *Ses* aren't just cute little copies of their more familiar relatives. Hence, Reindeerses don't always have antlers and Skunkses don't necessarily smell bad. (Gravee had actually said, "Skunkses arenae mingin'," but that's what he'd meant!) The important point is that every type of *Ses* somehow retains the **feel** of their larger relations, without being simple mirror-images of them.

Gravee had clearly found this concept particularly difficult to explain. In the end, he'd tried to illustrate his point with another example. Tigerses, he'd told them, don't all have big, sharp teeth or vicious, hooked claws, but there's nonetheless something essentially *tiger-ish* about each of them.

***

Next morning, Ben had woken early. The brightness of the light steeling into his bedroom between the curtains suggested the day was already shaping up to be another warm and sunny one.

Still, there had been rain in the night and the room had a slightly chilly edge to it. So Ben snuggled back into the pillows and duvet, enjoying their warmth, and listened to the muffled sounds of an Edinburgh dawn – bird song and distant traffic – coming in through his closed window.

He might even have drifted back to sleep, had not Sam burst into his room a few minutes later. Gravee followed Ben's little sister through the door, carrying a sandwich that was at least as big as he was.

"Och, ye make a braw piece, wee Sammie!" he'd been saying. "What did ye say was in it again?"

"Ham, peeny butter, mustard, cheddar cheese and marmalade." Sam beamed. "Oh, and mayonnaise."

Ben grimaced, but said nothing. He was used to his sister's creative approach to sandwich making. As far as Sam was concerned, whatever was within reach went in.

"Good mornin', laddie! Are ye no gettin' up today?" Gravee greeted Ben. "Wee Sam an' me have bin up for ages."

"Actually, I've been thinking about what you said last night," Ben said, by way of explanation for still being in bed. "There's something I don't understand."

"What's that then, wee laddie?"

Gravee was always calling Ben and Sam 'wee'. Ben found this a little odd, although he was far too polite to say so, since even Sam towered over the *Ses*. In fact, if Gravee was to stand in a coffee mug (although why would he?) he wouldn't be able to see over the rim. . . Not even on tiptoes!

"Well," Ben began. "You said there were *Ses* all over the world."

"Aye."

"So how come I'd never heard of them before I met you? Why haven't I seen them in books or on TV?"

"Och, well," Gravee said. "The first thin' ye need tae ken is that bein' *all over* isnae the same as bein' *common*."

"You mean, there are *Ses* everywhere," he replied. "But there's not that many of them."

"Reit!"

Ben thought about this a while, something obviously troubling him. "In school last term," he said finally, "We learnt about plants and animals. Our teacher taught us that each different type is called a species, and that some species are extremely common, but others are quite rare."

"Sounds aboot reit," confirmed Gravee.

"Well, our teacher also told us that some species are so rare that there are hardly any of them left. She called them *endangered*, and she said that if those few plants or animals die, then that species will be gone forever."

Ben paused and Gravee could tell they were nearing the boy's point. "What's bothering you, bairn?" he enquired gently.

"Gravee?" asked Ben, his eyes filling with tears. "Are the *Ses* endangered?"

Finally the little Ses understood his friend's concern. "Och laddie! Ye dinnae have tae worry yerself!" he said soothingly. "There arenae billions o' *Ses*, reit enough. But we're nae in any danger either."

Ben brushed an unshed tear from the corner of his eye. "Then why don't humans know about you?" he sniffed, still caught somewhere between dismay and relief.

"Och, that'll be the *blendin'*, that will."

"*Blending*?"

"Aye, *blendin'*."

"I've never heard of it," admitted Ben

"I'm nae surprised!" replied Gravee. "It's a *Ses* thing."

"But what does it *mean*?" asked the boy impatiently.

"Well, simply put, *Ses* can choose nae tae be seen by humans."

"Wow! So you can become invisible?" asked an impressed Sam, once again seeing to the heart of things.

"Nae really, bairn!" laughed Gravee. "It's mair like we can decide tae fade intae th' backgroond." he explained. "Sort o' convince people's eyes tae ignore us. Dae ye ken? We just call it *blendin'*."

"So how come we can see you?" asked Ben.

"Aye, well, it's reit unusual fur a human tae be able tae see a *blendin' Ses*, sure enough. But it does happen sometimes. We call 'em *Seers*."

The ticking of the hall clock counted off several seconds before Ben next spoke. "You mean Sam and me are *Seers*?" he finally asked in a hushed voice.

"Well... Yer half reit," smiled the *Ses*. "Th' fact is, yer the *Seer*, Ben."

Ben's grew wide with surprise. "Why me?" he whispered.

"I huvnae got a Scooby. Nobody does. Some folk are born *Seers*, that's all there is tae it."

As the initial shock subsided, Ben began to grin sheepishly, trying to contain the pride swelling inside his chest. Sam, on the other hand, looked completely crushed. Seeing this, Gravee awarded her an enormous wink.

"Och! Dinnae worry yerself, wee Sammie. There's nothin' I can dae aboot this greit eejit *seeing* me," the Ses admitted, indicating Ben with his thumb and pretending to insult him. "It's nae like he's doin' it on purpose, is it?

"But dinnae forget, you can see me 'cause I **allow** ye tae, ye being such a braw wee lassie an' all," Gravee continued. "Between ye an' me, I'd say that's much mair special than just bein' a plain auld *Seer!*"

At that, Sam too beamed with pride.

***

3. The Seer and the seen

Under a nearby tree, a pair of lion cubs, always so full of energy, begins to wrestle amongst their more lethargic elders. Showing little or no respect for the other members of their pride, they charge amongst – and occasionally **over** – the dozing adults like a furry beige whirlwind, snarling and clawing and pouncing at each other.

The sudden commotion is mirrored by a flurry of activity in the nearby Land Cruiser, as the humans reach for cameras and binoculars. The air is suddenly filled with gasps of delight and awe, the click of camera shutters and the whir of film advancing.[1]

All of this is clearly audible from where Jaspa the Giraffeses is sitting.

Except Jaspa isn't paying any attention to either the lions or the humans. Although he might **appear** to be looking straight at the tourist's vehicle, he's not really watching it. Instead, he stares unseeing into the middle distance, with a slightly glazed look in his eyes, completely unaware of the world around him.

Jaspa has more important things on his mind than the brainless antics of a couple of lion cubs or the unfathomable behaviour of a truck full of tourists.

For tomorrow, Jaspa is going home.

***

Jaspa slowly wakes from his daydream. He groggily rubs at his eyes, and then blinks a couple of times for good measure.

[1] Even in this digital age, amazingly some people still prefer cameras that use real film!

A sensation of discomfort creeps over him, as he realises that part of his brain has been trying to get his attention for some minutes now. Something **definitely** doesn't feel normal...

Someone is watching him!

Jaspa's senses prickle as they search for the source of his unease.

Everything seems peaceful enough. Insects buzz annoyingly in the heat and off in the distance a zebra is braying. Otherwise all is quiet.

Not far away to Jaspa's right, a secretary bird peers intently down at the ground beneath it, watching and waiting for the slightest movement. A movement that may well prove fatal for the animal that makes it.

While most other birds of prey hunt from aloft, effortlessly riding the wind, the secretary bird generally prefers to keep its taloned feet firmly on the ground. Yet its extraordinarily long legs, which give the secretary bird the appearance of a scrawny eagle on stilts, still enable it to scan the ground for prey from a height approaching five feet. The bird's odd name comes from its crest of long feathers, which look like the quills 19th Century office clerks kept tucked behind their ears.

Jaspa is well aware the awkward-looking raptor poses no threat to him. Still, for some strange reason that he can't put his finger on, his anxiousness refuses to go away.

***

Under the tree, the lion cubs continue to pounce on each other with mock ferociousness. In the truck, the tourists are all chattering excitedly, *ooh-ing* and *aah-ing* and taking photo after photo.

At least, most of them are.

Quite suddenly, Jaspa realises what's been bothering him.

If I didn't know better, he thinks to himself, *I'd swear that boy is looking straight at me!*

But clearly that's impossible. Humans can't see his kind when they're *blending*. Even the youngest *Ses* knows that!

***

The little creature looks up at Ben, making eye contact at last.

It's noticed me, thinks Ben excitedly.

"What was that, mate?" asks his dad.

"Oh! Nothing," he replies quickly, looking up at his father. Until then, Ben hadn't realised he'd spoken out loud.

"I bet you'd like to take one of those home, wouldn't you?" jokes Mr McRae, meaning the brawling lion cubs.

"I would! I would!" cries Sam, jumping up and down on her seat.

"Yeah," whispers her brother sadly, thinking of Gravee. "Me too."

***

Sorrow threatens to overwhelm Ben, as his thoughts settle briefly on Gravee. Almost immediately, however, he remembers the extraordinary figure sitting on the fallen branch.

Ben quickly returns his gaze to the broken bough. He's gripped with a sudden dismay and a wave of panic surges through him. A certainty that the tiny individual will have disappeared. Or that his grief for his missing friend has started playing tricks on him and he'd only imagined the branch's unlikely occupant.

Then a rush of pleasure replaces his passing fear.

The little creature is still sitting there. Still looking back at him.

Without knowing why, Ben winks at the branch's tiny occupant. A long, slow, exaggerated wink that causes half his face to scrunch up.

Almost immediately, the figure blinks back! Though, in truth, Ben can't be sure whether this is some sort of reply, an involuntary expression of surprise, or just a nervous tick.

***

Jaspa blinks in shock.

He's sure the boy in the truck just winked at him!

But again, that's simply not possible.

Not unless he's a *Seer*, and that's hardly likely, is it?!

And yet...

Despite himself, Jaspa finds his uncertainties beginning to evaporate under that steady, hopeful gaze, edged with sadness and a touch of desperation. Gradually his doubts and disbelief fade away, like shadows banished by the glare of the sun. With each passing moment he becomes more convinced that this is no mere coincidence.

The boy isn't just looking in Jaspa's general direction, he's looking right **at** him. Definitely. No question!

Jaspa's heard tales of *Seers*, of course. Legends of humans who could see *blending Ses*. He'd always thought they were just that... Legends. Myths. Stories told by mothers to make their children practice *blending*. The discovery that *Seers* might actually exist comes as quite a surprise to the bright young *Ses*.

Part of Jaspa's brain tells him he should be concerned. **Really** concerned!

So he's surprised to discover that, for reasons he can't begin to explain, he isn't. Perhaps it's the boy's honest face, but Jaspa no longer feels even the slightest bit worried.

In fact, it goes much deeper than that. The more Jaspa thinks about it, the more he realises that all of his anxieties have simply fallen away, to be replaced by an irresistible certainty that something life-changingly important has just happened.

And he finds just can't help grinning about it.

***

4. Danger Lurks

Jaspa continues to study the face of the boy looking back at him. It's a kind face, he decides. Open and thoughtful, but with a subtle hint of impishness to it. In many ways, Jaspa feels like he's looking in a mirror.

Yet there's something else clouding the boy's features. A deep and obvious sadness, which fills Jaspa with sympathy.

Suddenly, the Giraffeses' concentration is broken. Out of the corner of his eye, he catches a hint of movement off in the longer grasses beyond the secretary bird.

Or did he?

When Jaspa turns his head to look straight at the spot, the grass appears motionless.

He continues to stare the clump of grass, searching for whatever it was that attracted his attention. The seconds tick by and all seems quiet, though his sense of foreboding remains.

Even so, Jaspa's beginning to wonder whether it was just a breath of wind, or his mind playing tricks on him, when...

There it is again!

Unmistakable this time.

Something's definitely hiding in the long grass!

***

Jaspa slips down off the log and moves a few feet closer, hoping to get a better view of whatever is lurking there. He's a full 15 feet from the fallen branch before he eventually spies something between the tall stalks of grass. A pair of what look like bony humps, covered in sandy coloured fur.

He takes another couple of steps, sideways this time. And can finally make out the secretive skulker... A stalking lion!

In fact, it's a lioness, crouching motionless, her belly almost touching the ground. From this angle, Jaspa sees that what he took to be furry humps are actually the lioness's shoulders, sticking up above the curve of her back. Her head is held low, her face a picture of concentration.

She takes another, single step forward. The entire fluid movement is confined to her muscular legs, so that her body and head seem to float effortlessly forward. She pauses, making sure her intended prey hasn't observed her.

Jaspa follows the line of her deliberate gaze... Straight to the truck containing the boy!

"What 'ya looking at?" asks a loud voice in his ear.

***

To Ben's great dismay, the Giraffeses suddenly looks away, its attention clearly attracted by something else. A few moments pass, before it hops down off the log and begins to walk towards a patch of longer grass.

"Don't go," Ben begs softly.

As if it can hear him, the creature stops, apparently studying the grass.

Then, without warning, a second tiny figure is suddenly standing right beside the first!

One moment he's watching one Giraffeses, the next... **bang**... There's another one! As if out of thin air.

The unexpected appearance of the second *Ses* gives Ben quite a shock and he gasps out loud. Fortunately, everyone else is too busy watching the lions to notice.

Ben can't make any sense of it. Gravee had said that *Ses* couldn't make themselves truly invisible. And anyway, even if they could, Ben's a *Seer*! So, why hadn't he been able to see this second Giraffeses approaching?

That said, judging by reaction of the first *Ses*, Ben wasn't the only one surprised by the newcomer's sudden appearance.

***

Jaspa almost cries out in shock! Heart pounding, his head whips around to see the grinning face of his younger brother, just an inch or so away.

"Oh, sorry!" says Bisckits amiably. "Did I startle you?" He manages to keep a straight face for only a fraction of a second, before bursting into fits of giggles.

Bisckits is a little smaller than Jaspa and prefers to walk on all fours. His right ear has an upward quirk to it, which gives him a permanently quizzical expression. This is extremely appropriate, since Bisckits is curious about **everything**. A quality that all too often gets him into trouble.

"Be quiet!" hisses Jaspa crossly. "You nearly gave me a heart attack!"

"You don't say!" laughs Bisckits. "You should have seen your face! I thought...."

"Bisckits!" Jaspa interrupts. "This is serious! Pipedown and look over there!"

Slightly crestfallen, Bisckits glances towards where Jaspa is pointing. "It's a lion," he says sulkily. "So what?"

Jaspa sighs sharply in frustration. "But what's it **doing**?"

"It's doing what lions do. It's hunting..." Then, as he turns to look at the focus of the lioness' attention, he stifles a gasp. "It's hunting those people!"

"Exactly!" says Jaspa. "But that doesn't make any sense, does it? You know as well as I do that lions hardly ever attack humans, even when they're not protected inside a truck."

"We've got to warn them!" Bisckits exclaims, still watching the stalking lioness. Abruptly he starts off towards the tourist's truck.

Jaspa quickly grabs him by the shoulder and pulls him back. "What do you think you're doing?" he asks.

"Just what I said. I'm going to warn them!"

"And how are you going to do that?"

"Er..." replies Bisckits uncertainly. He looks back at the lioness. The tip of her tail twitches nervously as she slowly but relentlessly moves towards the truck and its occupants.

The younger Giraffeses turns back to his brother and pleads, "But Jaspa, we can't just watch and do nothing!"

"I know," Jaspa agrees. "And I think I've got an idea. Actually, I was about to try it just before you played your little trick on me."

Bisckits immediately looks uncomfortable.

For a fleeting second, Jaspa considers leaving it at that. It's definitely time his wayward little brother learnt a bit about responsibility. But the genuinely regretful look on Bisckits' face proves too much for Jaspa and he relents.

"Don't worry!" he reassures his younger sibling, clapping him on the back. "No harm done. Now, wait here... And keep your fingers crossed."

And he promptly disappears!

***

Eight days ago, Ben would have readily admitted he was hoping to see a *Ses* whilst in Africa. Four days ago, he would have had to confess to being extremely disappointed not to have seen one during their time in the Serengeti.

But that was before Gravee disappeared.

Since then, Ben has continued his vigilant watch for *Ses*, although the reason for his search has changed utterly. No longer is he driven by a desire to see exotic Rhinoses, Zebrases or Elephantses. Instead, Ben's spent every waking moment of the last 72 hours watching out for his friend, hoping and wishing and aching to see Gravee again. Unfortunately, despite his best efforts, he has no idea where Gravee might be. And that worries him deeply.

Even so, Ben can't help feeling a little bit excited. After all, in the last ten minutes, he's not only spotted two Giraffeses, but one of them has seen him, too! *I only wish Gravee were here to share this,* he thinks slightly guiltily.

The young boy gives his head a shake in an attempt to clear his gloomy thoughts, and looks back at the Giraffeses. The little creatures seem to be quarrelling about something.

As Ben watches, the newcomer gazes towards the patch of grass that the original Giraffeses seemed so interested in. After studying the grass for just a few seconds, the new *Ses* suddenly turns to stare, wide-eyed, straight at the Land Cruiser in which he's sitting. Ben holds his breath in anticipation...

To his great frustration the second Giraffeses looks away again, almost immediately. It didn't notice him!

Nevertheless, it's becoming quite clear to Ben that something about that patch of longer grass is worrying the two tiny figures.

And then, again without warning...

The first Giraffeses vanishes!

"No!" cries Ben in alarm.

***

Gravee had told Ben and Sam about how *Ses* can *blend*. He hadn't got around to telling the children that this isn't their only unusual ability.

You see, when the need arises, *Ses* are also able to move in a way that seems very peculiar to us non-*Ses*. Now, that doesn't mean that they bounce along on their heads or anything like that. (Well, it's possible that some might. People, whether human or *Ses*, do all sorts of odd things in the name of fun!) Rather, it's the way they can get from one place to another far quicker than would seem possible, and without ever having to resort to running. They call it *shifting*. And, before you ask, it's a mystery how they manage it.

Regardless of how it's done, *shifting* enables Jaspa to be standing right in front of the unsuspecting secretary bird in less than a handful of seconds. One moment the poor creature's minding its own business, busy hunting for a tasty snake or lizard, its favourite foods. The next it's peering along the length of its hooked beak at a little Giraffeses.

Jaspa waves up at it.

Although the bird towers almost five feet above him, the Giraffeses' sudden appearance gives it quite a shock. Predictably then, it does the only sensible thing...

It panics![1]

Raising its distinctive crest in fright, the secretary bird issues a coarse croak and jumps high into the air. A few moments later, it lands with a thump and, adopting the same method it would usually use to catch its prey, it begins stamping wildly but determinedly at the ground, trying to spear with its razor-sharp talons the vicious creature it believes is attacking it!

The sudden commotion triggers off a chain of events that occur so fast that, if filmed, they'd have to be viewed in slow-motion...

[1] Oh, come on now! Wouldn't you?!

...The lioness's concentration is broken and she instinctively raises her head to establish whether the abrupt uproar signifies imminent danger.

...In the Land Cruiser, the sleeping lions are suddenly forgotten, as everyone seeks out the source of the unexpected racket. All eyes fix on the secretary bird and its crazy hopping, although only Ben can see the tiny figure doing its own frantic dance between the bird's stamping feet.

...Andwele spots the lioness, still crouching in the grass, and points her out to the tourists.

...A young Thomson's gazelle bolts from the long grass between the lion and the Land Cruiser and races off across the plain, leaving a trail of dust in its wake. The incredibly fortunate little antelope had been resting in the false protection of the long grass, completely unaware that it, and not the humans in the vehicle, was the first choice on a lioness's menu.

***

Before the uproar even has time to die down, Jaspa *shifts* back to Bisckits' side, none the worse for his encounter with the highly-strung secretary bird. He looks at his younger brother and puts his hand to his mouth in embarrassment.

"Oops!" he says with concern. "I don't think that lioness will be very pleased with us if she ever finds out we were to blame for her dinner getting away!"

"You were to blame, you mean!" snorts Bisckits. "Don't go getting me involved!"

Jaspa continues to look worried for another half second or so. Then the feigned distress melts from his face and the pair of Giraffeses burst out laughing.

The lioness, however, is unconcerned. She unhurriedly rejoins the reminder of her pride beneath the acacia tree, safe in the knowledge that, before the day's out, there will be plenty of other opportunities to feed herself and her family.

***

The Giraffeses disappears again, although the ridiculous-looking bird continues its mad leaping for several more seconds. Ben looks back towards the broken branch, just in time to see the original

Giraffeses reappear beside the newcomer. To his relief, it appears to be unhurt after its baffling adventure with the bizarre bird. In fact, after a brief exchange, both little figures seem to burst into laughter!

The lioness saunters contemptuously past the stationary Land Cruiser, to the thrill of most of those within it, and collapses along with other cats beneath the acacia tree. Ben hardly notices, however, as he continues to gaze fixedly at the two tiny creatures only he can see.

***

Eventually, the Giraffeses laughter is replaced by the irregular breathing of two people trying to get themselves under control, punctuated by the occasional giggle of someone who's not quite succeeded yet.

Finally, Bisckits manages to ask, "Do you think we should be getting back? I'm guessing Uncle Mackee will be wondering where we've got to."

"Yeah, you're right," says Jaspa, wiping tears from his eyes. "Just... ow!... give my sides a second to stop hurting, first!"

Suddenly, he remembers the boy. He'd nearly forgotten about him in all the excitement.

The truck begins to pull away just as Jaspa looks up, but he's pleased to find the boy is still staring back at him. They consider each other for a few seconds more, human and Giraffeses, *Seer* and seen.

On an impulse, Jaspa raises his right hand and gives the boy a wave.

"Who are you waving at?" enquires Bisckits.

"A friend," says Jaspa distantly. "Just a friend."

***

To Ben's horror, the vehicle he's sitting in begins to move again. He's been willing the Giraffeses to look back at him, but now its too late. In his already emotional state, the disappointment fills Ben with an enormous grief, and he has to fight to keep tears from his eyes.

Just when he's about to give up hope, the original Giraffeses finally turns back towards him. It regards him solemnly for a moment.

And then, to Ben's absolute amazement, it waves.

The tears he's been holding back sparkle in Ben's eyes, but now they're touched with something more than sadness. He smiles and raises his hand slightly to the receding Giraffeses.

Although he knows it's completely crazy, Ben has the unshakable feeling this isn't the last time they'll see each other.

***

As they head off towards their camp, Bisckits is certain there's something Jaspa isn't telling him. Unfortunately, that's nothing new. For almost a year now, his elder brother has been prone to occasional, uncharacteristic bouts of evasiveness.

No. Not evasive... That sounds much too sinister.

It's just that he and Jaspa have never had secrets from each other. Yet Bisckits is sure his brother has been keeping something to himself these past ten months. Since just after Portia left on her *Journey*, in fact. Indeed, for a while he had thought Jaspa's peculiar behaviour was a direct reaction to their cousin's departure. They're extremely close, after all.

But Portia will be returning anytime now, and yet Jaspa's mysterious episodes continue, although admittedly nowhere near as frequently as they had been at the beginning. Bisckits concluded long ago that something else was behind his brother's odd actions, but after all this time he still has no idea what that *something* could be.

One thing **is** clear to Bisckits. Whatever Jaspa's secret is, it worries him.

No one else has noticed, of course. And Bisckits is convinced Jaspa believes he's successfully concealing his concern from his little brother, too. However, despite his happy-go-lucky demeanour, Bisckits is a lot more perceptive than most people give him credit for. Initially, he'd observed that whenever Jaspa thought he wasn't being watched, a look of intense concern, fear almost, crossed his face. After a few weeks this softened into what Bisckits now thinks of as a sort of occasional distractedness.

For a while, the nameless, one-sided barrier between them had really hurt Bisckits. But this young Giraffeses is also much more sensible and intelligent than most realise. Well, he'd really have to be, wouldn't he? The point is that Bisckits' had finally come to accept that when, or indeed if, Jaspa is ready to share his secret, he will. Until then... Well, Bisckits will continue to respect his brother's privacy.

Not that he doesn't still wonder what Jaspa's mysterious secret is, of course!

***

5. A fitful night

That evening, Jaspa and Bisckits relax back at their campsite, sharing a contented silence. They're camped just inside the eastern edge of the Lerai Forest, within the great crater of Ngorongoro.

The crater is a huge circular depression, over 12 miles across and 100 square miles in area. It's rimmed by a continuous wall of steep cliffs that, in places, rises more than 2000 feet above its floor. Ngorongoro was once an immense volcano, probably even taller than Mount Kilimanjaro is today. It towered above the surrounding landscape until, about two million years ago, it self-destructed in a cataclysmic explosion that turned the mountain inside out. By the time the dust settled, the volcano's soaring peak had been replaced by the vast crater that exists today. A geologist would more accurately call this type of crater a *caldera*. In fact, Ngorongoro is the largest unflooded caldera in the world!

But on this evening, as the sun slowly sinks behind the western crater wall, Jaspa finds it hard to imagine a more peaceful place as he mulls over the events of the day. A *Seer*, he marvels. *Wow!* He can still hardly believe it.

Almost as hard to believe is that he still hasn't told Bisckits about the boy in the truck. In all honesty, Jaspa isn't sure why. Perhaps he just needs time to think about it, before having to deal with the inevitable bombardment of questions that will follow the sharing of this latest secret.

Jaspa's pondering focuses on this last thought. Latest secret. **Latest** secret!

Hasn't it been difficult enough keeping **a**, as in singular, as in one, secret from Bisckits? There had been a time when he and Bisckits had **no** secrets between them. And now, here he is with not one *secret*, but *secrets*. Plural. It's crazy!

The weirdest part is that he never actually intended to keep the other thing from Bisckits. He'd just never found the right moment to tell him. At first he wasn't sure how his little brother would react, knowing his feelings on the subject. Then, as time had passed, it had only become more difficult to broach the issue because he'd also have to try to explain why he hadn't told Bisckits earlier.

It's such a mess. A stupid, awkward, heart-wrenching and, above all, unnecessary mess. The only consolation is that Bisckits is blissfully unaware of it.

Yet here he is starting down the same road again. And for absolutely no good reason. He must need his head examining!

***

Jaspa sighs and looks over at Bisckits. His younger brother and best friend is lazily building barriers out of twigs to provide an ever-changing obstacle course for an ant he is playing with.

"So where were you?" Jaspa asks eventually.

"Pardon?" enquires Bisckits, looking up at him with a slightly confused expression.

"Earlier on. Just before you decided it would be fun to give me a heart attack. Where had you been?"

"Oh. Then." Bisckits mumbles guiltily. "I was just having one last look at the watering-hole. I'm really going to miss watching the warthogs wallowing. They're so ridiculous!"

Jaspa's eyes narrow knowingly. "Watching?" he asks. "More like trying to flick mud balls into their ears, don't you mean?"

"Maybe!" admits Bisckits with an impish grin. "That too!"

The ant Bisckits has been annoying makes a break for freedom whilst its tormentor is distracted. It skirts around the latest twig construction and heads determinedly towards a nearby Wait-a-bit thorn tree.[1]

---

[1] Yes, this is a real tree!

"You know, it's probably a good thing we're going home tomorrow," says Jaspa, shaking his head slightly. "I don't think that old male with the missing tusk finds the game quite as entertaining as you do. I'm not sure he'd have tolerated it for much longer."

"Some people just have no sense of humour!" laughs Bisckits.

"Oh Bisckits!" Jaspa sighs. "Promise me you'll at least **try** to act a bit more responsibly on our *Journey*. Uncle Mackee won't always be there to get us out of trouble."

"We didn't need Uncle Mackee today, did we?" responds Bisckits, feeling suddenly argumentative.

"No." answers Jaspa quietly, trying to defuse the brewing situation. "No, we didn't. Then again, we weren't really in trouble, were we? As it turned out, not even the people we thought we were helping were in trouble! But we might be next time, and Uncle Mackee won't be just a shout away."

"No. But our *Rubani* will be!" Bisckits counters, refusing to let the issue drop.

Jaspa lets out a long, noisy breath. "Maybe. Maybe not." he concedes. "But you know that's not the point."

A long moment of silence draws out.

"You're right," Bisckits admits finally, looking at his feet. His gaze returns to Jaspa and his tone becomes serious and sincere. "You know how much I appreciate you waiting for me, don't you?"

The brothers stare at each other for a moment. Then the twinkle returns to Bisckits' eyes, "Wow, though! We're going to have so much fun!"

Jaspa's resolve weakens and he can't help smiling back. A great big, joyful, sun-bright smile. "Always," he agrees.

As Bisckits turns back to his previous diversion, the ant reaches the shade of the thorn tree. "Now, where did he go?" the younger Giraffeses wonders aloud.

***

Jaspa finds getting to sleep difficult tonight and it's well past midnight as he finally drifts off into a fitful slumber.

Bisckits, ever the more excitable of the pair, has even more trouble. Several times he almost captures the sleep that's proving so elusive, only to be jerked back to wakefulness by his anticipation of what tomorrow will bring. Eventually though, tiredness wins out over excitement, as it always does, and Bisckits also falls asleep.

***

Generations of Jaspa's tribe, known far and wide as the *Herd*, have chosen to live out their lives on the Short Grass Plains of the southeastern Serengeti in the shadows of the Shifting Sands. This strange pair of isolated, crescent-shaped, barchan sand dunes slowly wander around this part of the plain, slaves to the will of the wind. As they move, travelling up to 60 feet a year, the rubbing of sand grain on sand grain causes the dunes to *moan* softly and eerily.

Each and every *Herder* shares a deep-rooted love for the land they call home. All believe there can be no place on Earth as wondrous, and yet as comfortable, as their small corner of the Serengeti. Nevertheless, they're an open-minded folk, who also accept there are marvels to be seen and lessons to be learnt in the wider world.

It is this tolerant, unprejudiced attitude that forms the cornerstone of the *Herd's* most precious and ancient tradition.

The *Journey*.

Upon reaching a certain age, every young Giraffeses must leave the Shifting Sands behind for a short while to venture out into the world beyond. Following the migrating herds, they travel the Serengeti for the best part of a year, experiencing first hand the wonders of the wild lands beyond their home.

In many ways, the *Journey* mirrors the *walkabout* of Australian aborigines, which signifies the transition to adulthood. Both are voyages of discovery and adventure.

Nevertheless, the *Journey* can also be an extremely hazardous undertaking, particularly since the majority of youngsters set out wholly unprepared for the trials they will encounter along the way. Fortunately, Giraffeses are usually pretty level-headed and practical, although taking Bisckits at face value, you might not appreciate this. Long ago the *Herders* realised that some sort of training was required to prevent the *Journey* becoming **too** exciting.

And thus, for years uncounted, the *Journey* has been preceded by the *Schooling*, a short introductory trip under the watchful eyes of an older, more experienced Giraffeses. The *Schooling* serves two simple purposes: it softens the blow of being away from home for the first time, whilst at the same time enabling young Giraffeses to learn some of the fundamental skills they will need on the *Journey* proper.

***

This night marks the end of the *Schooling* for Bisckits and Jaspa. In accordance with *Herd* tradition, they've spent it in the magnificent Ngorongoro Crater. But with the coming dawn they will begin the trek home. There they will await the end of the *masika*, the 'long rains' that usually last from mid-March to May, which will announce the time has come for them to set out on their real *Journey*.

Customarily, Giraffeses are accompanied on their *Schooling* by one of their parents, but unfortunately this was not possible for Jaspa and Bisckits. Their father, Chief Cookees, couldn't bring them because, much to his and their disappointment, his responsibilities as head of the *Herd* made it impossible for him to be away for so long. Their mother, Sofee, unhappily didn't live to guide her sons through their *Schooling*. So instead, Sofee's twin brother, Mackee, volunteered to lead his nephews in their parents' place.

***

The brothers slumber on, their little chests rising and falling with each new breath.

In his dreams, Jaspa has already returned home to the dunes of the Shifting Sands. Floating free of his body, he looks down on a much younger Jaspa and Bisckits as they trudge up the side of the nearest dune. They finally reach the top and, without a moment's pause, fling themselves headfirst down the dune's steep face. Tumbling and rolling, the shadows of his memory slide back down again, laughing and shouting all the way.

***

The number of *Journeyers*, those Giraffeses embarking on the *Journey*, is usually around two or three, although it does vary from year to year. Portia was one of six to set out from the Shifting Sands last year and if Jaspa had accompanied them, as he was supposed to, there would have been a record seven *Journeyers*. In contrast, only Bisckits is coming of age this year, and if Jaspa hadn't waited for him he'd have had to make his *Journey* alone.

Actually, that's only half true. Although Bisckits would have been the only *Journeyer* this year, it doesn't mean he'd have been sent out to face the dangers of the Serengeti entirely on his own. For a Giraffeses' training for the *Journey* doesn't quite end with the *Schooling*. There's also the *Rubani*...

The initial stages of the *Journey* are usually pretty uneventful from a danger point of view. Surprisingly then, they're often the most difficult to cope with emotionally. Despite the *Schooling*, homesickness, lack of confidence, apprehension and general downheartedness are understandably common, especially in years when there are only one or two *Journeyers*.

In the distant past, there had been rare occasions when those first few weeks away from the *Herd* had proved so difficult for a young Giraffeses that they had abandoned the *Journey* almost before it had begun. Whilst the other *Herders* had placed no judgement on these few unfortunates, their self-imposed shame had tended to make them increasingly unhappy as they grew older.

But that was before Chief Barafu the Wise founded the *Rubani*. Since that day, not a single Giraffeses has failed to complete the *Journey*.

The *Rubani* is chosen from the previous year's returning *Journeyers*. He or she helps the young Giraffeses through their first challenging days away from the *Herd*, providing the support and comfort of someone who has recently been through the very same ordeals. Usually, the *Rubani* returns to the Shifting Sands after two or three weeks, leaving the new batch of *Journeyers* to continue on alone. However, it isn't completely unknown for them to choose to remain with their charges for the entire duration of the *Journey*.

***

Jaspa rolls over in his sleep. "Be patient," he murmurs vaguely. "Wait 'til you're stronger." He fidgets suddenly, a look of concern briefly crossing his slumbering face. Then the nightmare passes as quickly as it arrived, and he sinks back into more peaceful dreams.

Bisckits is fast asleep and so witnesses none of Jaspa's distress. Indeed, looking at him sleep, it's hard to believe he had such trouble dropping off. If not for his slow, rhythmic breathing, you'd swear he was a sculpture. Logs move more in their sleep than Bisckits does.

Of course, he more than makes up for it when he's awake.

***

Long before sunrise, Mackee is awake and dismantling his own campsite. It's set a short way off from that of Jaspa and Bisckits. Close enough to hear a call if they're in trouble, but far enough away to give them their independence. After all, they're supposed to be learning how to look after themselves in the wild, and they can't do that with their uncle constantly peering over their shoulders.

As he sets off through the damp grass towards the brothers' campsite, Mackee recalls their astonished faces as they had gazed down into Ngorongoro for the first time from the top of its western rim. He smiles to himself. Unfortunately, time had been pressing, and Mackee had only been able to let Jaspa and Bisckits savour the view from the crater's edge for a few short minutes, before insisting they begin their descent.

His thoughts drift away, into other memories of this wondrous place... The first time he saw it himself, all those years ago, when his father had brought him here for his own *Schooling*. And the last time he was here, only a year ago, when he had accompanied his daughter Portia on hers. She had left on her *Journey* almost ten months ago now, and although each day brings her return that bit closer, Mackee still misses his only child and wishes constantly for her safe return.

Upon reaching the crater floor, Mackee had led his nephews around the southern shore of Lake Magadi and past the northern edge of the Lerai Forest. By the time they arrived at the spot he'd chosen to erect their camps, the sun had already disappeared behind the crater wall to the west and the evening twilight was fading fast.

There had been no time to rest, but the boys had hardly grumbled when Mackee had immediately begun their training. That first evening he had taught Jaspa and Bisckits how to find water, before showing them how to construct a shelter from branches, leaves and grasses. By the time they had finally collapsed into their freshly constructed beds of moss, the night was already getting old.

It's hard to believe that was over two weeks ago and that the brothers' *Schooling* is already at an end. Jaspa and Bisckits have done well. Very well. And Mackee is certain they will be able to cope with any problems they might encounter on their *Journey*.

Yes, Mackee feels intensely proud of both his nephews. Nevertheless, he's been deliberately sparing with his praise during their time here. He doesn't want them to get too sure of themselves.

Mackee knows from experience that, although a lack of faith in your own abilities can often be dangerous on the *Journey*, overconfidence can sometimes be even more deadly.

***

6. Visitors in the dawn

All too soon, or so it seems to a very grumpy Bisckits, he is woken by an insistent shaking. "What?" he asks before his brain can quite figure out what's happening.

Slowly at first, but then more quickly as he emerges from the depths of sleep, Bisckits' senses take in the world around him. One dreamland is replaced by another. The stars are still bright in the clear, blue-black night sky, but in the east several of the peaks that make up the Crater Highlands are already silhouetted against the first hints of dawn.

The Crater Highlands rise to the east of the Serengeti, a cluster of volcanoes of which Ngorongoro is the largest. Most of them, including Ngorongoro, are now extinct. Only one remains active, Oldoinyo Lengai, which means *Mountain of God* in Swahili. It continues to erupt regularly to this day.

As the cotton wool feeling in his head begins to recede, Bisckits looks up at his tormentor.

"Jaspa!" he exclaims irritably. "What are you playing at? Can't a Giraffeses get any sleep around here? It's still the middle of the night!"

"Come on Bisckits. It's almost sunrise," Jaspa explains in the reasonable tone of someone used to Bisckits' early morning bad temper. "You'd better get a move on. You know Uncle Mackee wants to leave at first light."

"OK. OK!" groans Bisckits, collapsing back down and closing his eyes. "I'm up."

"So I see," teases Jaspa.

***

"Direct hit!" Bisckits exclaims triumphantly, though quietly, as he ducks back down behind a knot of tallish grasses. He pauses for a few seconds before risking another peek.

Ahead of him is a watering-hole in which three adult warthogs are bathing. Two of them seem content to just wallow in the mud. The third, however – a large male missing its right upper tusk – is shaking its head energetically. The motion makes the sizeable warts on its face wobble disgustingly. It appears to be trying to shake a gob of mud out of its left ear.

The warthog pauses in its task. It turns, slowly but deliberately, to look straight at the clump of grass in which Bisckits is hiding.

Suddenly, before the *Ses* has time to react, the warthog is running right at him at full speed. Bisckits stumbles backwards, tripping over a tree root as he does so, and the beast is upon him. He cries out in panic.

Instead of trampling him, the warthog begins vigorously rocking Bisckits from side to side with its snout. As it buffets the terrified little Giraffeses back and forth, the beast begins to repeatedly call out his name. "Bisckits!... Bisckits!... Bisckits!..."

***

"Bisckits! Wake up!"

"Arrrrgh!" Bisckits cries... And immediately feels very foolish for doing so.

For the second time that morning he finds Jaspa standing over him, shaking him. The sky is lighter than it was the last time his eyes were open, with only the very brightest stars still visible.

"Finally," says his older brother. "I thought you'd gone into hibernation! Now get a move on. You've had another quarter of an hour, but fair's fair. I need some help if we're going to be ready by the time Uncle Mackee gets here."

"Oh! Come on, Jaspa! Just five more minutes?" Bisckits pleads, though without much conviction. "Uncle Mackee's probably still in bed, anyway."

"No such luck for you, young Giraffeses!" comes the response. But not from Jaspa.

***

The Lerai Forest gets its name from its yellow-barked acacia trees, which the Maasai call *Lerai*. They're also known by a more dramatic name – fever trees – because they were once thought to cause malaria. This misunderstanding stemmed largely from the fact that they commonly grow near swamps, the home of the real culprits, disease-spreading mosquitoes. It's ironic then, that the recent expansion of nearby swamps is actually killing the fever trees of Ngorongoro's Lerai Forest.

Mackee steps around one of the acacias and into the circle of the boys' campsite. Light and open here at its edge, the Lerai Forest has some of the feel of an English parkland. Of course, in England the trees are not normally fever trees, and they rarely have leopards and vervet monkeys lazing around in them!

"Morning Uncle," says Jaspa, greeting his uncle with a small wave.

Anyone who spends even a little time with Jaspa can't help but notice his fondness for this particular gesture. Indeed, his grandfather affectionately calls him *Young Waver*. Many of the *Herd* proudly proclaim Jaspa to be *wavier than the sea*, even though most of them have never even seen the sea!

"Morning Jaspa!" replies Mackee. "Good to see at least one of my nephews has some sense of responsibility." He turns to look down on his other nephew. "Now then, Bisckits," he says. "Since **I'm** clearly not still in bed, why is it that **you** are? Have you decided to make your own way home?"

A sudden, loud trumpeting shatters the pre-dawn silence, saving Bisckits the embarrassment of trying to invent an excuse for his tardiness. All three Giraffeses can't help but jump at the abrupt, deafening noise.

Their surprise is short-lived, however. For over the last fortnight they've become used to this early-morning alarm call. Indeed, they've actually come to look forward to the dawn chorus and, more to the point, what it heralds.

Unfortunately, the same cannot be said for the flock of superb starlings, brightly coloured relatives of European starlings, roosting in the trees at the edge of the forest. As happens every morning at this time, the startled birds erupt into the air in a confusion of flapping wings and annoyed whining. Even in the half-light, the metallic blues and greens and rusty oranges of their plumage are magnificent.

A series of replying trumpets answers the first, some closer, some slightly further off. Jaspa, Bisckits and Mackee peer southwards towards the source of the calls, waiting for what comes next. A few minutes pass before Mackee spies something through the gradually brightening daylight.

"There!" he whispers, pointing between the trees.

At first, Jaspa can only determine several grey blurs shuffling about in the pre-dawn mist. But the vague shapes waddle gradually closer as the minutes pass, until he can finally make them out clearly.

Elephants! Five of them.

The group approaches across the dew-laden grass as a loose bunch. It's a bachelor herd, comprised entirely of males, each boasting an impressive pair of tusks. Occasionally, one of them will pause to rip up a clump of grass with its trunk. The grass is then transferred to its mouth where it is ground up, thoughtfully, as the bull shambles forward to catch up with the rest of the group.

Every morning the elephants undertake this expedition, from the crater rim where they spend the night, down to the Lerai Forest. A couple of times Jaspa and Bisckits have followed them deeper into the forest and watched them feeding on tree bark, which they strip off in long sheets, not caring if the tree is living or dead. Whilst the elephants seem to find the bark quite delicious, the trees are clearly less happy about the situation. Those trees that survive repair their damaged areas by growing thick, gnarly wound tissue, which even the elephants find unappetising.

Of course, elephants are a familiar sight near the Shifting Sands, yet the Giraffeses of the *Herd* nonetheless believe them to be somehow special. They consider elephants to be peaceful and wise, whilst at the same time strong and determined. The *Herders* respect, admire and value all of these qualities. So although Jaspa and Bisckits have witnessed this passage almost every morning for the last two weeks, they're nonetheless spellbound.

Alas, time is pressing and the brothers aren't able to follow the elephants this morning. Instead, they sit with Mackee and quietly watch as the gentle giants slowly lumber past. Far too quickly, they're lost from sight amongst the trees.

***

Although Jaspa is excited about seeing his friends and family again, he's going to miss the camp that has been their home for the last fortnight and he feels more than a little sad to be leaving.

Even so, as they finish dismantling their campsite and finally set off, he can't help smiling at the sound of breaking wood from deep within the forest. It reminds him that, much to the annoyance of the fever trees, the elephants are enjoying their breakfast.

***

7. Chance encounters

Whilst *shifting* enables *Ses* to cover ground extremely quickly, it's also incredibly tiring. As a result, they usually only use it over relatively short distances. Consequently, the sunrise finds Jaspa, Bisckits and Mackee making their way through the eastern fringes of the Lerai Forest on foot, plodding along at a steady pace.

They're heading for a dirt track that skirts around the edge of the forest. A track normally reserved for the rangers who watch over Ngorongoro and its wildlife.

The rangers are a little like modern-day versions of the old Wild West sheriffs, bringing law and order to a wild and untamed place. Their mission is to protect the animals of Ngorongoro from poachers and ensure the thousands of people who visit each year do as little harm as possible.

***

The transition from woodland to grassland is fairly gradual, the trees progressively giving way to more open vistas. By the time they reach the road, the Giraffeses have left most of the trees behind.

Just beyond the road stands a lone, ancient fever tree. The tips of its spreading branches reach out for the slowly climbing sun, perhaps 50 or 60 feet above the ground. However, these flimsy uppermost twigs would undoubtedly prove far too fragile to support the weight of the imposing bird perching down amongst the tree's lower branches.

In the still-gathering dawn light, it's difficult to make out any details of colouring or markings. That said, the bird's silhouette is more than enough for a still-sleepy Bisckits, who jumps as he first notices its menacing presence.

It's a large bird. Standing over two and a half feet tall, it must weigh at least ten pounds, perhaps even more. The long, finger-like primary feathers at the tips of its immense, folded wings add to a general sense of shaggy heaviness. Its stout, un-feathered legs end in large, powerful feet, which possess wicked talons that tightly grip the branch on which it's balanced.

But it's the bird's neck and head that capture Bisckits' attention. The base of the neck is rooted in a large hump between its shoulders. From there it seems to flow forwards, almost horizontally, before rearing up and over into the head, which terminates in a vicious, hooked beak. The overall effect like a downy serpent, with a grotesquely deformed head, poised ready to strike.

Bisckits shudders. "I hate vultures," he declares with considerable feeling.

Jaspa tenses, as if about to disagree with his brother. Instead he takes a deep breath, releases it slowly, and visibly wills himself to relax. Whatever he was about to express goes unsaid.

"That's odd," says Mackee, unaware of the narrowly averted argument. "It's a Ruppell's Griffon vulture, one of the six types of vulture that call the Serengeti home. But Griffons normally roost up in the Gol Hills, not down here in the crater. I wonder what it's doing here."

"Perhaps it's sick. Or got lost. Yes! Sick and lost!" blurts out Jaspa.

The other two turn to look at him, both somewhat startled. "Er... Are you feeling alright?" asks a surprised Bisckits.

An uncomfortable expression crosses Jaspa's face, clearly indicating he's just as shocked by his little outburst as his companions. "Oh! Um. Yeah. Fine. ...Er... Sorry!"

Mackee gives his nephew a final curious look. "Oh well. No time to stand about here discussing the finer details of vulture behaviour!" he says, diplomatically changing the subject. "Let's step it out a bit, we've got a lot of ground to cover today."

***

Half an hour later finds the three Giraffeses marching steadily along the rangers' road. So far this morning they've had it more-or-less to themselves. They're aiming for a picnic site located half a mile or so south of where they've been camping. Despite the fact that Mackee is setting a brisk pace, even Bisckits is enjoying their early morning walk... Now that he's finally properly awake. And recovered from the shock of their encounter with the vulture.

It's over 25 miles, as the vulture flies, from the Lerai Forest to the Shifting Sands. For those confined to the ground – and as incredible as they are, Giraffeses can't fly! – the distance that must be travelled is much greater, since a number of obstacles have to be overcome along the way. Not least of these are the soaring walls of the crater rim itself.

With the earlier, uncomfortable incident apparently forgotten, Jaspa hums under his breath, bobbing his head from side to side in time with the imaginary music. He stares up at the mist clinging to the upper slopes of the crater wall. Its delicate whiteness contrasts sharply with the blackened scar that runs down the slope and out onto the plain, towards them.

During their first few days in the crater, occasional wisps of smoke had continued to rise from the scorched earth, a clear indication that the fire responsible had occurred very recently. Bisckits, being Bisckits, had gone on and on about how he wished they'd witnessed the blaze, and how unfair it was that they'd arrived just a day or so too late. A small part of Jaspa had agreed with him, but on the whole he'd been glad they'd missed it. Fires, whilst undeniably exciting to watch, can be extremely unpredictable, not to mention dangerous.

Now, only two weeks later, the bright green of new shoots is already softening the harsh black of the burnt ground. Fresh, succulent grass is replacing the dry, inedible vegetation that the fire destroyed.

It's amazing really, thinks Jaspa, *the way nature can turn a disaster to its advantage.*

Jaspa's musings are interrupted by Mackee's hand on his shoulder. He turns to face his uncle, who points back the way they have come. A swirl of dust announces that something is coming towards them along the road. At first Jaspa can hear nothing, but as the dust cloud gets bigger he catches the sound of an engine.

"We better get off the track," Mackee tells them.

***

They quickly move off the road, to shelter behind a clump of red oat grass. Several minutes go by before the approaching vehicle comes into view.

"They're rangers," says Mackee almost immediately.

"How can you tell?" asks Bisckits.

"Good question!" the older Giraffeses counters. "How **can** I tell?"

Bisckits thinks for a moment before answering. "Because it's a ranger road?"

"Good answer! The most obvious answer is usually the correct one," Mackee says. "But how **else** can I tell they're rangers?"

Bisckits looks blankly at his uncle for several seconds, before Jaspa nervously suggests, "Because there are only three people in that truck?"

"So..." Mackee prompts him.

"Well, the tourists are usually crammed in like termites in a termite mound."

"Precisely. Well done! Plus, I doubt the gates have been open long enough this morning for any tours to have reached this deep into the crater yet."

Three dirt roads join the crater floor to the outside world: the Seneto descent road down the western cliff, the Lerai ascent road up the southern wall and the two-way Sopa road on the eastern side. Each is barred by a gate at the crater rim, which is closed during the night.

"I knew all that!" blurts out Bisckits defensively, before adding more quietly, "I just needed a bit more time to figure it out."

Mackee laughs and puts his arm around his nephew's shoulders. "Don't be so touchy, young Bisckits," he says reassuringly. "No one was making fun of you."

"Well.... OK, then." mumbles Bisckits, feeling slightly embarrassed at his outburst.

***

Unexpectedly, the vehicle begins to slow down, gradually rolling to a halt right in front of the three very surprised Giraffeses. Once again, Mackee is the first to figure out what's happening.

It appears that whilst the Ses were distracted by the rangers' approach, a solitary black rhinoceros wandered out of the forest to take up residence a little further along the road. There it stands in the middle of the track. Immobile. A living, breathing, one and a half ton roadblock, looking as though it doesn't have a care in the world.

Actually, even though this animal doesn't realise it, nothing could be further from the truth. Rhinos are Africa's most endangered large mammals, brought to the edge of extinction by poachers, who kill them for their horns. The larger white rhino is already extinct in East Africa, although the black rhino is the rarer of the two worldwide.

Black rhinos have a reputation for being unpredictable and prone to charging, so even the rangers who protect them tend to keep their distance whenever possible. The three men in the truck talk quietly to each other, as they wait to see what the rhino will do next.

Until this moment, Mackee had been planning to walk to the picnic area and there stow away on one of the many tourist vehicles. Then it would just be a matter of waiting until their tour left the crater, probably that evening. Tomorrow morning, they would have to hitch another ride, this time heading for the Oldupai Gorge, and from there yet another to the Shifting Sands.

But here before them, literally, Mackee sees a chance to sidestep the walk to the picnic area[1] and perhaps even make it to the crater rim before midday. If they're **really** lucky, they might even get part of the way to Oldupai this side of nightfall.

Seizing the opportunity, Mackee grabs hold of his two charges and drags them urgently towards the stationary vehicle. "Come on you two!" he yells. "Quickly now!"

Not understanding the sudden need to rush, Jaspa and Bisckits are momentarily stunned by their uncle's newfound haste.

Then Jaspa cottons-on and, as if emerging from a trance, shouts to his brother, "Come on, Bisckits. Get a *shift* on!"

[1]   No pun intended!

A couple of seconds later, three figures un-*shift* behind the rangers' vehicle. Mackee, who is significantly taller than his nephews, stands below the rear bumper and cups his hands together.

"Right!" he says, looking at Bisckits. "You first!"

When the boys are safely perched up on the bumper, Mackee hauls himself up. He leans back against the rear door of the Land Rover, letting his legs dangle over the edge of the bumper.

"Phew!" he declares to the world, still trying to catch his breath. "That was fun!"

Several more minutes pass before they hear the crunch of gears and the truck begins to slowly move forward. Apparently, the rhino has decided the rangers are no threat and has ambled off the road, though in its own good time, of course.

Facing backwards as they are, the Giraffeses are unable to witness this. But as they pass the spot so recently vacated by the rhino, with their driver picking up speed, they're able to catch a final, rearwards glimpse of the beast. It's trotting towards the Gorigor Swamp, Ngorongoro's largest wetland where rhinos love to take mud baths, swinging its tail behind it.

***

8. A lucky break

The rangers and their unannounced passengers pass the picnic site without stopping and continue westwards. Mackee now expects the vehicle to make for the ranger post situated south of the Lerai Forest.

This is going to make it harder to get aboard a tourist truck out of the crater, he thinks, suddenly worried that hitching a lift on the rangers' vehicle is going to end up costing time rather than saving it.

As it turns out, Mackee needn't have worried. To his great delight, they turn left after only a short distance, away from the ranger station and onto the Lerai ascent road.

At first, the track crosses the level, grassy area between the forest and the crater wall, but it soon begins to climb. The sides of the crater are far too steep to drive straight up and so the road zigzags up the slope, regularly doubling-back on itself in tight, stomach-churning loops.

Driving up a winding switchback road whilst clinging to the rear bumper of a truck and breathing in lungful after lungful of dust choked air is unlikely to make it into Jaspa's list of top ten favourite things to do in the morning. Even so, the views across the crater, albeit glimpsed through the dust clouds kicked up by the vehicle's rugged tyres, are breathtaking all the same. Although with the suffocating dust, Jaspa doesn't have too much breath left to take!

Through the scrub and grasses growing alongside the dirt road, Jaspa can now see out over the crater floor to the Lerai Forest. To the right of the trees he spots the ranger road skirting the forest, where less than an hour ago they'd seen the rhino. Down amongst the acacias, somewhere near that track, is the small clearing they've called home for the last two weeks.

Between the Lerai Forest and the northern sweep of Ngorongoro's cliffs is the stunningly beautiful Lake Magadi, an enormous silver mirror, reflecting the blue, cloud-dotted sky above. Beyond it, Jaspa can make out the dark green wall of the crater's opposite side and, rising another 560 feet above that, the forested southern slopes of another of the Crater Highlands' dead volcanic peaks, Mount Olmoti. Though covering a much smaller area than its giant neighbour, the summit of Mount Olmoti still reaches an altitude of about 10,160 feet. Think about it... That's almost two miles above the sea!

The waters of Lake Magadi are highly alkaline making them inhospitable to most forms of life, although no one seems to have told this to the flock of lesser and greater flamingos, which stains the eastern end of the silver-blue lake pink! The birds' pink colour comes from carotene, a substance present in the algae they feed on... and also in carrots. As Jaspa watches, the entire gathering suddenly takes to the wing, appearing almost to act as a single, complex creature.

Something must have spooked them, he thinks.

The birds circle once... Twice... Before returning to the shallow water at the lake's edge in a multitude of gentle splashes, the reason for their alarm apparently already forgotten.

***

At the top of the ascent road, the rangers once more turn westward and Mackee is sure they must be heading for their nearby headquarters. But luck is again with the three stowaways, as the Land Rover continues along the road following the crater lip clockwise.

Much of the time, the track actually runs just back from the crater's edge, so that the enormous basin itself is hidden from view. Looking south, down the steep wooded fall of Ngorongoro's outer slope, Jaspa can see yet another extinct volcano, Mount Oldeani. Beyond that, the land falls away towards the great scar of the Rift Valley, until the distance is swallowed up in the early morning haze.

The Crater Highlands, and the escarpment to the east, are only a tiny part of the African Rift Valley system, a 4000 mile long rip in the World, running down the east side of Africa from Lebanon to Mozambique. During the last 40 million years, this complex network of enormous parallel cracks in the Earth's crust, which geologists call *faults*, has been pulled apart by unimaginable geological forces. The land between the faults has sunk, to form the steep-sided, flat-bottomed African Rift Valley, which is between 25 and 250 miles wide, several thousand feet deep in places and, incidentally, the only geological feature on Earth visible from the surface of the Moon!

***

The Shifting Sands attract a steady, if modest, stream of tourists, so Jaspa and Bisckits are familiar enough with humans. Yet neither is prepared for what confronts them as they continue their dusty, bumpy trip around the southwestern segment of the crater rim. They stare open-mouthed – which proves a bad idea, given the dust – at the succession of lodges, campsites and other buildings huddled next to the road.

"I never knew there were this many people in all the World!" exclaims Jaspa.

Mackee laughs at his nephew's innocence. "I don't mean to shock you," he says, "But these are just places where a handful of the lucky ones come on holiday. Perhaps a few hundred at a time. Some of their cities, on the other hand, are home to **millions**."

"What's a hodilay?" asks Bisckits, not properly understanding.

"It's a...." Mackee begins.

"And what are cities?"

"A city is..."

"And how much is *millions*?"

"Whoa!" cries Mackee with a chuckle. "Give me a chance!"

"Er, sorry," says Bisckits.

"Apology accepted," says Mackee, bowing his head slightly towards Bisckits. "Right, ...um... Imagine how many termites there are in a really big termite mound. Well, a *million* would be a very useful number to know if you wanted to count them."

Termites are similar in size and appearance to ants, even though the two are unrelated. Like ants, termites also live in large colonies.

Many species construct towering mounds out of mud, glued together by their saliva, which in the Serengeti can be home to over a million insects.

"Come to think of it," Mackee adds, "A *city* is a bit like a termite mound, except it's for humans, of course. And the biggest cities can have **tens** of millions of people living in them."

Jaspa shudders.

"Finally," their uncle continues, "A *holiday* – not hodilay – is where humans go away from where they normally live for a short time."

The brothers stare at their uncle, appalled.

"Why would so many people want to live in the same place?" asks Jaspa, disbelievingly. "And if they managed to escape on one of these *holidays*, why on Earth would they go back again?"

"Hard to say," Mackee admits. "Humans are just strange, I guess."

"Or stupid," suggests Bisckits with conviction.

***

Following the curve of the crater's edge, the road gradually turns north, leaving behind the horrors of the human constructions as it does so. At Windy Gap, on Ngorongoro's western side near the top of the Seneto descent road, the rangers stop for a few minutes to talk to a group of tourists who are about to make an expedition down to the crater floor.

Covered with dust, inside and out, Jaspa is grateful for the brief pause.

Bisckits is clearly exhausted by the effort of holding on, and the gentle vibration of the still-running engine rocks him to sleep almost immediately. His head tips forward onto his chest and the little Giraffeses is snoring within a matter of seconds.

Jaspa is also shattered, but still can't resist the opportunity to gaze down on the mighty Ngorongoro Crater one last time.

***

The world explodes into a jarring, deafening, suffocating nightmare! Jaspa topples over against Bisckits, and only then realises they're moving again.

I must have fallen asleep too, he thinks.

Bisckits is again clenching his teeth, gripping on with all his strength. He looks at Jaspa, plainly far from happy, but says nothing. On Bisckits' other side, Mackee sits with head back against the truck's rear door, eyes closed, holding on determinedly.

Yet again, their vehicle travels more-or-less west, but now they're heading down the flank of Ngorongoro. To the south are two more of the peaks that make up the Crater Highlands, Mount Lemakarot and the even more oddly named Satiman Elgon. Below them, the Short Grass Plains of the Serengeti spread out into the distance, although Jaspa can't see this from his uncomfortable, rearward-looking vantage point.

In fact, Jaspa finds it difficult to see anything, since his eyes are apparently trying to jiggle their way out of their sockets. The Land Rover hurtles down the mountain, seemingly colliding with every rut and boulder the driver can spot. Nevertheless, even through blurred vision, the dark silhouette of the crater stands out starkly as a retreating, rising, horizontal line against the bright blue, early morning sky.

***

The journey down the mountainside seems to take forever, but they eventually reach Ngorongoro's lower slopes. As the road begins to level off, the buffeting becomes less intense and Jaspa is able to do something other than simply hold on for dear life. He looks around and spies a *boma*, a traditional Maasai village, set slightly back from the road off to his left.

A few minutes later the track comes to one of the many seasonal streams that reappear in the Serengeti each wet season. In the dry months, such streambeds are parched and empty, thin stony stripes crisscrossing the landscape like the ghosts of rivers. But at this time of year, vehicles must cross such temporary watercourses via drifts. 'Drift' is the local name for a ford, where a road passes straight *through* a river, crossing it without the aid of a bridge.

The passing of the Land Rover causes water to shoot sideways, as it rushes to evade the vehicle's chunky tyres. That stream water which fails to escape the wheels is sprayed high into the air behind them, blissfully drenching the three dust-coated Giraffeses leaning against the tailgate.

The next part of their ride proves to be relatively restful, especially compared to the alarm and discomfort of the drive down the side of Ngorongoro. The river they've just crossed flows into a wide, flat-bottomed valley, which is enclosed by steep sides and virtually blocked by the Olbalbal swamp a handful of miles downstream. The track follows the left bank of the watercourse for a while, before veering away from it to hug the steep headwall of the valley. After a couple more miles they reach a second stream, splash across it, and then zigzag up the far valley side to emerge on a wide plain.

***

Their unwitting transport sets out northwest across the plain. After one or two more miles, they come to a fork in the road and the driver bears right. Perhaps 20 minutes later they approach a small cluster of buildings, seemingly built in the middle of the plain. The rangers ignore the buildings, instead following the track that swings around behind them.

"Hold on!" shouts Mackee, and his two charges instinctively clutch more tightly to the bumper they're sitting on.

Almost immediately, the truck plunges over the edge of a chasm and down the precipitous slope beyond. Something cool and logical in the back of Jaspa's head informs him that this terrifying headlong tumble towards the centre of the Earth means they've reached the Oldupai Gorge.

The dirt track weaves back and forth across the steep face of the ravine. Jaspa grips the bumper so tightly his fingers are threatening to leave tiny dents in the metal. The small, familiar, rational part of Jaspa's brain – which the rest of Jaspa is finding increasingly annoying – smugly informs him that his body is screaming like a banshee.[1]

Just then, Bisckits loses his grip and starts to slide off the bumper. Thankfully, Mackee manages to grab him at the very last instant and hauls him back to safety.

***

To Jaspa's relief, and Bisckits' great surprise, they finally reach the base of the slope without further incident or major injury. As the

---

[1] A banshee is a female (ban) Sidhe (shee) who haunts a long-established family, wailing loudly and terrifyingly when one of them is about to die!

vehicle slowly splashes through the river flowing through the bottom of the gorge, Mackee turns to them.

"OK," he announces. "This is our stop! When we get to the other side of the river we're going to jump for it."

Jaspa and Bisckits both look at him wearing their best *you've got to be joking* expressions.

"Come on boys!" Mackee encourages them. "It'll be fun!"

"Easy for you to say," exclaims Bisckits. "You're five times bigger than we are!"

"You'll be fine," says Mackee reassuringly. "Just aim for a patch of grass and don't forget to roll when you land! Now, don't think about it just...

"...JUMP!"

***

9. The Oldupai Gorge

Jaspa looks up at the cloudy sky and the bright orange rain. Everything feels kind of fuzzy. Vague. Wrong.

The calm part of his brain is trying to get his attention again, although it's becoming increasingly frustrated, because the rest of him is too distracted to listen. Orange rain! Now, that can't be right.

They're petals.

"Sorry?" says Jaspa.

It's not rain, they're petals.

"Petals?" asks Jaspa

Aloe petals, to be more precise.

"Oh."

You're lying under an Aloe plant.

"Oh."

You knocked its petals off when you crashed into it.

"Oh." says Jaspa absent-mindedly. "Er... Who are you?"

I'm you.

"Me?"

You.

"So, I'm talking to myself?" asks Jaspa, starting to worry a little.

Yes... And no.

"Care to explain that?" says Jaspa. The speaker is beginning to get on his nerves.

And then it comes to him. "Oh! I get it! You're the voice I hear in my head whenever I'm scared or worried."

Exactly.

"Oh."

You say 'Oh' too much. The voice sounds irritated.

"Oh. Er... Sorry!" apologises Jaspa. "Wow. This is well weird!"

Not really. Everyone locks away a small part of their mind to do the thinking when the rest of them is too frightened or pre-occupied. Most people just don't realise they're doing it.

"Oh... I mean... Er... Oh."

Silence.

"So, um, were you trying to tell me something, then?" asks Jaspa, trying to fill the awkward pause.

Yes. The voice now seems exasperated.

"Er... What was it?"

You can't breathe.

"Can't I?" asks Jaspa curiously.

No.

"Oh... Why not?"

Because Bisckits is lying on you.

"Oh. Is he?"

YES!

"Oh!" says Jaspa.

***

Jaspa tries to take a breath, but can't. Something heavy is squashing his chest. Tiny fireworks explode inside his bulging eyes. Then the words of the voice come back to him.

With a great effort he heaves Bisckits off his upper body and sucks in a two marvellous lungs-full of air. The dust in the air makes him cough, but he breathes in again. And again.

Bliss!

Finally, his breathing begins to become more regular and Jaspa lies back on the ground. Tilting his head to one side, he looks at Bisckits, who's groaning.

"You alright?" Jaspa asks between breaths

"Just winded." Bisckits replies, holding his stomach. "Give me a minute."

"Uncle Mackee?" Jaspa calls.

"Over here."

Jaspa lifts his head up and looks around for his uncle.

Mackee is getting to his feet a few feet away, brushing the dust off himself as he does so. He walks over to the brothers, wearing a concerned expression. "Are you both alright?"

"I think so," says Jaspa.

Mackee lets out an explosive breath and collapses back down, next to Jaspa. "I guess that wasn't such a great idea, after all," he confesses with an awkward grin.

***

It takes the three of them several minutes to recover. Surprisingly, it's Bisckits who stirs first. "Where are we?" he asks.

"The Oldupai Gorge, I think," replies Jaspa, also sitting up.

"That's right," confirms Mackee. "That's the museum up there."

The brothers look up at where Mackee is pointing. The museum is the same small cluster of buildings they had driven around just before this latest misadventure began. To anyone approaching them along the road from Ngorongoro, they appear to be in the middle of a relatively unremarkable stretch of the Serengeti Plains.

From this angle, however, the buildings perch precariously on the very edge of a deep, steep-sided ravine... The Oldupai Gorge, a 30 mile long, 300 feet deep wound that cuts across and into the southeastern Serengeti Plains, passing within one and a quarter miles of the Shifting Sands.

Across the river from where the three Giraffeses are recovering, the side of the gorge climbs sharply up to the museum at its crest. In places, Jaspa can see where reddish-brown vertical cliffs, which are covered with horizontal stripes, break up the steep slope.

To Jaspa, the setting has a strong feeling of heavy permanence. Unchanged and unchangeable, since the dawn of time. But he couldn't be more wrong. The entire landscape is none of these things. Geologically speaking, it came into being relatively recently... Born in a melting pot of fire and water. Although, since the Earth is over four and a half **billion** (4,500,000,000) years old, pretty much everything is *relatively recent*, geologically speaking!

Over the last four million years, the volcanoes of the nearby Crater Highlands have periodically belched ash across the whole Serengeti, repeatedly turning the plains into a dust-covered wasteland. Fortunately, the rains that followed each trial by fire, transformed the resultant desert into a fertile, green oasis. Furthermore, about two million years ago the entire area around the present Oldupai Gorge was a huge alkaline lake.

The stripes Jaspa is admiring were created when these seemingly unrelated events collided. For they are actually layers of lake sediment – all the stuff that gradually collected at the bottom of the lake, such as sands, silts, clays and the remains of dead plants and animals – sandwiched between sheets of volcanic ash, blasted out of the Crater Highlands' volcanoes during a particularly violent and fiery episode in their history.

Eventually the lake drained, and ever since the Oldupai River has been cutting down through the sediment and ash layers, producing the current gorge and revealing two million years of geological history in the process. In the meantime, water has eaten away at the exposed cliffs and slopes, scoring them with a multitude of gullies and fissures. However, much of the removed material didn't make it very far, collecting directly below these gullies, as a string of cone- or bell-shaped piles of earth and debris along the valley sides.

***

Jaspa can't help noticing there's far more vegetation down here within the gorge than up on the plain above. The slopes and debris cones are covered with plant life. Aloe, like the one he's sitting under, stand out because of their bright orange flowers, but acacias and grasses are also plentiful. And then there's the wild sisal the Maasai call *Oldupai*, a pointy-leaved plant that's so common here the tribe named the gorge after it. For many years, the gorge was mistakenly known it as 'Olduvai', thanks to an early European misspelling of the Maasai name.

"What's a *museum*?" asks Bisckits.

"Weeell," says Mackee, thoughtfully. "Usually it's a building full of old things. Although not always. I suppose you might say it's where humans put things they think other humans will be interested in seeing."

"This seems like a bit of an odd place to put one of these museum things," says Bisckits, screwing his nose up. "There's nothing here! Certainly nothing old, anyway."

"Ah!" replies Mackee. "That's where you'd be *very* wrong!"

Jaspa smiles quietly to himself. He's heard this story before.

"Many, many, **many** years ago, long before Giraffeses found the Shifting Sands, other creatures lived here. They lived here and they died here. But when they died, echoes of their lives remained. These *memories* were locked away in their decaying bodies and, sometimes, in the belongings and other things they left behind."

Mackee's enthusiasm is contagious and Bisckits sits statue-like, a fascinated picture of concentration. Jaspa, familiar as he is with the story, is nonetheless captivated by his uncle's obvious passion for the tale.

In fact, it almost feels as if Oldupai itself is listening. Remembering its own past and those who once called it home. Recalling a time before there was even a gorge. A time of shallow alkaline waters and ash raining from the sky. A time when clouds in the east glowed red in the reflected light of erupting volcanoes.

"Now about a hundred years ago, a human called Wilhelm Kattwinkel came to Oldupai looking for butterflies. Instead he found the ancient remains, or fossils, of these creatures. Since then lots of humans have spent decades digging in the Oldupai dirt, most famously Louis and Mary Leakey.

"Some of the fossils they've found are of animals still alive today, like... oh, I don't know... um... crocodiles, hippos, tortoises, hares. All sorts of things... It's a long list.

"But other, far stranger beasts have also been unearthed. Some of them could have come straight from a fairytale... Like the ferocious sabre-toothed cat,[1] a bizarre three-toed horse called 'Hipparion', a strange hippo whose eyes stood out on stalks, and a fantastic elephant called 'Deinothere', which had downward-curving tusks growing out of its lower jaw."[2]

---

[1] Sabre-toothed cats are most definitely not tigers!

[2] Honestly, the remains of all these real animals have been discovered at the Oldupai Gorge.

Bisckits looks around nervously, causing Mackee to grin slightly as he continues, "All these animals lived here, once upon a time. Although, they're all extinct now, of course."

"Of course!" repeats Bisckits, just a little too quickly. "Extinct! Of course! I knew that..." His voice trails off into silence, but the rest of him relaxes noticeably.

Mackee smiles at his younger nephew, then gives Jaspa a wink, before picking up the tale once more. "Now, as remarkable as these creatures may be, they're not the real reason people keep coming back to Oldupai.

"You see, most humans are far more interested in themselves than in, well, just about anything else! That's why they consider the Oldupai Gorge to be one of **the** most important places in the world. Because here they've discovered evidence of some of their earliest relatives. They've found their ancestors' bones, tools they made out of stone, and even traces of their homes. They get quite excited about it all!"

In fact, the bones of **four** different types of hominid – the scientific term for humans and their closest relatives – have been found at Oldupai. The oldest are 1.8 million years old. The youngest, a measly 17,000 years old, are of a creature called *Homo sapiens...* The scientific name for you and me.

"I remember when I was a young Giraffeses," Mackee continues. "Not much older than you two are now, I suppose. We heard that Mary Leakey had found some incredibly old footprints down at Laetoli, near the edge of the escarpment above Lake Eyasi. If you can believe it, these footprints were twice as old as any of the remains found here at Oldupai. The humans got so worked up about it that your father and I decided we wanted to see them for ourselves!

"Laetoli's only about 25 miles south of here, but it took us a week to get there. Mind you, it was worth it. The tracks stretched for perhaps a hundred feet and we could see, clear as day, where two people had walked across the plain, with a third following in the footprints left by the biggest of the first two.

"The footprints looked so fresh, like they'd been made just a day or two earlier. I was amazed when I later learned they'd been made by early humans a staggering 3.6 million years ago. I still find it hard to believe they were already ancient when Ngorongoro blew its top! No wonder human scientists sometimes call this region the *Cradle of Mankind.*

"But the most important and interesting discovery made at Oldupai is largely overlooked by most humans, of course," sighs Mackee, changing topic slightly and shaking his head sadly. "They're too wrapped up in their own affairs. Most of them haven't even heard of a Sivatherium!" The Giraffeses' tone clearly reveals he considers this to be an unfathomable oversight.

Unwilling to admit to Uncle Mackee that **he's** never heard of one either, Bisckits nudges Jaspa in the ribs. "What's *silver hairy bum?*" he hisses.

Jaspa clasps his hand over his mouth, stifling his giggles. "A *Sivatherium*, not a *silver hairy bum*, cloth ears!"

"Whatever!" says Bisckits, going red. "So Mr Smarty-Giraffeses, what is one, anyway?"

"Sorry," says Jaspa. "Um, it's an extinct type of giant giraffe. Except it looked more like an antelope, I think. It had stocky legs, a short neck and great big hand-shaped horns." He places his hands on his head to imitate antlers, and wiggles his fingers making his brother laugh.

"Cooool!" says an impressed Bisckits.

Sivatherium really is a kind of extinct giant giraffe, which looked much like Jaspa describes it. They're thought to have lived between two million and six thousand years ago, possibly surviving until even more recently.

***

"Right!" says Mackee, standing up. "We've been especially lucky today and we've made brilliant time so far, but we can't sit around here all day telling stories. The Shifting Sands are still four miles or more away, so we'd better get a move on if we want to make it home before nightfall."

As Jaspa and Bisckits get to their feet, a voice behind them suddenly calls, "At last! I was beginning to think you were going to sit there all day, blathering on like three old men!"

The *three old men* swivel round as one, looking for whoever is taunting them. But there appears to be no one there.

Maybe 20 feet further up the slope, a handful of tourists are standing next to a parked truck listening to a woman talking. It seems Mackee isn't the only one telling stories about the Oldupai Gorge this morning. Other than that there's not a living soul in sight.

The boys look at Mackee questioningly, but he can only shrug, equally bewildered.

"Good grief!" the mysterious, yet oddly familiar, voice says. "Do you want a lift or not? At this rate, these tourists will have left before you've made up your minds. And then you'll find yourselves **walking** back to the Shifting Sands!"

Mackee and his two nephews look back at truck and for the first time notice the small, smiling figure perched atop the spare wheel.

"Portia!" they gasp in unison.

***

Mackee drops to his knees as Portia jumps down off the vehicle and practically flies into her father's waiting arms.

After a long, long time, he gently pushes her backwards, until they are as far apart as possible with her right hand still tightly clasped in his left. "Let's have a look at you," he says, his voice sounding slightly gruff through his emotion.

Portia stands with her weight on one leg and her left hand held behind her back, looking up into the joyful face of her still-kneeling father, smiling shyly back at him.

Mackee gazes at his daughter for several seconds. "You've grown," he finally sniffs, his eyes glassy with unshed tears.

"That's what you always say." Portia teases tenderly. Then she holds him to her once more and whispers, "I've missed you!"

"I've missed you too, darling."

Eventually she looks up at her cousins, who've been hanging back, content to allow father and daughter this special moment together. "Are you two just going to stand there, or what?" Portia demands. "Don't I even get a hug?"

***

Portia embraces Bisckits first, before stepping back and ruffling his mane. "How's the aim, Bizzee?" she enquires. Portia has called her little, hyperactive cousin 'Bizzee Bisckits' for as long as they can all remember. "Still practicing with those mud balls?"

Bisckits grins broadly. "Go and ask the warthogs down in the Crater!" he boasts.

Then, at long last, Portia turns to Jaspa. "And how have you been, Waver?" she asks, giving him a great big Bearses hug.

"Pretty good," he replies. "Pretty good. All the better for seeing you again, though!"

"It's great to see you too, Waver. It's great to see all of you! I've been waiting for..."

But they never find out how long Portia had been waiting for.

Because, completely out of the blue, she's abruptly interrupted by an unexpected and agonised wail from Mackee. Jaspa and Bisckits look up in alarm. And are shocked to discover their uncle is crying. **Really** crying. His tears of joy from only a moment ago have been replaced by real, pain-drenched tears of pure dismay.

Suddenly looking much, **much** older, Mackee gingerly takes hold of his daughter's left wrist, lifting it towards his tear-soaked face.

"Portia!" he cries. "What happened to your poor hand?"

Jaspa immediately looks down at Portia's left hand. The hand Mackee is lovingly cradling in his own. The hand, Jaspa suddenly realises in horror, which is missing two fingers!

***

10. Confessions

Later that evening Jaspa and Portia sit side-by-side atop the eastern dune of the Shifting Sands. A short while earlier they had climbed the dune, talking excitedly about the last ten months. Now they sit in silence, each engrossed in their own thoughts, both staring unseeingly at the sun as it begins its daily descent towards the western horizon.

A deep rumbling brings Jaspa back to the here-and-now. He has a passing sensation of being slightly cross-eyed, before he finally manages to focus his eyes on something.

There, directly in front of them, is the source of the noise he just heard. An enormous thunderstorm, towering above the grasslands like a mountain ripped free and floating above the Earth. The shadow-darkened base of the storm seems to hug the plain, supported by the pillars of rain pouring from it. The *cumulonimbus* cloud above – as scientists would call it – builds in vast, white, sun-drenched billows. Higher, ever higher, until its top is perhaps six or seven miles above the plain. Up there, high-level winds tear at a storm's top, drawing it out eastwards like someone pulling on candyfloss, to produce the distinctive anvil shape. The arc of a rainbow and an occasional fork of lightning appear to anchor the entire monstrous structure to the land beneath.

With a deep breath, Jaspa takes the plunge and broaches the subject that has remained tactfully unmentioned until this moment. "So." he asks quietly, "How did you hurt your hand?"

Mackee had been so distraught at the sight of Portia's disfigured hand that, without a word passing between them, Jaspa and Bisckits had given the others as much space as possible on the drive back to the Shifting Sands. Once they were safely inside the truck, Portia had gently led the stunned Mackee to a quiet spot beneath a seat at the rear. There, father and daughter had talked quietly and intensely, their heads close together.

The two brothers had settled themselves in a corner on the other side of the vehicle. Neither of them had attempted to overhear the conversation between their uncle and cousin. But from their body language it was clear that Portia was comforting her father and not the other way around.

At first Jaspa had found this strange. Yet as they rattled along the dirt road towards home, he had realised that, judging from the healed look of Portia's hand, she'd had several months to get used to the missing digits, whereas Mackee's emotional wounds were fresh and raw.

Gradually, Mackee's tears had subsided and eventually Portia had motioned her cousins to join them. The subsequent conversation had remained casual and slightly brittle, as each of them carefully avoided any further reference to Portia's damaged hand.

"It was ridiculous really," begins Portia, after a short pause. "I came through so many dangers on the *Journey* without so much as a scratch. I crossed rivers so full of crocodiles you could hardly see the water. One time, I even had the wildebeest I was riding ripped out from underneath me by a lion, for goodness sake."

"And this?" She held up her hand and looked at the space where her fingers should have been. "I did this collecting firewood!"

"What?" exclaims Jaspa. "Did you hit your hand with and axe or something?" Many aspects of daily *Ses* life are very similar to our own, including their use of tools.

"Ha!" Portia snorts in something approaching disgust. "Nothing so dramatic, I'm afraid. Well, not in the way you mean, anyway.

"No, I was just gathering loose sticks and my mind wandered from the task at hand. Wandered a bit **too** far as it turns out. Without realising it, I grabbed a branch... Which actually turned out to be a snake. It bit me on the hand, one fang in each of these." She flexes the knuckles where her missing fingers would have met her hand, making Jaspa feel a little queasy.

"By the following morning they were completely numb. The day after that I passed out. And when I woke up, several days later, my left hand was short two fingers!"

"I don't get it," confesses Jaspa.

"Well, it seems they got infected, or the poison started to... well... do whatever poison does. I don't really know myself. And to be honest, *why* doesn't seem so important anymore.

"The fact of the matter is, my fingers had to be amputated. Apparently it was either them or me!" Portia stops and considers this for a moment. "Hey! That does sound pretty dramatic after all, doesn't it?" she adds with a grin.

"Anyway, I'm told Tabora, our Gnuses guide, did it himself," Portia concludes with a touch of pride.

Jaspa looks horrified. "Didn't it hurt?"

"Not at the time. As I said, first they went numb and then I was unconscious. Of course, it hurt like nobody's-business for a week or two after I woke up.

"But do you know what the strangest thing was?" Portia asks.

Jaspa shakes his head, eyes wide.

"My **hand**... the bit I still have... **never** hurt. All the pain seemed to be in my fingers, even though they were gone. To be honest, even now it sometimes feels like they're still there. Weird, huh?"

"Weird!" agrees Jaspa.

They both consider Portia's phantom fingers for several moments. "Anyway, that was almost eight months ago. Most of the time I hardly even notice they're not there anymore."

"Really?" enquires Jaspa, curious despite himself.

"Really!" Portia responds firmly. Then she seems to reconsider this for a moment before adding with a smile, "Of course... It makes counting **much** harder!"

And with that the matter is closed.

***

From their vantage point up on the dune, Jaspa and Portia can see at least six storms cells slowly scything their way across the Short

Grass Plains. An unstoppable line of soaking ferocity, relentlessly heading in their direction.

Every few seconds, one or other of the storms glows briefly from within, like an immense light bulb, evidence of the gargantuan forces raging inside it. The overall effect is like a string of very big – no... make that *gargantuan* again – like a string of gargantuan Christmas tree lights, twinkling above the never-ending plains and the multitude of animals that have congregated on them. Although Jaspa's never seen Christmas tree lights, of course. Or even heard of Christmas, for that matter.

Throughout the dry season, the plains of the southern Serengeti are dry, dusty and virtually deserted. There's almost no water to be found at the surface, and those animals that do remain must be able to survive on what little moisture they can obtain from their food. Giraffes, incidentally, are one of the Short Grass Plains' most conspicuous dry season inhabitants, which is perhaps a clue to why the *Herd* settled at the Shifting Sands in the first place.

The coming of the rains brings about a miraculous change, as sun-baked, dried-out grasses give way to fresh, tasty, green shoots. News of this grazer's banquet travels fast, and the Short Grass Plains soon become the temporary home of immense herds. From up here on their dune, Jaspa and Portia can only see a fraction of the total herds, yet they still stretch from horizon to horizon, literally as far as the eye can see.

First and foremost among the herds are the wildebeest. Over one and a quarter million of them! Wildebeest, which are also known as white-bearded gnus, are actually a type of antelope, although they look more like long-legged, dark grey, curly-horned cows. . with beards! Some people have claimed that they either *look like they were assembled by committee* or that they were *the last animals to be made, using the bits left over after all the others were finished.*

Accompanying the wildebeest hordes are roughly 200,000 Burchell's zebra and about a quarter of a million Grant's and Thompson's gazelles. Told you the herds were immense. Or perhaps that should be *gargantuan*, since that's already almost two million animals accounted for! And that doesn't even include the whole host of other herbivores that tag along.

And following this walking larder come the predators, hungry for meat and intent on turning the feasters into the feast!

The unimaginable mass of herbivores spends the wet season milling around the area northwest of the Shifting Sands, all the while feeding on the lush grasses. If the thunderstorms are like the lights on a Christmas tree, then the endless herds are like the presents beneath it. OK. . So they're furry, four-legged presents, and with no wrapping paper, but you get the idea.

It's during this time of plenty that most wildebeest calves are born, the seasonal fertility of the Short Grass Plains ensuring the new mothers have an endless supply of nutrient-rich grass from which to make milk. Calves can walk within seven minutes, but unfortunately nature isn't always cute and cuddly, and the newborns are still easy pickings for the predators. Happily, the synchronised birth of about 400,000 calves between late January and mid March means plenty survive, even after the hunters have had their fill.

***

Portia is a little taller than Jaspa and her coat is somewhat browner than his, less yellowish. In the few short hours since their reunion, Jaspa has noticed that his cousin **has** grown during her time away from the *Herd*, but in a way that has nothing to do with inches. It's more like the *Journey* has given her a confidence and maturity that wasn't there before... A fact clearly reflected in the way adult *Herders* are already treating her differently. Jaspa wonders how much the ordeal with her fingers played a part in shaping this new-and-improved Portia.

Out loud he says, "Tell me more about your *Journey*. What was it like?"

"It was amazing! I loved every minute of it!" Then Portia gestures to her left hand, "Well, almost every minute.

"Oh! But you should have been there, Waver!" she declares wistfully, caught up in the memories she wished Jaspa could have shared.

Then Portia sees a look of anguish flash across Jaspa's face and silently scolds herself for being so thoughtless. After all, by rights he **should** have been there.

Instead, Jaspa had remained behind last year, keeping the promise made to his mother, her Aunt Sofee, shortly before she died. It must have been so hard for him to watch her and the others begin their *Journey*. What should have been Jaspa's *Journey*, too. Portia knew it had been horrible for her to have to leave without him, but it must have been so much worse for Jaspa.

As you already know, there were no other Giraffeses born to the *Herd* in the same year as Bisckits. Thus it had always been known he would one day have to undertake the *Journey* on his own. This had caused his parents no end of concern, especially given Bisckits' somewhat impetuous nature. And so, as Portia's Aunt Sofee lay dying, Jaspa had promised her he would delay his own *Journey* by a year, and thereby accompany his little brother.

That was four years ago.

When the time came for the *Journeyers* to leave last year, Bisckits had begged Jaspa to go. But Jaspa – big-hearted, selfless, noble Jaspa – had refused to break the promise he made to his mother and so had watched Portia and the others leave without him.

"Oh, Waver! I'm sorry!" Portia apologises. "That was so insensitive of me."

"Don't worry," replies Jaspa. "It wasn't your fault. I mean, I won't say I wasn't disappointed, but I made a promise and..." His voice trails off.

***

There's another flash of lightning and, a few seconds later, a rumble of thunder punctuates the silence. During the wet season, thunderstorms occur almost every evening. Still, it's been three days since the last one, which leads Jaspa to think the rains may be coming to an end early this year.

Jaspa sighs heavily. For him and Bisckits the end of the rains will signal much more than just the start of another dry season. It will also announce the time has come for them to once more leave the Shifting Sands. To set out on **their** *Journey*.

"Do you know what bothers me more than anything else?" he asks Portia suddenly.

She looks at him questioningly, but says nothing.

"I'll tell you what..." Jaspa says, raising his voice slightly. "Everyone knows that most *Herders* go on the *Journey* because it's tradition. Because they're expected to. Not because they truly want to."

Portia nods her agreement.

"But you know as well as anyone that I've always looked forward to mine. I've always **wanted** to go!

"Everyone said it was only one more year to wait... But... But I still was so disappointed I couldn't go with you and the others last year..." It's as if a dam has burst inside Jaspa and all the frustration he's bottled up inside himself comes flooding out in an unstoppable stream of words.

"And now it looks like the rains will end early, so I won't even have to wait that full year... But now you're back and... And you were hurt and... And I've missed you and..." The torrent fuelling Jaspa's outburst has run its course and his words peter out. "...And..." With an effort he quietly finishes his thought, "...And I can't say goodbye to you again... Not already... I just can't!"

Not knowing what to say, Portia places her good hand to Jaspa's face. "You'll be fine, Waver," she manages to say, but the words sound hollow even to her. "At least you'll be with Bisckits," she tries again. "I've had to put up with Parree for the last ten months!"

Jaspa sniffs and, with a great effort, smiles. "Say! Perhaps they'll make you *Rubani* this year, and the three of us will at least get a couple more weeks together."

"I wish," says Portia wistfully. "But we've all known for years that Frankee's going to get that honour."

"Yeah." agrees Jaspa in a resigned tone. "I guess you're right." And the pair of them slip back into gloomy silence.

***

Lightning flashes beneath the storm directly in front of them and Jaspa, taking control of himself once more, begins to steadily count out loud, "One Giraffeses. Two Giraffeses. Three Giraffeses. Four Giraffeses. Five Giraffeses. Six Giraffeses. Seven Giraffeses. Eight Gira..."

A deafening thunderclap explodes all around them, so loud it dislodges a few sand grains from the crest of the dune. They tumble down the dune's steep side, bumping into more along the way, creating a mini avalanche.

"What are you doing?" Portia shouts above the continuing rumble.

"I got to seven and a half Giraffeses." Jaspa calls back.

"So?"

"Oh! Well, you can tell roughly how far away a thunderstorm is by waiting for a lightning flash and then counting Giraffeses," explains Jaspa in a more normal voice, as the thunder's grumbling dies away.

Portia looks at him doubtfully. "Giraffeses?"

"Yeah," laughs Jaspa. "You're actually counting seconds, but most people count too fast. So I count Giraffeses instead, because it takes about a second to say 'One Giraffeses' out loud," he explains. "Besides, it's more fun that just going: One... Two... Three..."

The look on Portia's face clearly announces she still thinks her friend is playing a trick on her.

"No really!" Jaspa protests. "For every five Giraffeses you count, the storm is roughly one mile away. I got to seven and a half Giraffeses, which means the storm is about a mile and a half away."

"Hummm!" says Portia uncertainly. "If you say so."

"Honestly!" Jaspa assures her. "It's true!"

Actually, it is. Thunder and lightning result from gargantuan (sorry!) energy releases inside storms. Lightning travels at the speed of light, an incredible 186,283 miles a second, reaching your eyes almost instantly. Thunder takes a lot longer to get to your ears, because sound only travels about 0.2 miles a second, which is still impressively fast! So, next time you're in a thunderstorm, count the seconds – or Giraffeses! – between a flash and its bang, divide this by five, and you'll know roughly how far away the storm is. Try it... It really works!

"I guess we'd best be getting back then," replies Portia, still not totally convinced, "otherwise we'll end up swimming home."

***

They half run, half slide down the face of the dune. As they near the bottom Portia loses her balance completely and toboggans the last few feet on her front, feeling very undignified. Jaspa laughs so much he almost joins her, but manages to control himself just enough to remain upright.

When he reaches his cousin's side, Jaspa bends down, offering her his hand. Portia takes it and pulls herself upright, spitting out sand as she does so. Unfortunately, this sends Jaspa into yet another fit of giggles... For which he is rewarded with a solid thump on the arm.

***

The thunder continues to crash around them, assaulting their ears and making the very ground shake. The approaching thunderclouds cast vast shadows, which plunge huge areas of the plain into semi-darkness. Gleaming shafts of sunlight pierce down between the storm clouds. Where they strike the ground, the earth seems almost to glow from within, making the shadows appear even darker by contrast.

The two Giraffeses march hurriedly along under the gloom of the closest thundercloud, in the vain hope they'll get home before the rain hits. Over and over again, sheet lightning replaces the false twilight in which they're now walking with an intense, flat, shadowless imitation of daylight. Each time the lightning flashes Jaspa and Portia both start cheerfully counting Giraffeses aloud. The number of Giraffeses they manage to count before each thunder crack shrinks rapidly as the storm comes ever nearer.

They're not even half way home when they first hear the sound of falling rain. Less than five minutes later the downpour arrives. It smashes into them like a tidal wave,[1] a sudden wall of water that makes Portia shriek in surprise.

"Over here!" she shouts, running towards a nearby group of wildebeest.

If you're a cow-sized animal living in the middle of open grassland, you have little choice but to simply endure whatever weather Mother Nature throws at you. Knowing that, perhaps it's not so surprising that the wildebeest under which Jaspa and Portia shelter more-or-less ignores the torrential rain. In fact, if it wasn't for the occasional jerky movement from one or other of the nearby

---

[1] A scientist would use the Japanese word tsunami (pronounced t-sue-naa-me, with the 't' almost silent).

calves, as they struggle to get into better suckling positions, you might start to believe the cousins are taking cover amongst a group of wildebeest statues.

Come to think of it, perhaps phrases like *sheltering* and *taking cover* are just a bit misleading. The near-horizontal rain pays about as much attention to Jaspa and Portia's wildebeest-cum-umbrella as the animal does to it. Rainwater blasts between its skinny legs and hammers sideways into the two poor Giraffeses.

That water which does reach the ground, hits it with such force that it bounces several inches back into the air, further soaking the already-drenched cousins. And if all that wasn't bad enough, the tiny amount of rain actually falling on their wildebeest's back – and therefore **not** on Jaspa and Portia – trickles around the animal's flanks to its belly. From here it continues its temporarily interrupted journey to the ground as big, fat water droplets.

"Urgh!" exclaims Jaspa, as one of these drops lands on his neck.

Lightning flashes and Portia's response is lost in the thunderclap that follows almost immediately. The heart of the storm is now zero Giraffeses away!

"Pardon?" shouts Jaspa.

"I said 'Staying here is pointless!'" repeats Portia in a loud voice. "I'm soaked through anyway. We might as well make a run for it!"

"When you're right, you're not wrong!" agrees Jaspa. He laughs and immediately starts running, calling back over his shoulder, "Last one home's a Baboonses!"

***

Part 2

The Journey Begins

11. Éxodus

Today the *Herders* come together to celebrate the *Exodus of Childhood*. This annual festivity, which coincides with the end of the long rains, is a bittersweet occasion. On the one hand it symbolises the end of a young Giraffeses' childhood, whereas on the other it marks the day they must leave the safety of the *Herd* and set out on the *Journey*. It also heralds the approach of the dry season, a time of extreme hardship in the southern Serengeti.

This year, the *Exodus* is being held earlier than usual, for the rains are failing prematurely. The zebra herds have already left and now the wildebeest are starting to move on. And so, Jaspa and Bisckits must also depart.

As is traditional, the whole *Herd* has congregated for the *Exodus*, on the summit of the western dune of the Shifting Sands, to bid farewell to those about to embark on the *Journey*. The roughly 300 strong gathering is arranged sitting in a circle around a central, open area. Chief Cookees is addressing the assembled Giraffeses, reminding them, as custom dictates, of the *Journey's* purpose and the significance of the ceremony they are about to witness.

***

Jaspa has been looking forward to this morning, and his *Journey*, for as long as he can remember. He recalls how incredibly difficult it was to look on last year, as his friends disappeared into the distance. Without him!

He'd continued to watch until long after they were out of sight, his heart close to breaking. Yet now, only minutes away from his own departure, he feels a panic rising inside him...

He's not ready to leave!

Thoughts chase each other through his head, like tiny fishes in a shoal: *My family, my friends, my home! How can I leave them all behind? – Bisckits! How can I look after Bisckits? I'm not even sure I can take care of myself! – And Portia! How can I say goodbye to her again so soon? – It's all too much!*

Suddenly the school of little thoughts takes flight at the menacing, relentless approach of a single, colossal shark of realisation, looming up out of the dark depths of Jaspa's growing panic...

I can't go!

Any second now, he's going to be called forward by his father, Chief Cookees, to be presented to the entire *Herd* as a *Journeyer*. Jaspa begins to feel sick. He's going to look so stupid when he tells them all he's not going. He trembles at the thought of how ashamed of him his mother would have been.

***

Portia is sitting next to Jaspa. She sees him shudder out of the corner of her eye and turns to look at her friend. His face has gone very pale. Very pale indeed.

She leans over and whispers, "Tell me."

Jaspa lowers his gaze to the ground, but makes no reply.

"Waver?" she tries again.

No response.

Portia is just about to ask a third time, when her cousin nervously asks, "How did you feel before your *Journey*, Portia?"

She gently chews at her bottom lip and gives him a knowing look. "It's perfectly normal to feel scared, if that's what you mean?"

Jaspa looks a little shocked, but continues to stare at the sand between his knees. "Is it that obvious?" he asks.

"Only to anyone who isn't blind!" Portia laughs quietly.

"Jaspa! Jaspa! Jaspa!" she exclaims in a hushed voice. "You worry too much. *Everybody* is at least a little scared before their *Journey*."

"Really? I thought it was just me... I thought I was just being a coward!"

"Don't be daft! Believe me, being completely separated from the *Herd* for the best part of a year is a big, big deal. For everybody. You'd have to be mad not to feel a bit nervous. I hardly slept at all the week before I left. I was terrified!"

"But everyone was really impressed by how calm you were!" protests Jaspa, a little too loudly. A couple of the nearby adults give him disapproving looks.

"Shhh!" hisses Portia before continuing, "It was all an act, Waver. All an act. I tell you," she adds in a whisper so quiet even he can hardly hear it, "in all honesty, I was absolutely petrified the morning of my *Exodus*."

Finally, Jaspa looks up at his best friend after Bisckits. He can tell from her expression that she's telling him the truth. "I'm sorry," he says quietly. "I never knew,"

"Exactly!" she says. "You weren't supposed to know. Nobody was! By convincing everyone else I wasn't scared, I half persuaded myself. Do you understand?"

With Portia's confession, Jaspa's fears begin to fade away.

But that doesn't mean he's about to pass up the golden opportunity she's just presented to him! He looks her in the eye and with exaggerated seriousness whispers, "Sorry, I haven't a clue what you're talking about. In fact, I think you must have got too much sun on your *Journey*, because you seem to have gone completely mental!"

"Oh, you little..." she exclaims, laughing under her breath and punching him on the arm.

Then their tomfoolery is cut short, as Cookees announces, "Jaspa. Bisckits. Please come forward to be presented to the *Herd*!"

***

Chief Cookees is an imposing figure. He's not quite as tall as Mackee, but what he gives away in height, he more than makes up for in sturdiness. He stands straight and proud, lightly resting his huge hands on the shoulders of his two sons, who stand nervously on either side of him.

"Fellow *Herders*," he begins in his strong, confident voice. "It has been my privilege to stand before you all many times at the *Exodus of Childhood*. On those occasions I have presented a great many of you to the *Herd* as *Journeyers*." Quite a few heads nod in unspoken agreement.

"I trust none of you will be offended, however, when I say that today's *Exodus* will always have a particularly special place in my heart!" A ripple of amusement runs through the seated throng.

Cookees smiles and is obliged to temporarily raise his voice, in order to be heard over the gentle laughter, "For today..." He then continues at his original volume, "...For today, I have the greatest honour a father could wish for. Today I would like to present **both** my sons to you, as *Journeyers!*

"With this *Exodus of Childhood* we say goodbye forever to Jaspa and Bisckits, the children. And whilst we are saddened by their departure, at the same time, we look forward to welcoming back Jaspa and Bisckits, the adults!"

The two brothers look a little sheepish as, again in accordance with tradition, the whole *Herd* stands to applaud the latest *Journeyers*. Portia gets a little too carried away and whistles, loudly. Realising what she's done, her left hand flies to her mouth and she looks around self-consciously, as if wondering where the whistle could have come from. But her embarrassment is short-lived and she's soon clapping enthusiastically once more.

***

Cookees raises a hand and the applause gradually dies away. "Of course, before they can commence their *Journey*, they need a *Rubani* to accompany and lead them."

A hush falls on the crowd. Then, as expected, Cookees calls Frankee forward.

Knowing murmurs of approval break the silence.

Frankee strides out into the centre of the circle, directing a wink at the still-grinning Bisckits as he walks. Approaching Jaspa, Frankee reaches out and grasps his good friend's left forearm with his right hand. Jaspa does likewise, clasping arms in the traditional *Ses* greeting.

A tall, handsome and popular Giraffeses, Frankee seems to excel at whatever he turns his hands to. Yet his kind and modest nature ensures this is a source of delight for others rather than a reason for jealousy. Many *Herders* believe he will one day become their Chief, so it comes as no surprise to hear him named as *Rubani*.

What happens next, however, comes as a shock to almost everyone!

"In a slight break with tradition," Frankee announces, "although in keeping with our honourable Chief's fondness for occasional theatrics, I've been asked to **reveal** this year's *Rubani*." He turns and nods to Cookees, who returns the gesture with an expansive smile.

Several of the assembled Giraffeses grasp the significance of his words immediately. Others take a little longer. But eventually everyone deciphers what he is saying.

Frankee **isn't** the *Rubani*!

"As is our custom," Frankee continues, "The *Rubani* has been chosen jointly by the Council of Elders and last year's *Journeyers*. And our decision was unanimous!

"The ability, leadership and compassion... not to mention bravery... of one of my fellow *Journeyers* stood out amongst the rest. It gives me great pride, therefore, to announce the *Rubani* who will accompany Jaspa and Bisckits is..."

The whole *Herd* holds its collective breath, although more than a few of them have already worked it out.

"...Portia!"

***

Amidst an onslaught of congratulations, Portia makes her way towards the gradually increasing group at the centre of the gathering.

Frankee picks her up in an affectionate hug. "Congratulations!" he almost shouts above the cheers.

"Thanks," Portia calls back, as Frankee puts her down. She turns to her cousins. Neither one of them has moved, both apparently rooted to the spot in shock.

"Since my sons seem to have lost their manners, I suppose I should say something," laughs Chief Cookees, also hugging his niece and clearly enjoying himself. "Well done, Portia!"

"Thank you, Uncle."

Finally, Jaspa finds his tongue. "You knew!" he accuses her. "You knew, and you didn't tell me!"

"It was only decided last night," replies Portia defensively. "And I wasn't allowed to tell you." She sticks her nose in the air in mock indignation, adding primly, "I could always turn it down if you like!"

Jaspa does a double take and Bisckits looks aghast.

"**No!**" they both cry in unison.

"Are you mad?" exclaims Jaspa, who is now grinning like a demented person. "This is perfect! Absolutely perfect!"

***

Several minutes later, Chief Cookees crouches on one knee in front of Jaspa and Bisckits. Around them the whole *Herd* buzzes with excitement.

"I wish your mother was here to see this," he tells his two sons, "She would have been so proud of you." He sighs. "Well, I guess it's time for you to leave. I'm going to miss you both. Look after your brother, Jaspa."

"Of course, Father."

"And you, Bisckits! Do as Portia tells you. And **try** to keep out of trouble!"

"Yes, Father."

Cookees hugs first Jaspa then Bisckits, before motioning Portia over. She finishes bidding farewell to her own father, who appears a confused mixture of pride and worry, before joining them.

"Are you sure you want to do this, Portia?" her uncle asks.

"I've never been more sure of anything in my whole life," she replies firmly.

"Good!" says Cookees decisively, before standing up and calling the *Herd* to order.

It takes the Giraffeses a little while to reform the circle. When peace finally descends, Portia steps forward, and in a clear, steady voice, formally intones, "I, Portia, humbly accept the duty of *Rubani*. So doing, I claim the honour of leading the *Exodus of Childhood*."

She turns to face northwards and a break appears in the ring before her. The *Herders* on either side shuffle away from the widening rift, until the circle is transformed into a 'U' shape. Once the 'U' has finished forming, Portia strides purposefully forward, announcing as she does, "Those Giraffeses who would be *Journeyers*, the moment of your departure is upon you!"

Jaspa and Bisckits fall in behind their *Rubani* and, without looking back, follow her on the *Exodus of Childhood*.

Jaspa's *Journey* has begun at last!

***

12. Cheetah's Kopje

The *Rubani* leads the two *Journeyers* northwards. Away from the Shifting Sands. Away from their home. Away from their family. Away from their friends.

Yet despite all this, Jaspa marches forward with a spring in his step. Now that he's finally on the move, he discovers he's never felt happier! The fear that haunted him as he waited to be presented to the *Herd* has completely evaporated, like a distant, hazy nightmare banished by the morning sunlight.

He can't quite believe it. **This** is his *Journey*. Right here. Right now. It's incredible! And his **best** friends and **closest** family – with the exception of his father, of course – are with him to share it. Life doesn't get much better than this!

Jaspa's reverie is interrupted by Bisckits, who enquires, "So, where are we heading?"

"Just as far as Cheetah's Kopje," Portia responds.

Kopjes (pronounced 'copy') are small rocky mounds, scattered across the plains, which provide some relief from the otherwise flat grasslands. Cheetah's Kopje is what the *Herd* call the bare, isolated hillock that rises out of the plain a bit more than half a mile north of the Shifting Sands.

"Oh!" says Bisckits, sounding slightly disappointed. "Why?"

"That's where we're meeting your guide."

"Our guide? I thought you were our guide."

"Nooo. Not me, Bizzee. I'm just here to make sure you don't get into too much trouble in your first five minutes!" she teases.

"So, who's our guide?" Bisckits quizzes her eagerly, ignoring her taunting.

"Well, your actual guide is called Tabora, although you'll be travelling as part of his tribe. But that's all I'm going to say on the matter. You'll just have to wait and see!"

***

Jaspa understands Bisckits' initial disappointment. Cheetah's Kopje has been part of his everyday life for as long as he could remember. An eternal and insignificant outcrop of rock, silhouetted against the distant Gol Hills. He must have visited it a dozen times, probably more. And if Jaspa is honest, he'd also expected a more exciting start to their *Journey*.

On the other hand, unlike Bisckits, he's heard all about Tabora from Portia, and can't wait to meet him.

Unexpectedly, one of the proverbs that *Herder* parents teach their children comes back to him. Down through the years, he hears his mother's voice, as clear as if she was standing right beside him, "To see what's beyond the horizon, you first have to reach it."

And finally he begins to properly understand it. Cheetah's Kopje might be familiar, but up until now it has marked the horizon of Jaspa's world. A world that is about to get much, much bigger. A world that, with any luck, is also about to become a **lot** more exciting!

***

Even with the occasional *shift*, it takes the trio almost two hours to reach Cheetah's Kopje. By the time they get there, it's almost noon and the day is growing hot. They puff up the gentle slope of the knoll and collapse under an acacia near the summit.

Although the kopje isn't very high, hardly more than a bump in an otherwise flat landscape, Jaspa's view from the top is nonetheless stunning. Immediately to the south are the Shifting Sands, with the Oldupai Gorge running west to east just beyond, like a scar slicing the Earth in half. To the east, the Crater Highlands tower a mile above where the little Giraffeses is sitting (and more than one and a quarter miles above the Rift Valley, on their far side), whilst to the north stand the more modest Gol Hills.

But dominating the entire panorama, surrounding Jaspa's vantage point upon Cheetah's Kopje, is a boundless expanse of grass...The flat, smooth, unending plains.

To the northeast this sea of grass forms the Mamen and Salei Plains that surge between the Crater Highlands and the Gol Hills, forever dividing the two uplands. To the south it floods across the Engusoro and Kimuma Plains, until it spills over the edge of the Great Rift and into the shallow, alkaline Lake Eyasi – over 30 miles long but on average only six feet deep – more than 3000 feet below.

But to the west this green sea becomes an ocean. An ocean stretching **further** than the eye can see. The infinite Serengeti Plains themselves. Whose very name comes from the Maasai word *Siringit*, meaning *place of endless space.*

***

Cheetah's Kopje gets its name from the pair of male cheetahs that claim the area around the small hill as their realm. Cheetahs are usually solitary, jealously guarding their territory from others of their kind, but it is not unknown for two, three or even as many as six to live together, forming a kind of gang. When Jaspa, Bisckits and Portia arrive at the kopje, its rulers are stretched out on one of the rocky outcrops that pepper its slopes, lazily scanning the plain to the east for their next meal.

For whatever reason, *blending* only works on humans. Fortunately, however, even though they can see *Ses*, most animals more-or-less ignore them. Very occasionally, a *Ses* may fall victim to a particularly hungry carnivore, but such instances are, thankfully, rare exceptions. So, whilst both cheetahs briefly look up as the three Giraffeses approach, they almost immediately return to their search for larger prey.

***

Without warning, one of the cheetahs stands up, arches his back in a lo-o-o-ong stretch, and drops off the rock. He slowly heads down the side of the kopje and out onto the plain, clearly being careful to stay downwind of a small cluster of Thompson's gazelles, or *Tommies* as they are often known, which has broken off from the main herd.

The gazelles are predominately sandy brown in colour, but bear distinctive black bands down both sides of their bodies, which contrast sharply with their white bellies and throats. Characteristic black and white stripes also run along the length of their faces, and their black tails stand out starkly against their white rumps.

As with deer, a male gazelle is called a buck whereas a female is called a doe. This little breakaway group is made up of young adults, both bucks and does. Each stands about 24 inches tall at the shoulder, though the bucks are slightly bigger than the does.

Evidently, the cheetah believes he has spotted a weakness in one of the grazing animals, and a gamble of life and death is about to begin. If he is correct, he will have the edge in the imminent hunt and the two cats will shortly be dining on gazelle. If he is wrong, the little antelope will be able to stay ahead of him, and the cheetah will be forced to abandon the chase. If that happens, the cats will go hungry and the Tommie will escape with its life.

At first, the cheetah gives his intended prey a wide berth, circling around to the other side of the Tommies, feigning disinterest. Yet all the while it tries to calculate whether an attack will prove worthwhile. After several minutes, the cat seems to decide the odds are in its favour... And starts his approach.

Cheetahs are famous for being the World's fastest land animals, able to reach speeds in excess of 70 miles an hour in a sprint. However, what's less well known is that once a cheetah commits to top speed, it must catch its prey within about 800 feet. If it doesn't, the energy expended in the chase is more than the cheetah will get from the meal, and so it will give up. Logically then, the closer the cheetah can get to its prey before the real chase begins, the more chance he has of catching the gazelle before he becomes too exhausted to continue.

Consequently, the pursuit starts in slow-motion. The cat unhurriedly stalks the group of Tommies, gradually reducing the distance between him and them. Carefully, the cheetah advances, his chances of success increasing with every step. The gap shrinks from 700 feet to 500 feet... To 300 feet... 250 feet... 200 feet. Jaspa, who has been watching the drama unfold, realises he is holding his breath.

When the cheetah is only 150 feet from the Tommies, one of them starts to slowly trot forwards. Its long, parallel, slightly curved, strongly ridged horns identify it as a buck. Abruptly, the little gazelle leaps high in the air, all four legs held stiff and straight beneath him, like he has suffered a great electric shock. The buck seems to float for several moments, frozen in mid air, but when his feet eventually hit the ground he immediately breaks into a run, accelerating rapidly away from the danger.

The buck's strange jump, the purpose of which isn't fully understood, is called *stotting*. If you find that expression a little too silly, you could use its other scientific name... *pronking*!

Perhaps warned by their companion's distinctive leap, the other Tommies also take flight, racing off in all directions, like the separate trails from the head of an exploding firework. One of them, a smallish doe, appears to be limping slightly, unable to put her full weight on her front left leg. It quickly becomes obvious that this is the weakness the cheetah has spotted. He ignores all the other Tommies and pursues the injured doe with a grim single-mindedness.

The gazelle streaks across the grass, back legs kicking, her white rump flashing in the bright sun as her black tail bounces up and down in time with her strides. Jinking left and right, she tries to throw off the pursuing beast, but the cheetah follows her dodge for dodge, gaining all the time. The sleek, graceful power of the cheetah is unrelenting, matching the gazelle's every stride, ruthlessly reeling her in. Her only hope is to keep going, to stay ahead of her tormentor just long enough for it to abandon the chase.

The Tommie makes an unbelievably sharp left turn, and Jaspa thinks she must get away. But as well as being extremely fast, the cheetah is also supremely agile. It leans into the corner, angling so far over its left shoulder appears to almost touch the ground, like a racing motorbike taking a bend at full throttle. The cat's back paws slide slightly, throwing swirls of dust into the air. Then its claws bite the dry earth and the hunter is upright once more. And still closing. The gazelle makes turn after impossible turn, but her pursuer is determined. Relentless. Hungry.

The distance between hunted and hunter continues to shrink, until only about three feet separates them. This close, the bunching and stretching of the animals' bodies as they run is enough to make the gap change noticeably. It contracts and extends, contracts and extends repeatedly with every stride.

The oscillating gap closes one final time... And suddenly, the doe is falling. The cheetah has managed to hook a single claw around her hind leg, tripping the Tommie. Her speed does the rest, sending her tumbling head over heels. Within two more strides, as the gazelle rolls end over end through a dust cloud of her own making, the cat is upon her.

Unable to watch any longer, Jaspa looks away quickly.

"Serengeti glorious place, Friend Giraffeses," says a deep voice behind him. "Beautiful and full of wonders. But also full of dangers and ugliness. Life and death forever intertwined. Harsh it is. But often one animal must perish for others to survive. This nature's way.

"You must accept this, before your *Journey* is done. But don't fear. Tabora promise he guide Friend Giraffeses safely and faithfully."

***

13. The Nomads' Tale

Look up.

Tonight is the Dark of the Moon. The last glow of sunset has all but drained from the sky. It's tempting to say something dramatic like 'the heavens are an inky-black canvas pierced by countless pinpricks of light." But if you've ever experienced a moonless night in a place far from any streetlights, you'll know just how inaccurate this is.

Whilst it's true that every star[1] does seem so much brighter than normal. So much sharper. So much clearer. This also goes for all those stars you don't normally see. All those stars that, on other nights, are drowned-out by moonlight and streetlights. The faint stars **between** the familiar stars, which are only visible on the darkest of nights. But on those nights they shine for all they're worth, filling the would-be blackness with their faint white glow.

***

Look down.

With no stars to dilute the night, the Earth is actually **much** darker than the sky. The black is broken only by a single, small, reddish light, glowing and spluttering in the distance.

***

Approach.

The orange glow resolves into a fire, hunched figures silhouetted against its smouldering embers.

[1] In fact, many of the 'stars' we see in the night sky are actually entire galaxies, each made up of billions of stars.

***

Approach.

A log cracks as fire devours it. It slumps down slightly, and the movement sends a shower of ash and sparks into the warm evening air. Flames dance briefly, dividing and reuniting, their light shimmering momentarily on the tiny faces huddled around the fire.

***

Approach.

"You know what?" says Jaspa thoughtfully, his features lit by the fire's orange-red glow. "I don't think my back hurts **quite** as much this evening. Not as much as it normally does at this time of the day, anyway."

"Huh!" snorts Bisckits, flexing his shoulder blades. "Count yourself lucky then. My bum's still so sore I can hardly sit down!"

Tabora chuckles. "Giraffeses still complaining?"

"Well, it's alright for you," protests Bisckits. "You're used to riding these things. I prefer my own four feet!"

Tabora laughs again. "Great Migration over 500 miles, Friend Bisckits! And that not include constant search for good grass and water... Here and there, backwards and forwards..." He emphasises each direction with sweeping movements of his arms. "...Round and round, east and west, north and south. Never stopping." He pauses slightly, before nudging Bisckits with a good-natured elbow, "I think legs of Friend Bisckits wear away with so much walking! Best he rides," Tabora concludes, nodding in mock seriousness.

Bisckits snorts again.

"Come on Bisckits. Cheer up!" Jaspa says encouragingly. "I reckon we're starting to get the hang of it at last. After all, we hardly fell off at all today."

"Tell that to my poor ribs," groans Bisckits.

Jaspa turns to their guide. "What do you think, Tabora?"

Tabora is a Gnuses (pronounced 'G-noo-ses'). He's a sniff taller than Jaspa and has a shaggy grey coat. His chest is broad, but so skinny you can make out his ribs, and his limbs are impossibly slender. His face appears stretched and narrow, though it ends in big lips and a long straggly beard. Upon his head, above his ears, he carries an impressive pair of horns, which begin by growing sideways and then turn upwards, tapering to sharp points.

"For sure, Friend Jaspa," agrees Tabora seriously. "You and Friend Bisckits better riders every day."

"See!" Jaspa beams proudly at his brother.

Jaspa's smile is contagious and, try as he might, Bisckits can't quite suppress a lopsided grin in return.

"For sure. In seven, maybe nine months," Tabora continues, "You both be good as Friend Portia..."

Portia, who has been quietly contemplating the flickering flames, smiles modestly, but says nothing.

"... She **nearly** good as Bwananuke, daughter of Tabora," their guide concludes.

The smiles disappear from the faces of all three Giraffeses. "Oh!" says Portia, looking crestfallen. At only seven weeks old, Bwananuke is Tabora's youngest daughter.

Tabora laughs once more, a deep, pleasant, belly-laugh. "Friend Portia! Friend Jaspa! Friend Bisckits!" he says, putting a fatherly arm around each of them in turn. "Do not be upset by Tabora's joke. He promise he make *Nomads* of you by end of Great Migration!"

***

"Please Father, pleeease!" begs Togora for at least the hundredth time!

Tabora lets out an explosive breath. "Oh! Very well!" he declares in pretend annoyance. Togora, Tabora's eldest son, grins and his father gives him a conspiratorial wink as he gets to his feet.

Portia prods a dozing Bisckits. In reply, Bisckits just about manages to half-open a single, sleepy eye. He raises the corresponding eyebrow questioningly.

"Tabora's going to tell the *Tale*," Portia whispers.

"The what?" asks Bisckits sleepily.

"The *Tale*! The story of how the Great Migration began."

The effect on Bisckits is little short of miraculous. In less than a heartbeat, he's sitting up straight, watching Tabora eagerly. Jaspa, who has been nodding on Portia's other side, shakes off the sleep that has also been threatening to claim him.

Tabora stands motionless, head bowed. A gradual hush settles around the campfire. Children fidget excitedly and receive stern, disapproving stares from their parents. The onlookers hold their collective breath, waiting for Tabora to begin.

After what seems like an age, with his head still lowered, the *Nomad* begins to speak.

***

"When World still young, desert covered whole land." *The storyteller holds his right hand close to his waist, palm down, and moves it from right to left, signifying the flatness of the plain.*

"But then..." *he raises both hands until they are in front of him at arm's length, palms still facing down but fingers now stretched wide* "...come first rains..." *he glides his hands slowly from right to left, wiggling his fingers ever so slightly, imitating rain* "...bringing wonderful green grass..." *he rapidly drops his arms to his waist, then slowly lifts his now upward-facing, cupped hands in a way that suggests something growing* "...and then trees..." *his hands start low, palms together, then curve up and apart, like the spreading branches of an acacia tree* "...and banishing desert."

"Grass smell sweet, and beasts soon follow..." *hands held in front, fingers curved down, he repeatedly 'walks' one hand over the other.* "First come grass-eaters..." *hands low, imaginary grass is chewed between 'mouths' made by fingers and thumbs* "...then tree-eaters..." *left hand holds right elbow, right forearm is vertical like a long neck, enabling the 'mouth' of his right hand to 'eat' the highest leaves of a pretend tree.*

Portia leans over to Jaspa and breathlessly hisses, "That's my favourite part!" Her cousin smiles briefly and nods his agreement, but Tabora's storytelling is so captivating he is quite unable to look away.

"...And then meat-eaters!" *The storyteller spits out the last word and, in the same instant, suddenly lifts his head for the first time. His eyes are wide, his lips pulled back in a snarl to expose clenched teeth. His hands are claws, held on either side of his mouth. The firelight stains his face the colour of blood, although some parts remain in deepest shadow. His eyes, nostrils and mouth are black pits, his* horns the stuff of nightmares, his long beard ripples like flames. The flickering fire causes his features to shift and change alarmingly.

It all proves too much for one youngster, who screams in terror, then begins to sob into the comforting arms of her mother.

And then...

Tabora is standing before them once again. His face relaxed, the snarl vanished, the claws no more. He continues, "And with the beasts come Gnuses. Our first ancestors..." *a pointing finger traces a circle, starting at his own chest and taking in all those listening* "... the *Settlers*!

***

"For countless years grass-eaters thrive on plains and numbers increase. And first among them are our cousins, the gnus." Tabora continues his story, accompanying his words with hand movements and facial gestures more descriptive than any drawing or photograph.

"Even meat-eaters are content to prey only on sick and infirm. All is balance on plains." Tabora holds his hands out to the side, palms up, to resemble a set of scales. "All is good. And *Settlers* prosper.

"This was time when *Settlers* first learn to ride gnus." He gives Jaspa and Bisckits an almost imperceptible wink.

"But nature's way is change. Always change. And one year rains not come. Without them, soil too thin and grass not grow and plains become like desert. Dust blows everywhere and nourishing grass dies. Beasts die too if they stay.

"Yet Gnuses sense water in west and so guide gnus to find it. To find survival. And other beasts follow. Even meat-eaters. After this *Settlers* without proper home... and so change name. Become first *Nomads*!

"In west, beasts find rivers and pools and springs. There grass grow without rains. But grass not as sweet as on home plains. So *Nomads* keep gnus moving. Turn them northwards. And other beasts follow.

"All face many dangers along path. Drought. Disease. Even rivers filled with monstrous meat-eaters who devour all they can. Many die, but eventually Gnuses discover Mara and decide it good place."

In many ways, the lush grasslands of the Maasai Mara are simply the northernmost part of the Serengeti. However, because they lie outside Tanzania, in the neighbouring country of Kenya, we humans feel the need to give them a separate name. Whatever it's called, the Maasai Mara also represents the northward limit of the Great Migration.

"Mara grass long and plentiful when beasts arrive. But too many grass-eaters, and after few months only roots left. So beasts must again move on, if they to survive. All seems bleak...

"But wondrous thing happens, just when hope almost gone... Gnuses feel return of rains! They lead beasts back south. In distance, clouds build and build. Until at last they can hold their water no longer. And rains break!

"Now beasts can smell rains themselves. Smell new grass growing. And race towards it. When they finally reach home plains again, beasts and Nomads find beautiful green carpet of fresh young grass. All has come full circle.

"This is our *Tale*! Tale of first Great Migration. Tale of how our ancestors stopped being *Settlers* and became *Nomads*. Tale of how Gnuses saved all beasts of Serengeti. Great Migrations uncounted have followed since then, but so it began.

"And so we not forget, in every generation one is charged to remember *Tale*. That is honour of Tabora's family, for we are tribe's *Talekeepers* and *Taletellers*."

It's unfortunate that 'telling tales' has such a negative meaning for us, because Tabora's family are **very** proud to be *Taletellers*!

Tabora Talekeeper lowers his head and walks away from the light of the fire, into the darkness of the night. Behind him, he leaves a silence broken only by the crackle of the flames.

As with most legends, there is a lot of truth in the *Nomad's Tale*. Every year the wildebeest herds, accompanied by the zebras and gazelles, really do undertake a 500 mile migration in search of food and water. Fossils found at the Oldupai Gorge suggest this was already happening over one million years ago.

Other questions, concerning how the wildebeest find their way, and whether the Gnuses really are responsible for the whole thing, remain unanswered.

***

14. Tempers fray

Jaspa and Bisckits, accompanied by Portia, joined Tabora Talekeeper's family when the rains began to fail, a little over two weeks ago. Shortly thereafter, with the Short Grass Plains around the Shifting Sands no longer able to support them, the herds had broken-up and headed off in search of better grazing. The Great Migration had begun once again.

Tabora's *Nomads* guided their wildebeest north, skirting to the west of the unpronounceable hills of Olongoijoo and Oldiang'ar Ng'ar. At Nasera Rock, a 260 foot tall island of granite that rises out of the Short Grass Plains, which is believed to have provided shelter for prehistoric humans for thousands of years, they turned eastwards. From there the Gnuses had cut across the western end of Ang'ata Kiti – which means *Small Plain* in Maasai – to reach their goal: the mysterious sounding Hidden Valley.

Throughout the wet season, water collects within the bowl-like confines of the Hidden Valley to form a wide, shallow, temporary lake, nestled in the Gol Hills. When the rains come to an end this natural reservoir offers a brief sanctuary from the harshness of the looming dry season, providing water for plants and animals alike.

Jaspa has witnessed the annual arrival of the wildebeest herds to the plains around the Shifting Sands many times, yet he was totally unprepared for what awaited him in the Hidden Valley. For a short time each year, up to half a million wildebeest and zebra crowd into this idyllic vale, to take advantage of its extended opening hours. Jaspa had never before seen so many animals in one place.

Unfortunately, even the riches of the Hidden Valley cannot sustain such numbers for long. With so many animals competing for its resources, all too soon its grasses are eaten, its water drunk. Finally, the herds must once more move on. Or perish.

Sad to say, many do perish. Just as described in the *Nomad's Tale*, which recounts the first Great Migration, thousands of those animals that leave the eastern plains at the start of the dry season each year never return to taste their sweet grasses again. This is simply part of the great circle of life. In the end, the hunters and scavengers must also eat.

***

"Vultures give me the creeps," declares Bisckits fervently.

Soaring over the land, tirelessly searching for their next meal, vultures are perhaps the most noticeable of the Serengeti's scavengers.

It's mid-morning and the three Giraffeses are once more being lead past Nasera Rock by their Gnuses guides, although this time they're heading westward. Behind them they leave the exhausted pastures and shrunken lake of the Hidden Valley. Before them lies their destination, the distant Moru Kopjes on the far side of the Long Grass Plains, about 40 miles away as the vulture glides.

Bisckits' announcement is in response to the flurry of activity currently taking place in the shadow of Nasera Rock, where a group of vultures is squabbling over the remains of a zebra. The absence, at least so far, of lions or hyenas suggests the animal died of natural causes... although falling prey to a carnivore **is** natural causes in the Serengeti! Occasionally, a vulture's head or leg protrudes from the teeming mass of feathers that otherwise, thankfully, hides the carcass from Bisckits and the others.

"I've never understood why you hate vultures so much," says Jaspa, evidently trying to sound casual. "What makes them different from any other scavenger or hunter?"

"Oh, I don't know!" replies Bisckits, defensively. "The bare heads. The bloody faces. The hanging around waiting for other animals to die. The fighting over dead bodies. It's all so... so... so icky!"

"Icky?!" exclaims Portia, half smiling.

"Don't make fun! I just don't like them, alright!"

"Alright, alright!" chuckles Portia, holding up her hands in mock surrender. She looks over at Jaspa to include him in the joke and is surprised to find he isn't smiling. In fact, if she didn't know him better, she'd swear Jaspa has taken his brother's comments personally. Portia's smile also fades as she studies her cousin's face.

"What's wrong, Waver?" she enquires, concerned.

"Nothing," he replies, though this is clearly far from the truth.

A golden jackal approaches the dead zebra, but the vultures' feeding frenzy makes it impossible for it to get close enough to claim a share of the meal. It creeps up behind a lappet-faced vulture, the largest and most aggressive of the Serengeti's vultures, with a wingspan of about ten feet and weighing over 15 pounds. The jackal grips the bird's tail in its mouth and tugs, hoping to distract the scavenger long enough to steal a mouthful of meat.

Unfortunately, the vulture is too focused on feeding to pay any heed to its much smaller tormenter. After five or six unsuccessful attempts to goad the lappet-faced, the jackal gives up and moves on, only to be chased off completely by several white-backed vultures. Smart enough to realise when it is beaten, the jackal slinks off in search of less dangerous pickings.

***

After a few minutes, Jaspa finally breaks the silence. "You know, I agree vultures aren't exactly the prettiest things in the world," he says with exaggerated calmness. "And admittedly their eating habits leave a bit to be desired. But I still think they get a lot of undeserved bad press."

"How so?" asks Bisckits scornfully.

"Weeell..." Now Jaspa struggles to find the right words. "Well, you have to admit that they're fantastic flyers, even for birds. You've got to give them that."

Sunlight warms up some parts of the Earth's surface more, or faster, than others. In turn, such hotspots heat the air above them, producing a column of warm, rising air known as a thermal. If a bird or plane (or anything else for that matter) stays within a thermal, it is lifted ever higher into the sky.

Each morning of their short stay in the Hidden Valley, Jaspa had watched hundreds of Ruppell's griffon vultures leave their nesting sites in the nearby Olkarien Gorge and effortlessly ride the thermals on motionless, outstretched wings. Up and up the vultures spiralled, higher and higher, until they became unrecognisable dots in the sky. From up there, the birds scanned the ground, using their keen eyesight to seek out their next feast.

What Jaspa doesn't know is that a Ruppell's griffon vulture has the unfortunate distinction of holding the world record for the highest documented bird flight, reaching an altitude of 37,000 feet, or about seven miles. The bird was unfortunate because the 'recording device' was Boeing 747 Jumbo Jet, which 'documented' the bird's height by colliding with it! Needless to say, the poor vulture didn't survive to have a celebratory party!

What's more, since their method of flying requires very little flapping, vultures can cover great distances without burning up too much energy. In fact, the griffon vultures from the Olkarien Gorge frequently travel over 125 miles a day in their search for food, coming back to the gorge each night to sleep and care for their young.

"And vultures can't help the way they look, any more than we can," Jaspa continues, warming to his subject. "They're just born that way. Because of the job nature has given them. There's nothing they can do about it!

"And just consider what the Serengeti would be like without them! Most vultures never actually **kill** anything. They just clean up after the lions and hyenas and cheetahs and leopards and wild dogs and all the other predators! Or get rid of the bodies of all those animals that die from thirst or hunger in the dry season, or from injuries or disease. Think about it. Without vultures and all the other scavengers the Serengeti would be covered with rotting corpses!"

Once again, Jaspa's quite correct. Predators are only responsible for about 30 percent of deaths in the Serengeti. Drought and sickness are far bigger killers.

Portia is taken aback by the passionate tone of Jaspa's voice. The strength of his conviction is obvious, and she rapidly realises that her cousin's outburst is more than just some throwaway observation on an insignificant matter. This is clearly very important to Jaspa. A subject he has thought about long and hard.

But before Portia can respond, Bisckits snaps back his own heated reply, "Can you actually hear the rubbish coming out of your mouth!?"

"Well, it's clear **you're** not listening!" Jaspa retorts sharply.

"What's the point? You're talking complete nonsense!" Bisckits yells. "Let me spell it out for you. Vultures!... Are!... Vile!! End of story!"

"Bisckits! Jaspa!" bellows Portia, instantly ending their argument. The fact that she uses their real names, instead of her nicknames for them, shocks the two brothers almost as much as her anger. "That's enough. From both of you!"

Jaspa and Bisckits stare down at the neck of the wildebeest they are riding, both looking somewhat shamefaced. Yet neither replies and clearly neither of them is willing to back down.

Portia breathes out in exasperation, hard and loud. "What's got into the pair of you?"

"He started it!" murmurs Bisckits.

"Yes... Well, I'm finishing it!" Portia says firmly, anger creeping back into her voice. "What would your father say? Even worse, what would your mother say? You should both be ashamed of yourselves, bickering like brainless starlings. Now, clasp arms and apologise to each other... Right now!"

Even in the midst of their argument, Jaspa and Bisckits are mindful of their cousin's wishes and feelings. For this reason – and this reason alone – they do as she instructs. But not once do they make eye contact as they clasp arms. Nor do their mumbled apologies betray any hint of sincerity.

Portia sighs inwardly, painfully aware that this quarrel is far from over.

***

Bisckits hates arguing with his brother. But he can't understand why Jaspa is being so Pigses-headed. As far as he knows, Jaspa has never even met a vulture, so why does he like them so much? It makes no sense!

Deep down, Bisckits knows he's being childish. Even deeper down, he knows that Jaspa is right. That vultures **are** just doing what they need to do, in order to survive. Yet for some inexplicable reason, the part of Bisckits at the surface refuses to admit he's wrong.

Perhaps it's because he's far away from home and hiding the fact he's feeling homesick. Perhaps its because he aches all over from riding this wretched wildebeest everyday. Or maybe he's simply in one of those moods where, for no good reason at all, you feel all frustrated and stubborn and confrontational and you want to argue with the whole world. Bisckits doesn't know. But whatever the reason, Bisckits does know he's unable to give in.

***

Jaspa hates arguing with his brother. But he can't understand why Bisckits is being so Pigses-headed. As far as he knows, Bisckits has never even met a vulture, so why does he hate them so much? It makes no sense!

Jaspa knows he should just let it go. Or at least, agree to disagree with Bisckits. Yet this time he can't. He just can't. Sometimes you just have to stand up for what you believe. For what is right!

Besides, anything less would be disloyal. And Jaspa couldn't bear feeling like a traitor.

***

15. The wisdom of Tabora Talekeeper

Jaspa blinks slowly, trying to get the sticky sleep out of his eyes. As he does so, he raises his hand to his forehead in an attempt to shield his face from the day's glare. It's actually not that hot. Temperatures in the Serengeti are nowhere near as high as most people imagine, and remain fairly constant throughout the year, in comparison with other parts of the world, averaging between about 60° and 75° Fahrenheit (15° and 25° Celsius). However, it's been almost a month since the last significant rainfall and the incessant pounding of the sun is beginning to take its toll on Jaspa.

He's not the only one suffering, either. The gloominess that has settled over him, like a smothering blanket he can't quite manage to throw off, seems to be shared by all those around him, even the wildebeest and other animals. And the dry season has hardly got into its stride!

Jaspa often dreamed of the time he would set out on his *Journey* and cross the mighty Serengeti. In his mind's eye he'd imagined the excitement of travelling the endless green plains, under an infinite blue sky, surrounded by the innumerable wildebeest, zebra and gazelle of the limitless herds... Jaspa the Giraffeses, brave explorer, boldly confronting whatever the Serengeti threw at him, with a spring in his step and a smile on his face.

But the reality was so much more... boring! Yesterday they had finally arrived at the Moru Kopjes, after trudging wearily around the plains for well over a week. They could have covered the distance between the Hidden Valley and here in a fraction of the time if they had taken a more direct route. Instead, the Gnuses had led them on a winding path, back and forth across the increasingly desiccated and shrivelled grasslands, on a seemingly pointless, endless trek to nowhere.

Of course, Jaspa knows the route Tabora chose wasn't really pointless. Far from it. He knows the entire Great Migration is driven by a single, simple, basic need: the constant search for edible grass and drinkable water. Generations of Gnuses have discovered, and passed down, the locations of those rare, special places where the grass remains green and nutritious for a few, crucial days longer than on the rest of the plains, or where water persists for a short while after all the other sources have dried up. Tabora's *Nomads* have led the wildebeest in their care to each of these fleeting sanctuaries, one after another. If charted on a map, their plotted path would resemble a particularly complicated and angular join-the-dots puzzle, each *dot* representing a single, short-lived oasis surrounded by rapidly withering grassland.

***

Somewhere in the area near the isolated, tree-covered Naabi Hill, the Short Grass Plains of the southern Serengeti gradually gave way to the Long Grass Plains of the central area. Too preoccupied with other things, Jaspa hardly noticed. In part, this is because his shaken, aching body continues to protest at being forced to ride a wildebeest all day, every day, and often half the night, too . But the main reason for his persisting melancholy mood is his ongoing feud with Bisckits.

Not that you can really call it a feud, thinks Jaspa. After all, a proper feud would require... well, more feuding! At least then there'd be some contact between them. But there's none. Instead, there's just this dreadful, uncomfortable silence. No bickering. No arguing. No fighting. They never speak to each other. They never even make eye contact.

To make matters even worse, if that's possible, his continuing quarrel with Bisckits is also placing an increasing strain on his friendship with Portia. Unwilling to take sides, and unable to convince them to make up, she finally washed her hands of the pair of them, telling them both to *'grow up!'* in frustration. Since then she has remained coolly distant from the two brothers.

The only minor consolation is Portia's decision to stay with them for the remainder of their *Journey*. She'd originally planned to head home as they passed through the Lemuta Kopjes, where their meandering path took them within just two days travel of the Shifting Sands. But when the time came she had felt unable to leave them. Unfortunately, this was apparently only because *'it wouldn't be fair to leave Tabora to deal with my two blockhead cousins alone'*, so this dubious silver lining feels more than a little threadbare and tarnished.

***

Jaspa is perched on one of the rocky outcrops that together comprise the Moru Kopjes. If the grassland plains of the Serengeti can be described as seas, then the granite kopjes that protrude from their otherwise flat surfaces are like islands.

In truth, the correct geological term for a kopje is an inselberg, a German word that literally means *island mountain*. The kopjes are actually the tips of the highest peaks of ancient mountains that were all but buried when ash, ejected from the volcanoes of the Crater Highlands, fell thick across the Serengeti to form the plains. In certain areas, these lonely remnants of a long gone landscape group together for company. The Moru Kopjes, located at the western edge of the central plains, are one such cluster.

The rock upon which Jaspa is sitting is hardly more than a boulder, really. As he stares east from its sun-warmed, rounded dome, over the top of the massed wildebeest herds and across the boundless Serengeti Plains, Jaspa realises that somewhere beyond the horizon are the Shifting Sands. Home.

The thought makes him feel slightly sick. Back there, Bisckits and Portia had both been his friends. Yet here he is, surrounded by more than a million other creatures, and he's never felt so alone.

***

"Still so sad, Friend Jaspa?" asks Tabora, sitting down beside him. The Taleteller's tone mirrors his evident concern. "It not good for you to fight with Friend Bisckits and Friend Portia. They both miserable too. Why not you be first to say sorry and end sadness?"

"I'd like to, Tabora. I really would. More than anything," replies Jaspa hopelessly. "It's just..." He realises he doesn't know how to express his feelings, and his explanation tails off.

"Mmm," responds the Gnuses, perhaps in understanding, perhaps not.

For a time they sit together in silence. Then, quite suddenly, Tabora stands up and brushes himself off. He turns to Jaspa and announces, "Tabora can't sit here whole day. He must pay respects to Friend Oripot. Friend Jaspa should come too. Maybe Friend Oripot cheer him up."

Despite his bleak mood, Jaspa feels his curiosity spark. "Who's Oripot?"

The *Nomad's* eyes sparkle mischievously. "Come with Tabora and see," he answers mysteriously. Then, without another word, he jumps down off the kopje and heads out into the long grass, motioning Jaspa to follow.

***

Sitting on the kopje, looking down from above, the so-called *long grass* hadn't actually looked that long. Why, the wispy vegetation barely reached above the wildebeests' knees! But down here among the stems, it's a different story. Suddenly the grass seems far taller and **much** more tightly packed.

Being as small as he is, Jaspa finds it difficult forge a path through the thickly gathered blades. But Tabora, although barely bigger than Jaspa, has no such problems. He scythes through the foliage with practiced efficiency, as easily as a jungle explorer cuts through the forest undergrowth – and without the aid of a machete! Every so often the Gnuses pauses, allowing Jaspa to catch up, before ploughing on once more through the dense vegetation.

"Where... are... we... going?" asks Jaspa, each word punctuated by a laboured breath.

"You see. You see!" comes the uninformative answer.

Tabora weaves between the legs of the wildebeest and, occasionally, the odd zebra. As Jaspa slogs through the dry, unyielding grass, trying to stay close to the Gnuses, a thought occurs to him. Something he half remembers Tabora telling them as they passed Naabi Hill.

"Tabora?" he pants, "Didn't you say we'll only be staying here at Moru for a couple of days?"

"Ah!" replies the *Nomad*, "So Friend Jaspa listening, after all! He so miserable, Tabora thinks he only hear what inside his own head."

"I'm sorry," says Jaspa unhappily, "I've just got a lot on my mind."

Tabora stops so suddenly that Jaspa almost runs into the back of him. The Gnuses turns to face his companion, before clasping his arms and looking him straight in the eye.

"Friend Jaspa must find way to make things right with Friend Bisckits," he says seriously. "But first he must make things right with himself. Being so sad whole time not good for *Ses*. Dangerous to wallow in sadness too long. Tabora knows it hard, but Friend Jaspa must try to lift heart. Only then can he make peace with brother."

The *Nomad's* sincerity leaves Jaspa lost for words. He finds that he can only manage a nod, to indicate he understands what Tabora has said. Although *understand* is perhaps still something of an exaggeration.

As abruptly as he stopped, Jaspa's guide heads off again, picking up their interrupted conversation over his shoulder, "Friend Jaspa correct. Tabora did say *Nomads* only stay near Moru Kopjes for few days."

"But why?" asks Jaspa, finding his tongue again, as the discussion returns to less awkward matters. "There's plenty of grass here. And there's water in the Mbalageti River. Why can't the wildebeest stay for the dry season? In fact, why can't they stay here all year round?"

"Oh, Friend Jaspa! Tabora wish it so simple!" the Gnuses says, longingly. "But Tabora explain... First: Mbalageti today run east of Moru Kopjes. But in few weeks, with no more rain, it become more like long string of unconnected pools. No more water flow. Then pools get smaller and smaller, taste worse and worse. In end, they dry up, or are too poisoned by dead animals and dung to drink."

Jaspa shudders at the thought.

"Second: even if water remain, and stay fresh, look at grass here... Long and tough. Too tough for wildebeest. And wildebeest must be Gnuses' first concern. This grass already dry. Too dry. And never as nourishing as short, sweet grass. Not like grass near Shifting Sands." He winks at Jaspa, who smiles at the peculiar compliment. "So Nomads lead wildebeest on Great Migration and wait for rains to return to southern plains. And for short grass to grow again."

***

They continue to push through the resistant vegetation. As they labour forwards, Jaspa suddenly becomes aware he is in the midst of a swiftly growing and darkening shadow. He looks up, searching for its source...

Straight into the open, slobbering and, most significantly of all, **rapidly** approaching mouth of a wildebeest!

Frozen by shock, Jaspa is unable to even think, let alone react.

Without warning, Tabora crashes into him, shoving him sideways. For a moment Jaspa is lifted completely off his feet, before he thumps back down to Earth, banging his right elbow painfully. He turns to Tabora, just in time to watch, incredulous, as the *Nomad* slaps the wildebeest hard on the snout!

Jaspa waits for the animal to retaliate. He's sure that the provoked wildebeest, herbivore though it is, will strike back, and that Tabora is about to become horribly well acquainted with its teeth.

Instead, the giant stares stupidly down the length of its face at the tiny Gnuses... Who is now telling it off!

"...is Friend Wildebeest doing?" shouts Tabora. "She must use eyes more! Nearly hurt Friend Jaspa!"

More like 'Nearly ate Friend Jaspa!', thinks Jaspa, nursing his elbow and shaking slightly.

"Now go. And be more careful in future!" orders the Nomad. The wildebeest blinks dim-wittedly and then, to Jaspa's amazement, shambles off.

Jaspa lets out the breath he's been holding. "That was incredible!" he stammers. "I didn't know Gnuses could actually **talk** to wildebeest! I mean, back home I've tried talking to giraffes a couple of times, but they just looked at me and then went back to whatever they were doing." Then an idea comes to him, "Or maybe they did understand me after all!" he murmurs, though mainly to himself.

Jaspa's pondering is cut short by a great laugh from Tabora. "Friend Jaspa honours *Nomads*! But alas Gnuses like all other

Ses... We cannot speak with animals!" Then, leaning close to Jaspa, he whispers, "And between Tabora and Friend Jaspa, nor can Giraffeses!" The *Nomad* grins to show his teasing is good-natured.

"But I saw you speak to it!" Jaspa protests.

Tabora's face becomes serious for a moment. " *Her*, Friend Jaspa," he corrects, gently but firmly. " *Her*, not *it*. **Never** *it*."

Jaspa blushes, embarrassed by the unintended offence he has caused, but Tabora's smile returns immediately and he continues, "Anyway, Tabora not speak **to** her, he speak **at** her."

Seeing the look of confusion that crosses Jaspa's still-reddening face, Tabora attempts to explain further. "Gnuses love wildebeest cousins. But, if Tabora honest, they not smartest creatures in World. They also very nervous. But you nervous too if you dish of day on most predators' menus! Tabora's slap surprise wildebeest so she not accidentally bite him. Then his loud voice make her go away, find less noisy grass! But she not understand Tabora's words."

The kindly Gnuses, aware of Jaspa's growing discomfort, concludes a change of subject is needed. He bends aside a thick tuft of grass to reveal they are standing at the base of another kopje. "So, Friend Jaspa," he says, "Now we must climb!"

***

Few trees grow out on the central plains of the Serengeti, since their roots are normally unable to penetrate the hardpan, a dense, waterproof crust that often forms just beneath the surface in arid and semi-arid regions. In contrast, many of the kopjes are peppered with fissures, which provide tree roots with solid anchorages and, even more importantly, access to the water otherwise trapped beneath the hardpan.

Trees aren't the only things to take advantage of the kopjes in this way. A wealth of other plants and a host of animals also gather round them, like moths attracted to a candle's flame, turning these barren rocky outcrops into havens of amazing diversity.

The kopje to which Tabora has guided them is much larger than the one they have just left. Its smooth sides soar high above the two *Ses*. The Gnuses leads Jaspa clockwise around its bulk, hugging the kopje's bare flanks, which tower over them like a sheer wall of rock. After only a short distance, they come to a place where the roots of a large candelabra tree, so called because it looks just like a multi-branched candlestick, reach the ground.

"We climb here," Tabora says. "It easier than trying to go up smooth rock. But take care not to break or cut tree. White sap of candelabra tree **very** dangerous. It burn skin, blind eyes."

Without waiting for a response to this rather worrying announcement, he begins to scale the tree's overhanging roots.

Feeling more than a little nervous, Jaspa follows the Gnuses up the rock-face. In the end, though, the climb proves much less difficult than he expects. No disfiguring white sap comes oozing out of their makeshift ladder to burn his skin or blind his eyes. Nor does he lose his footing and fall to a messy end on the ground far below. At one point, their passage does startle a bare-faced go-away-bird into noisy flight, but even this incident hardly seems worth mentioning.[1]

Eventually the rock *wall* of the kopje's side decides to find out what being a *floor* is all about, and quickly levels off into a wide and, most importantly from Jaspa's perspective, relatively horizontal surface. At this point, the rock-hugging roots of the candelabra tree transform into branches, which stretch up towards the sky.

Able to walk upright once more, the *Ses* take their leave of the tree and head off across the kopje's crown.

***

Vegetation clusters thickly around the kopje's base, most notably in the form of numerous candelabra trees. But up here on its top there are almost no plants. Instead, the smooth, bare rock is covered with... Other, smaller, smooth, bare rocks. Most of these are round, or at least fairly round**ed**. And *smaller* doesn't necessarily mean *small*. In fact, just to Jaspa's left is a group of three enormous rocks, shaped like three giant potatoes, each of which must be at least 15 or 20 feet tall.

But one particular rock stands out from all the others, on account of its unique shape. Tabora walks straight up to it, turns to Jaspa, and declares, "We're here!"

Jaspa looks around in bewilderment. "We're where?" he asks.

---

[1] Yet again, this isn't a joke... There really is such a thing as a *bare-faced go-away-bird!* It gets its name because its call apparently sounds like it's saying *go away!*

16. Oripot

Now, Jaspa has never seen an orange, let alone a segment from one, which is a shame, because *the same shape as an orange segment, lying on its curved side* would be the perfect way to describe the object currently in front of him. Admittedly, the orange in question would have been about ten feet in diameter and made of stone, but hey...

The two flat surfaces of the crescent-shaped, rock wedge – as Jaspa would probably have to describe it[1] – are covered with shallow pits, the biggest of which are about the size of real oranges. Several of these larger pits have rounded, orange-sized stones resting in them, such that it is immediately apparent that the orange-sized stones have been used to make the orange-sized pits on the sides of the orange segment shaped rock. Although, this is perhaps overdoing the whole *orange* thing!

But to Jaspa it's just a big, oddly shaped rock. "I thought we were going to meet your friend Oripot!" he exclaims, baffled.

"So we are, Friend Jaspa. So we are. And this front door of Friend Oripot," replies Tabora cryptically.

***

Jaspa is feeling increasingly confused. He'd naturally assumed that *Friend Oripot* was another *Ses*, but he's starting to wonder. In fact, he's beginning to doubt that Oripot even exists. Perhaps Tabora

---

[1] See... Isn't the *orange segment* description much clearer? Not to mention more poetic!

is playing a joke on him, in an attempt to cheer him up. If so, the Gnuses has a strange idea of what's funny... Leading Jaspa on a wild Ostrichses chase through an almost impenetrable forest of grass; nearly getting him eaten by a wildebeest; making him climb up a sheer, towering rock wall using a tree filled with flesh-devouring sap as a ladder; and finally telling him this huge, bizarrely shaped rock is some sort of door.

"Do not worry, Friend Jaspa," says Tabora, as if reading his mind. "Soon everything clear."

The Nomad reaches down and picks up a large pebble. He takes a few steps backwards... before hurling it, with all his considerable might, at the curiously shaped rock.

Tabora's missile hits the larger rock about a foot and a half from its base, catching in one of the lowermost pits. The curve of the pit sends the pebble ricocheting off at an unpredictable angle, narrowly missing Jaspa. But the young Giraffeses hardly notices...

Because the strange rock has begun to sing!

***

Upon being struck by Tabora's pebble, the enormous crescent-shaped rock emits the clearest, most beautiful, high-pitched ringing tone that Jaspa has ever heard. Through his feet he can feel a faint resonance in the stone beneath him, as if the entire kopje is answering the humming rock's song. Known as *Gong Rock* for obvious reasons, it was once used by the Maasai to announce tribal meetings.

Jaspa stands awestruck as its reverberations gradually die away. Only then does he notice the other, more familiar sound. At first Jaspa can't quite put his finger on what it is. Then he realises it's a voice, but a voice distorted by echo upon echo.

It doesn't sound very happy.

"Bloomin' tourists ...rists ...rists ...ists ...ists ...ss!" mutters the voice crossly. "I hate bloomin' tourists ...rists ...rists ...ists ...ists ...ss! Always banging on the gong ...gong ...gong ...ong ...ong...ng. Think they're so bloomin' clever ...clever ...lever ...ever ...ver."

The voice adopts a mocking tone, "'Oh, look Marjory, a ringing rock! ...rock! ...ock! ...ck!' Fools! ...ools! ...ls! ...s!"

The speaker concludes its opinion of tourist behaviour with a shout... "It's not a bloomin' toy! ...toy! ...y!

"Now, is there anyone out here actually worth speaking to?"

Jaspa realises that as the speaker's irritated rant has progressed, the echoes have gradually become less pronounced. In fact, hardly any accompanied this last question.

The Giraffeses turns around, searching unsuccessfully for the source of the voice. He's about to give up, when he spies the smallest *Ses* he has ever seen, standing in the shadow of the middle potato-like rock, looking at him expectantly.

"Well?" it enquires impatiently.

***

The *Ses* under the rock stands upright on its back legs like Jaspa, but is still barely a third his height. Its body is well-rounded, conveying the impression its owner doesn't miss too many meals, and is covered in wrinkly grey skin. Two immense, floppy ears adorn the sides of its head, and in place of a nose it has a long, flexible, fleshy tube.

"You're an Elephantses!" breathes Jaspa, realising too late that he's spoken the words out loud.

"And you're a Giraffeses!" comes the curt response. "So what? What do you want?"

"Er..." Jaspa is at a loss.

Fortunately, Tabora saves him any further embarrassment by stepping out from behind a smallish rock that has been concealing him from the Elephantses. In an instant, the little figure's demeanour transforms from annoyed martyr to delighted host.

"Tabora!" it cries. "I was wondering when you'd stop by! I was talking to Hembe about you just this morning. Oh! She'll be delighted to see you!"

Without giving the *Nomad* chance to reply, the Elephantses turns back to Jaspa. "But why didn't you say you were with Tabora?"

"I..."

"Any friend of Tabora's is a friend of mine! And of Hembe too, of course!"

"I don't mean to be rude," says Jaspa, finally managing to squeeze a word into the, until now, one-sided conversation, "But, who are you?"

"Why, I'm Oripot!" the tiny Elephantses declares with a bow. "At your service!"

***

"Good to see Friend Oripot," says Tabora, clasping arms with the little *Ses*. "It long time since we last meet!"

Oripot laughs and, shielding his mouth from Tabora with his hand, confides to Jaspa in a loud whisper that the Gnuses is plainly meant to hear, "He says that every year!" Then, in a louder voice, he address Tabora directly, "So, what brings you here?"

"Oh, just passing through!" Tabora grins broadly at his joke and gives Jaspa a wink. The Giraffeses can't help feeling he's suddenly found himself in the middle of a circus act. Clearly, this is something of a routine between the two older *Ses*.

"But where are my manners?" enquires Oripot of himself. "Come in. Come in!"

Beckoning them to accompany him, he turns and heads towards the rock behind him. Jaspa has barely enough time to wonder where on Earth he could be leading them, when the Elephantses disappears!

For the third time that day, Jaspa finds himself rooted to the spot in shock. Whilst a shifting *Ses* may **seem** to disappear to a watching human – assuming that human is a *Seer*, of course, otherwise they wouldn't be able to see the *Ses* in the first place – they **always** remain visible to other *Ses*. And every *Ses* knows that there's no such thing as magic, it's just something invented for children's stories. Yet Jaspa has just seen – or more to the point, hasn't *seen*! – Oripot disappear before his very eyes!

Tabora, who is standing behind Jaspa, places a friendly hand on the stationary Giraffeses' shoulder. "Friend Jaspa not coming?" He takes three strides towards the rock, stoops slightly...

And also vanishes!

Keep calm, thinks Jaspa to himself. *Don't panic. There's a rational explanation for this. Now, if I can only figure out what it is...*

***

After the brightness of the surrounding day, it takes Jaspa's eyes a little while to become accustomed to the shade here under the rock. Slowly, however, amidst the boulder's shadow, a patch of even more intense darkness gradually begins to emerge. A pitch black hole, leading straight into the rock, like the gaping mouth of night itself.

Gathering his courage, Jaspa walks forward and steps into the dark opening...

...And immediately bangs his forehead hard on the rock!

Jaspa clasps his left hand to his head, squinting against the pain. He breathes in sharply between clenched teeth.

"That wasn't the smartest thing I've ever done!" he hisses softly to himself. Under his palm Jaspa can already feel a lump forming, and when he takes his hand away it feels slightly sticky from the trickle of blood that is gently oozing from the small cut on the bump's crown.

Clearly, the unlit tunnel in which Jaspa finds himself was made with smaller *Ses* in mind. He again cups his left hand over his growing lump and, ducking slightly, he gingerly shuffles forward into the absolute darkness, guiding himself along the wall of the tunnel with his other hand.

The passage slopes steeply upwards until, after 15 or 20 steps – it's difficult to count steps accurately when you're shambling forward like a blind, and very nervous, zombie – it makes a sharp turn to the right, almost doubling back on itself. As Jaspa rounds the corner, he becomes aware of a faint glow ahead, which grows steadily as he continues up the tunnel towards it. Still climbing, but gaining confidence with every step, he no longer needs to feel his way along the wall.

After a further dozen steps, the passage makes another switchback, this time to the left. This third length of tunnel obviously runs parallel to the first, although at a considerably higher level within the rock.

But that's not the first thing Jaspa notices. The first thing he notices is the glare. He stands blinking, like a rabbit caught in a car's headlights. For the faint glow he had seen from around the corner is only a reflection of the bright light coming from the far end of this newest stretch of tunnel.

Going from darkness into light, Jaspa's eyes adjust much more rapidly, so that as he walks forward he's soon able to see shapes through the dazzling brightness. But not until he reaches the tunnel's mouth can he make any sense of them. The sight that greets him as he steps out of the passage is noting short of miraculous.

Before him is a vast chamber, carved out of the very rock. Numerous other chambers, great and small, are visible through wide airy passageways, on this level and higher up. Without knowing why, Jaspa is suddenly certain that the whole enormous rock is hollow. Not empty like the shell of an egg or a nut. More like a honeycomb: an incredibly complicated network of interconnected cavities and tunnels, chambers and passageways, rooms and corridors. Jaspa later learns that all three of the enormous potato-shaped rocks are hollow, the two outer ones linked to this middle one where the rocks touch, by means of tunnels not visible from outside.

Outside the rock, the Serengeti dry season is proceeding unchecked. Yet in the middle of the entrance chamber is a wide stone bowl full of water. At the centre of this basin is a fountain that reaches almost to the ceiling, perhaps two feet above. Jaspa has never seen a fountain before, which makes it all the more impressive to him.

Everywhere he looks are Elephantses, dozens of them. Some moving about purposefully, others just standing around chatting, but all contributing to the energised hum that echoes off the rock walls of the chamber, filling the air.

Jaspa drifts forward towards the central bowl, rotating slowly as he goes, taking in the spectacle. He reaches the edge of the basin and dips his fingers into the cool water. Leaning forward, he uses his hand to scoop some of the liquid into his mouth. It tastes wonderfully crisp and refreshing. Unable to think of suitable words to describe his amazement and wonder, he finally settles for just one. An old favourite the World over.

"Wow!" he says.

"So you like it?" asks Oripot, who is standing just behind him, smiling. Then he bows deeply as he formally adds, "Allow me to welcome you to Elephantu."

***

17. Family troubles

"Ah!" exclaims Jaspa, wincing slightly.

"Oh, you poor dear!" murmurs Hembe sympathetically, as she dabs at the lump on his forehead with a cool, damp cloth. Hembe is even shorter than Oripot and so, even though Jaspa's sitting on the floor, she has to stand on a stool to examine his cut. Given his initial surprise at how small Oripot was, Jaspa is even more astonished to discover he's actually quite tall for an Elephantses.

"Well, I'm afraid you're going to have quite a bruise for a couple of weeks. But the cut isn't too bad, so at least you won't have a scar."

They're in the main, oval room of the chambers that Hembe and Oripot share. Behind them are several small arches that lead to the Elephantses' other, more private rooms. By contrast, in front of them is a much larger, rounded opening that fills almost the entire wall. It provides them with a breathtaking, unobstructed view of the Entrance Hall and its fountain. Out in the hall, in the wall immediately to the left of these chambers, is the doorway to the entrance tunnel.

If *Herders* hold elephants in high regard, they have even more respect for Elephantses, considering them to be the wisest and most steadfast of all the *Ses*. Jaspa has never met an Elephantses before, and so finding himself in one of their villages, especially one hollowed out of several giant boulders, takes a bit of getting used to.

Whilst Hembe has been tending to Jaspa's injury, Tabora and Oripot have been catching up. From what he can hear of their exchange, Jaspa gathers it's actually been two years since they last met.

The main route of the Great Migration varies from year to year, changing to take advantage of things such as a recent rainfall or an area of fresh grass. In addition, rather than always moving as one enormous herd, the Gnuses often split the wildebeest into several, really big herds, each following a slightly different path. Jaspa gathers that last year Tabora's route had taken him through the Seronera Valley, too far north of the Moru Kopjes for him to make his usual annual visit with his Elephantses friend.

Taking advantage of a short lull in the conversation, Jaspa asks a question that's been bothering him. "Oripot, did the Elephantses build Elephantu?"

"Erm... Not exactly. Curiously, many of the caverns you can see appear to be natural. In any case, they were already here when we discovered the Three Rocks. We Elephantses have simply modified what we found. We've enlarged some chambers, combined others, and even excavated a few new ones. Of course, we had to construct the tunnels connecting the rocks together. Oh, and we also had to block up the original entrance cave, and replace it with the passageway you entered through... To stop the light escaping, you understand."

Jaspa finds he does understand. Even a human couldn't miss a light shining out from beneath a rock, and they'd bound to become curious. So the sharp turns in the entrance tunnel were designed on purpose: to prevent light escaping from inside the rock.

Yet there's still one thing Jaspa doesn't understand. "But where does the light come from in the first place?!" he asks, voicing his puzzlement. "Surely the inside of a rock should be as dark as night."

"Quite so! Quite so!" Oripot replies. The Elephantses turns to Tabora and says, "He's a sharp one, isn't he?" Jaspa can't quite suppress a self-conscious grin.

"Friend Sofee and Friend Cookees of the *Herd* his mother and father," says the Gnuses meaningfully.

"Indeed?" exclaims Oripot delightedly. "Well, that explains a lot!"

"Anyway, where was I? Oh yes. The light... Well, fortunately the Three Rocks are riddled with a special type of crystal. In the dark it glows faintly, filling Elephantu with a gentle light at night-time. But when exposed to sunlight it shines brightly, as you can see."

"But there **is** no sunlight inside a rock!" Jaspa politely protests.

"Ah, well that's the trick, isn't it...?" Oripot leans towards Jaspa in a conspiratorial manner and confides, "...I'm afraid we Elephantses have cheated slightly! We made thousands of tiny pinpricks to let the sunlight in, all over the tops of the Three Rocks. You can't see them unless you climb up on top and look really, **really** hard. The crystals do the rest. They filter the daylight to every part of Elephantu, magnifying it in the process."

"Cool!" says Jaspa. "And the water?"

"Oh, that's just channelled from a natural spring underneath the kopje."

"And the singing rock?"

Oripot again turns to Tabora. "Sharp **and** inquisitive! He truly is Cookees' son!"

Turning back to a bemused Jaspa, the Elephantses replies, "It's actually called Gong Rock. I'm afraid we don't really know why it rings like that. It just does.

"We discovered its... er... curious properties shortly after we arrived here. Since then our friends have used it to announce their arrival. They sound the gong, then await the Keeper of the Gong, who goes out to greet them."

"So you're the Keeper of the Gong?"

"Quite so! Like my father was before me, and his mother before him. In fact, the position has been handed down through my family ever since Elephantu was first established," Oripot declares with humble pride.

Then a change seems to come over the Elephantses, and he sighs unhappily. "Unfortunately, it's not like it used to be. Humans discovered the Gong, you see."

As he continues to explain, an uncharacteristically bitter tone creeps into Oripot's voice, reminiscent of the annoyance Jaspa had heard in it just before they first met. It's almost as if a completely different, less jovial person is speaking.

"Oh! To begin with it wasn't so bad. The Maasai would occasionally use it to announce tribal gatherings and the like... But then came the tourists. Every year, more and more of them. All banging on the Gong. Morning, noon and night. Like it's some sort of novelty act!"

Oripot sighs again, even more deeply this time. "I do hate the bloomin' tourists," he murmurs.

As if on cue, a wondrous note fills the air, reverberating through the very rock. Jaspa is once again filled with awe, but in contrast Oripot looks deflated. He gets to his feet and turns to his guests. "Excuse me, please," he requests, before heading off towards the entrance tunnel.

***

"Please forgive my husband," says Hembe after Oripot has left. "The constant trek up and down to answer the Gong is beginning to wear him out."

"Why doesn't he just ignore it?" asks Jaspa.

"He can't. It's his duty. Whenever the Gong is sounded, the Keeper of the Gong **must** answer. He used to consider it a great honour, but these days it's more of a burden... What with several dozen humans arriving everyday, each wanting to ring the Gong themselves."

"Can't someone else answer it?"

"No, I'm afraid not. It's our tradition. Only the Keeper may answer the Gong. Still, he's not as young as he used to be and soon, tourists or no, he'll have to pass the title on to Mageshe, our eldest daughter. I know she'll be happy to take the responsibility off his hands, but she has a family of her own and Oripot feels guilty about adding to her daily troubles."

For just a moment a hush comes over the room, then Hembe composes herself and changes the subject. "So, Jaspa, tell me about yourself!" she says brightly.

Her unexpected enquiry takes Jaspa by surprise, and all he can manage is "Oh! Er..."

She smiles kind-heartedly, and offers him a lifeline. "Did you know Oripot and I were fortunate enough to meet both your parents when they were on their *Journeys*?"

"Um... No, I didn't."

"Oh, yes! I remember them well. Sofee was so intelligent and gentle. I was so sorry when I learned she'd passed away."

"Thank you," whispers Jaspa.

Not wishing to dwell on this, Hembe goes on. "Now Cookees, I recall, was full of good-natured mischief, inquisitive about everything, always getting into scrapes." She laughs warmly, "Who'd have believed he'd end up chief!?"

"Sounds just like Friend Bisckits!" chuckles Tabora, who's said nothing since Oripot left the room.

"And who is Bisckits?" Hembe asks Jaspa.

"My younger brother."

"Excellent!" coos Hembe in motherly delight. "Is he much younger than you?"

"Just a year," replies Jaspa.

"Wonderful! I **do** hope to meet him when he makes his *Journey* next year!"

Suddenly sure that the conversation is about to take an awkward turn, Jaspa nonetheless feels obliged to answer. "Actually... er... I promised Mum... before she died, that is... er... that I'd wait for Bisckits... I mean, that we'd do our *Journeys* together."

Hembe thinks about this for a second, before asking, "Then where is he?"

Unable to answer, Jaspa feels the warmth begin in his ears and then spread to his whole face, as he begins to blush.

"Friend Bisckits and Friend Jaspa had argument almost two weeks ago," explains Tabora on his behalf. "Still not speaking."

Thanks Tabora, thinks Jaspa.

"Not speaking?" asks Hembe, clearly horrified. "**Still** not speaking after two weeks? And this when you're travelling together?"

"Actually, it's more like a week and a half," mumbles Jaspa.

"But that's terrible!" says Hembe, ignoring him.

"Tabora say same, but Friend Jaspa and Friend Bisckits not listen." Then, as if it's an afterthought, the *Nomad* innocently adds, "Friend Portia say they stubborn blockheads! She wash hands of both."

Jaspa feels his already burning face get even redder. *You're enjoying this aren't you?* he thinks, giving Tabora an exasperated look.

"And who's Portia?"

"Cousin of Friend Jaspa and Friend Bisckits. She travel with them as *Rubani*."

"Well, I have to say she sounds **very** sensible! I'm sorry not to have met her last year." Hembe returns her attention to Jaspa. Even though she has to look up into his face, her firm, though not unsympathetic, gaze still makes him feel like the small one.

"Jaspa, my dear. I'm sure that whatever your argument with your brother is about, it seems to be of the utmost importance to you both. But there's something you must understand. There is nothing... **Nothing!**... more important than family and friends. Never forget that Jaspa. Never."

Hembe shakes her head sadly. "If you and Bisckits are to work this out, one of you has to make the first move. From what I remember of your parents, if Bisckits really does take after your father, like Tabora says, he's unlikely to back down first. I can only hope, therefore, that you've inherited your mother's good sense. I'm sorry, but it looks like this responsibility rests on your shoulders."

Part of Jaspa wants to shout: *No! That's not fair! You don't understand! You don't even know what the argument is about! I'm the injured party here! I'm the one standing up for what's right!*

Another part of him, that rational part that had saved him in the Oldupai Gorge, says: *Listen to her Jaspa. She's right! You know she's right. After all, she's an Elephantses. She's wise. She knows! She might not actually know **why** you're arguing, but she still **knows!** Perhaps Bisckits will never come around to your way of thinking, but are you honestly willing to lose him over a difference of opinion? And are you really prepared to throw away your friendship with Portia, too? It makes no sense! Hembe's right, Jaspa. It's up to you!*

Out loud, he simply whispers, "I know."

***

When Oripot returns about five minutes later Hembe says nothing, but just gives him an enquiring look. "Oh! It was the Hyraxses again," he answers her unasked question, sounding slightly frustrated and weary.

Hyraxes are small herbivores, which look a bit like large guinea pigs. Three types of hyrax live in the Serengeti: rock and bush hyraxes both live on the kopjes, whereas the tree hyrax – wait for it – lives in woodland. Sometimes it's all in the name.

"Now, now, dear!" Hembe calms her husband. "At least it wasn't tourists!"

"You're right, of course." Oripot takes a deep breath, which seems to restore some of his good cheer. "It's just that these days they just seem to be here all the time."

"What did they want this time?" his wife asks.

"Oh, the usual. I sent them over to speak to Makindu again. He enjoys chatting with our *new found cousins*, as he puts it. Personally, I think he encourages them too much."

As he explains, Oripot gestures through the main opening of the chamber towards a group of four *Ses* standing near the fountain. One of them is an Elephantses, who Jaspa correctly assumes to be Makindu. He sports a large, genuine smile beneath his trunk as he clasps arms with each of his guests in turn.

Jaspa reckons that all three newcomers are probably slightly taller than Makindu, though their hunched posture and rounded backs makes it hard to be certain. Their bodies are covered from head to foot in silky, light brown fur. They hold delicate forelimbs close to their pleasant, intelligent-looking faces, much like a squirrel does. Their faces, which are topped by small, rounded ears, lack even the slightest hint of a trunk.

In short, looking from Elephantses to guests, Jaspa finds it hard to imagine two types of *Ses* who look **less** alike.

Tabora, in his usual straightforward fashion, puts into words precisely what Jaspa is wondering. "Cousins?" he asks curiously.

Hembe and Oripot exchange a brief glance, and then share a faint, resigned smile. "Well," begins Hembe, "It seems that some humans are claiming that they can prove that the hyrax – together somethings called a sea cow, whatever that are – is the elephant's closest living relative. Although it sounds crazy, these scientists claim to have found fossils of a hyrax the size of a hippo! Somehow the Hyraxses have learnt this and..."

"...And now they think they're our long lost cousins!" finishes Oripot. He wrinkles his trunk in uncertainty.

"Don't misunderstand us," continues Hembe. "They're all really rather pleasant. At least the ones we've met." Oripot repeatedly nods his agreement. "And, to be honest, it might be nice if they really are family. Family is extremely important to Elephantses." She gives Jaspa a meaningful glance. "It's just..." She looks over at Oripot for help.

"It's just..." he stumbles, "...Well, the fact of the matter is they do tend to go on a bit! I mean, we Elephantses like a nice chat as much as the next *Ses*. But Hyraxses... they can talk the hind leg off a bloomin' Zebrases!"

"Oripot!" his wife scolds him gently.

"Oh! Sorry, er... off a Zebrases."

Hembe indicates her approval of his revised wording with the slightest nod of her head.

"On top of that, once they get an idea in their heads, they're like a hyena with a bone. They're always here, wanting to discuss what it **means** to be family... Not that Makindu minds. He loves a good debate.

"But I swear, those Hyraxses sound the Gong almost as much as the bloo... as the tourists! I have to go up and down the tunnel so often it's worn my legs down to stumps!" Grinning, he leans back in his chair so his feet are off the ground, and wiggles his distinctly elephant-like back legs at Jaspa, who giggles.

"Still, there's no harm in them... And, as I say, Makindu enjoys the company," he concludes.

***

The *Journeyer* and his guide stay with the Elephantses for most of the afternoon, during which time Oripot gives the awestruck Giraffeses a tour of Elephantu. When Tabora finally announces they have to be going, it is with a heavy heart that Jaspa says goodbye to his newfound friends.

"We know *Herders* don't usually leave the Shifting Sands again, after their *Journey* is completed," says Oripot sincerely, clasping arms with Jaspa. "But if you **do** ever pass this way again, please come and visit us."

"I'd love to," replies Jaspa.

Hembe gives Jaspa a big, caring, parting hug. "Don't forget now, Jaspa. It's up to you to make peace with Bisckits and Portia!

"I know," he assures her quietly. "I will."

Replaying Hembe's last comment in his head, something occurs to Jaspa. "Hembe... You and Oripot did only meet my parents once, didn't you? I mean, when they were young and on their *Journeys*?"

She looks at him quizzically, clearly wondering where this is leading. "Yeees..."

"But you both seem to remember them, and everything else, so well."

"I suppose so..."

"So it's true then... Elephantses never forget?"

"Ah!" says Hembe, understanding at last. She laughs. "I'm afraid not, Jaspa. That's just elephants!

"But!..." she adds purposefully, "It **is** true that Elephantses never forget **family**!"

***

18. Bisckits the Bold

It's almost dark by the time Jaspa and Tabora arrive back at the *Nomad's* camp. The sun has already set, but the sky to the west remains a deep malevolent orange, the colour of a flame's heart. The silhouette of a lone flat-topped acacia stands out starkly against the fiery sky, its dark, cloud-shaped canopy supported on bare, black branches. Above them, the dome of the heavens changes from orange in the west, through deep blue, to black in the east, where the stars shine for all they're worth.

In contrast to the kaleidoscope of colours overhead, the world below takes on the flat, grey, washed-out hue of twilight. Down amongst the long grasses, colour becomes a thing of the imagination. A dream of cheerful brilliance stolen by the approaching night.

Before they even reach the campsite, Jaspa senses that something's wrong. Everything is too quiet... No shouting. No laughing. No singing.

Evidently Tabora feels it too, for he suddenly breaks into a run without even waiting to make sure Jaspa is following.

When they reach the clearing about the campfire, Jaspa's sense of uneasiness increases... This side of the circle is almost deserted. The *Nomads* are all clustered on the other side of the fire, looking out into the night.

At that moment, sounding unnaturally loud in the ominous, leaden silence, a single, calm voice says, "Keep calm. But whatever you do, don't move."

***

Jaspa forces his way through the Gnuses. He's surprised to find they're arranged in a broad, loose, U-shaped arc around a stick that someone has stuck into the ground, end first. The open end of the 'U' is barred by a small kopje, which has a deep cleft running through it from top to bottom.

The stick in question is wide and flat at the top, but tapers rapidly towards the base. Strangest of all, though, is that the *Ses* seem to be keeping a **very** respectable distance between themselves and the focus of their attention. All of them are at least ten feet from the stick.

All except one.

A lone figure stands within the open circle defined by the Gnuses and the kopje...

Bisckits!

Like the *Nomads*, his eyes are focused on the shiny, black stick. This is particularly odd, since he appears to be talking quietly to someone next to the kopje. Jaspa can't see this second person, because the stick is blocking his view.

Driven mostly by an understandable curiosity concerning everyone's strange behaviour, but also in part by his new resolve to heal the rift between himself and his brother as soon as possible, Jaspa calls out "What's going on, Bisckits?"

His brother looks around at him.

And, startlingly, so does the stick!

***

The *stick* considers Jaspa, decides he poses no threat, and snaps its attention back to the front, all in the space of a heartbeat.

"Jaspa!" says Bisckits in a level voice. "Stay back!"

What Jaspa has mistaken for a stick is, in fact, a black-necked spitting cobra. It's impossible to tell how long the snake is, because most of its body lies knotted in loose coils on the dry earth. One thing is certain, though: it's big! Black-necked spitting cobras are usually between four and a half and six feet long, but exceptionally large individuals can exceed eight feet.

The front part of the snake is raised up off the ground, swaying slightly as it concentrates on something at the base of the kopje. The snake's normally slender neck is flattened to form the menacing, blood-chilling hood characteristic of cobras.

Disregarding Bisckits' advice, Jaspa takes three quick steps to his left. The snake ignores him. From this angle, the firelight glistens on the back of the cobra's head, neck and hood, picking out the delicate, diamond detail of its scales.

Jaspa's attention, like that of the snake, is captured by the small, terrified figure the reptile has pinned against the rock. A shiver runs up Jaspa's spine and he feels suddenly sick, for the person trying desperately to squeeze further back into the cleft that runs down the kopje's side is...

***

"It's got Portia trapped," calls Bisckits calmly.

"I can see that!" says Jaspa, trying to get a grip on himself. "OK. Er... Don't panic! We should try to..."

"Jaspa. I've got this covered!" Bisckits interrupts him, firmly. "But I could use your help..."

"What's your plan?"

"Please! We don't have much time, here."

Jaspa is about to argue, but thinks better of it. "What do you want me to do?"

"Right," says Bisckits. "On the count of three, see if you can distract the snake, just for a second or two. But be careful, don't forget these things spit venom if they think they're in danger! Are you ready?"

"Ready!" says Jaspa without hesitation.

"Here we go then... One... Two... Three!"

Jaspa shouts loudly at the snake, clapping his hands noisily at the same time. As he had hoped, the cobra's head swings around to face him for a second time.

Wishing only to distract the snake, not aggravate it, Jaspa immediately falls silent and stands perfectly still. The reptile regards him with cold, emotionless eyes for a second, giving Bisckits enough time to snatch up a large pebble. The snake's tongue darts out towards Jaspa, tasting the air. Once. Twice. Before it again dismisses him and returns its gaze to Portia, who's still cowering at the foot of the kopje.

"OK! Good!" says Bisckits. "That was great." As he's talking, he fidgets with the stone in his hand, searching for the most comfortable position.

"Now comes the tricky part! This time... This time I need you to provoke it into attacking you!"

"You need me to **what**?!" exclaims Jaspa.

"I need you to get the snake to attack you. While it's facing Portia, it can see me too. But if you can get it to look away from us for long enough, I can do the rest."

"What are you going to do?"

"Jaspa. Trust me!"

Even through his fear and worry, Jaspa hears a steely undertone in Bisckits' voice, one he's never heard before. He takes a deep breath. "Alright, Bisckits. We'll do it your way. I just hope you know what you're doing!"

"So do I!" Bisckits mutters to himself. Then, louder, he says, "No problem!"

Someone taps Jaspa on the shoulder, making him jump with fright.

"Sorry!" says an unfamiliar Gnuses behind him. "Didn't mean to scare Friend Jaspa."

Jaspa has been so focused on Portia and Bisckits he'd practically forgotten about the other onlookers.

The Gnuses hands him a flaming branch, taken from the fire. "Thought this might help," he says.

"Er, thanks." says Jaspa, uncertainly.

"Friend Jaspa wave it. Attract cobra," explains the Gnuses. "*Nomads* help too!"

Jaspa looks at the *Ses* behind him and finally registers that at least a ten of them are holding similar branches, which are also alight.

"Thanks!" Jaspa repeats, but with more feeling this time. *OK*, he thinks to himself. *Waving I can handle!*

He turns back to his brother. "Alright Bisckits. Ready when you are... Let's do this!"

Bisckits exhales hard. "Right then! On three again! OK? One..."

Jaspa draws a deep breath, and prepares to shout.

"...Two..."

Sensing the Gnuses gathering at his shoulders, making good on their offer of support, Jaspa grasps the burning branch in both hands, and makes ready to wave it.

"...Three!!"

***

Jaspa bellows for all he is worth, but his voice is all but drowned-out by the riotous roar that explodes on either side of him. As he waves the blazing foliage backwards and forwards in front of him, the *Nomads* step forward, flanking him, so he doesn't have to face the danger alone.

Their courage humbles him. After all, why should they risk their lives for three Giraffeses? But at the same time their bravery inspires him and he steps forward, shouting louder and waving harder than ever.

The sudden explosion of noise catches the cobra completely unaware, just as Bisckits had hoped. It whips around, and its surprise increases at the sight of the thing attacking it from behind.

Unable to distinguish the individual *Ses* amongst the swirling flames of their spinning, burning branches, the snake sees only a fire-breathing creature bearing down on it. Startled into panic, instinct takes over and the reptile reacts as only a spitting cobra can. It pulls its head right back... Then suddenly lunges forward, fast as a rapier.

As the striking beast's head comes forward, it opens its mouth and pumps venom into its fangs, hissing like an enraged cat. Spitting cobra fangs have venom holes in the front, rather than in the tips like other in snakes. This enables them to spray blinding venom up to eight feet into the eyes of their attacker. So it is that the pressure behind the poison, combined with forward motion of the snake's head, sprays two fountains of the unstoppable venom towards Jaspa and the Gnuses.

***

Initially everything goes exactly as Bisckits planned it. More-or-less.

The noise made by Jaspa and his unexpected backing group attracts the attention of the snake. Then the fright of the advancing flames goads the creature into attacking Jaspa and his partners.

But as the cobra pulls its head back its head to strike, things begin to go wrong... Because, for a split second, Bisckits also succumbs to panic.

What have I done? he thinks. *What was I doing, asking Jaspa to stand in front of a vicious, poisonous snake and force it to attack him? What if he gets hurt? I can't believe I've been so reckless!*

But then, out of the corner of his eye, he sees Portia, petrified, wedged into the crack in the rock, weeping uncontrollably. And his determination and certainty come flooding back.

The cobra **is** going to kill her.

This **is** her best chance.

He gauges the weight of the pebble in his hand, takes aim at the back of the snake's head... And launches the stone at his enemy with every bit of strength he can muster.

***

The pebble seems to crawl through the air, moving slower than a fly in amber. Bisckits and the watching Gnuses hold their collective breath as the rock creeps towards its target. Until...

BANG!

The missile slams into the back of the snake's head with a sickening thud, knocking it instantly unconscious! As it collapses, the cobra's trade mark hood deflates and the creature's suddenly limp body crumples to the ground in a tangled heap, like a length of wet rope.

But the venom is already in flight. It spurts towards the Jaspa and his decoys faster than a bullet. Faster than a thought. So fast you couldn't even lift your hand in time to shield yourself!

But then, **you're** not a *Ses*!

***

As soon as the cobra is committed to its attack, Jaspa and the Gnuses *shift* left and right, out of its direct line of fire. Moving far faster than most other animals could even imagine, the *Ses* manage to escape the worst of the snake's weaponry.

Unfortunately, the spitting cobra's *spit* doesn't exactly move slowly either. In the fraction of a second it takes the venom to reach its intended victims, the two concentrated jets have dispersed into a relatively unfocused spray. Even though they're *shifting*, Jaspa and the two Gnuses closest to him can't quite move quickly enough to avoid the outermost droplets of this poisonous cloud.

Luckily, black-necked cobra venom is only dangerous if it gets under the skin or into an eye, and all three of them are able to safely wipe the dew-like poison off their coats.

It's been less than two seconds since Bisckits' count reached "Three!"

***

Jaspa and Bisckits look each other straight in the eye for the first time in almost two weeks. Both wear expressions of relief. And not only because they're all still alive.

Then current events catch up with them. "Portia!" they yell in unison, looking towards the kopje.

But Portia's not there anymore.

The two brothers are instantly beside themselves with worry. They break into a run, dashing headlong for the rock. Happily, their fears are cut short by a curt shout.

"Friend Jaspa! Friend Bisckits!" calls Tabora. "Over here!"

***

Later, the Giraffeses learn that on arriving back at the camp, Tabora had quickly realised what was happening. He'd skirted left, around the back of the gathered *Nomads*, until he'd reached the kopje. At that point he was as close as he could get to Portia without attracting the cobra's attention. The Gnuses had been about to *shift* across in front of the snake and, hopefully, grab Portia on his way past, when Bisckits had announced he had a plan.

Now, no one in their right mind intentionally runs in front of an attacking snake with razor sharp fangs that can spit venom up to eight feet, unless they really, **really** have to! Especially when that snake is 20 or 30 times bigger than they are. Thus recognising the gaping pitfalls of his own scheme, Tabora had decided to trust that Bisckits had a better one. Nevertheless, as soon as Jaspa and the Nomads had drawn the snake's attention away from the stricken *Rubani*, Tabora had seen the opportunity to resurrect his own idea as a sort of contingency plan.

So while Jaspa played matador with a six foot long, highly aggressive, venomous snake, and Bisckits embarked upon some target practice on the same six foot long, highly aggressive, venomous snake, Tabora had darted in, scooped up Portia, and darted back out again... Just to be sure!

***

"I froze!" declares Portia between sobs. "I saw the snake, and all of a sudden everything that happened last time came flooding back. And I just froze! I couldn't move!"

"Don't worry Friend Portia," says Tabora soothingly. "Snake unconscious. *Nomads* already drag it far away. When it wake up, snake slither other way. Cobra too smart to attack Friend Bisckits and Friend Jaspa again!"

Jaspa and Bisckits smile weakly, but both are too worried about their cousin to celebrate their victory just yet. Still, the fact she's talking at last is progress. For a full ten minutes after the attack, Portia was so badly shaken that she wouldn't even release her vice-like hold around Tabora's neck.

Tabora's words finally sink in and Portia looks up at the concerned brothers. "You saved me?" she sniffs.

"Well, we had a lot of help," replies Bisckits.

"It was Bisckits' idea, actually," adds Jaspa.

"Yeah, but it was you and the Gnuses who risked your lives."

"Well, maybe... But you threw the stone!" suddenly caught up in the story despite himself, Jaspa turns back to his cousin. "You should have seen it Portia. Wham! He got that snake right in the head. It didn't even see what hit it!"

"Whoa! What's all this about throwing rocks and risking lives?"

"Er..." say Jaspa and Bisckits together.

"At least you two are talking again," says Portia, trying on a small smile for size. She finds it fits, after all.

"I guess so," replies Jaspa, a bit sheepishly.

"Yeah," confirms Bisckits, with a grin. "For now, at least!"

"Friend Bisckits and Friend Jaspa heroes!" announces Tabora.

"So it seems," says Portia. She sits up, sniffs once more, wipes her eyes on the back of her hands and smiles again, more broadly this time.

"You'd best tell me all about it!"

***

19. The Western Corridor

Next morning, the *Nomads* and their followers turn their backs on the endless plains of the central Serengeti and move into the Western Corridor. From the Moru Kopjes, Tabora leads them northwest, following the southern bank of the Mbalageti River, through the wide gap that separates the hills of Niaroboro and Oldoinyo Rongai. As they travel, the wildebeest herd stretches out to form a loose chain of animals several miles long.

Originally, Tabora had planned to remain around the Moru Kopjes for a couple more days. But everyone, especially Portia, is so uneasy after the events of the previous evening that he decides it's best to get going without further delay.

"It probably good thing anyway," he confides in Jaspa. "Other herds already gone. Tabora's *Nomads* last to leave plain. Don't want to fall too far behind."

This all leaves Jaspa somewhat confused. "I don't understand," he admits.

"What Friend Jaspa not understand?"

"Well, you talk about not getting behind and other herds and **Tabora's** *Nomads*. You mean there are others?"

Tabora laughs. "Has Friend Jaspa **seen** wildebeest herds? They many more than one million beasts! One small *Nomad* and his tribe cannot lead **all** of them!"

He places a fatherly hand on Jaspa's shoulder. "There actually seven *Nomad* tribes. We each lead our part of Great Herd on separate route handed down by ancestors. But all tribes meet twice each year, once on Short Grass Plains and once on Mara, to exchange news, have fun, and for young boy and girl Gnuses to meet each other!"

Tabora grins meaningfully at Jaspa, and then thoughtfully adds, "Perhaps Friend Jaspa has girlfriend back at Shifting Sands?"

The question hits Jaspa like a charging rhino, catching him completely unaware and unprepared. One second they're talking about *Nomad* customs, the next **that**! Bang!

Weren't adults ever young? Don't they remember how embarrassing it is when your mum, or aunt or grandmother goes on and on and on about whether you've got a girlfriend – or boyfriend – yet?

He feels his face redden and, unusually, instead of providing a laid-back and reasonable answer, his mouth seems to be doing a rather convincing impression of a goldfish... opening and closing without any actual words coming out.

Tabora holds his inquisitive expression for a few seconds more... And then roars with laughter.

"Oh! Tabora just joking Friend Jaspa!" he apologises, brushing the tears away from his eyes. "Friend Jaspa not worry, Tabora not really expect answer!

"Young Giraffeses just like young Gnuses. Would rather fight ten spitting cobras than talk to adult about love life! But Friend Jaspa's face...!"

The *Nomad* bursts into fresh peals of laughter.

For once, however, Jaspa's sense of humour temporarily fails him. He sits and stares straight ahead, between the horns of the wildebeest he and Tabora are riding, with an uncharacteristic scowl on his glowing, red face!

***

The Western Corridor of the Serengeti National Park is like a finger of land, pointing towards the sunset. Through it flow the Mbalageti and Grumeti Rivers, on their way to Lake Victoria. Covering a staggering area of almost 70,000 km^2, Lake Victoria is Africa's largest lake. Only Lake Superior, one of the five Great Lakes of North America, is bigger. At its eastern end, the Western Corridor is perhaps 60 miles across, but by the time it approaches the papyrus reeds on the shore of Lake Victoria, over 60 miles distant, it has narrowed to about seven miles.

After the monotony of the infinite plains Jaspa finds the beautiful and varied scenery of the Western Corridor a feast for the eyes. The region is a patchwork of different landscapes and vegetation. Rocky hills rise above smaller, more modest plains, which are in turn broken up by frequent patches of acacia scrub and woodland.

Through all this meander the Mbalageti and Grumeti Rivers, their banks obscured by dense riverine forests. These forests grow thick and lush along the banks of the Serengeti's larger rivers, supported by sub-surface water that is ever-present, even when the rivers themselves dry up. In the relatively cool and moist conditions beneath the trees live a host of plants and animals found nowhere else in the Serengeti.

His mood uplifted, Jaspa soon puts Tabora's teasing behind him, along with the tedium of the endless grasslands.

***

On the morning of their third day in the Corridor, the Giraffeses ride with spirits soaring. For the first time, the three cousins are being trusted to ride together on the back of a wildebeest, without a Gnuses babysitter... And they're all feeling pretty chuffed about it! Perhaps Tabora has some faith in their riding abilities, after all.

In truth, they're not really having to do very much, except stay on the wildebeest's back. All the work is being done by a handful of *Nomads* up at the front of the column, who are leading the way. Everyone else is taking it easy, leaving their wildebeests to instinctively follow those ahead. The pace of the march is leisurely, slowed by the animals' constant need to graze. The wildebeest often spend 16 hours a day munching away on grass.

An incessant cow-like grunting accompanies the herds. "Gnu... gnu... gnu..." Wherever they go, whatever they do. "Gnu... gnu... gnu..." Day and night. "Gnu... gnu... gnu..." Running, jumping, standing still. "Gnu... gnu... gnu..." Five minutes with a herd of wildebeest leaves you in no doubt about how they got their nickname... The gnu!

Jaspa rather likes the sound. He finds it soothing. His brother, on the other hand, has a host of less flattering words to describe it: annoying, boring, brainless!

Bisckits is becoming so complacent about his riding skills that he's stretched out on his back, sunbathing. Sheltering his eyes with his hand, he tilts his head to look around them. "They're funny looking things, aren't they?"

"What are?" asks Jaspa, taken off guard.

"Wildebeest! I mean, look at them... What with their long, sad faces, funny-shaped horns, spindly legs, and a back end that seems to be several sizes too small. I just think they're a bit, well, odd."

Portia giggles. Bisckits gets the distinct impression she's laughing **at** him, not **with** him.

"What?" he asks, sounding slightly affronted. "What have I done now?"

The particular *funny looking thing* they're riding comes to a halt in the shade of a fever tree. It bends down and begins cropping a small patch of short grass it's spotted growing there.

"Bisckits," explains Jaspa slowly. "We've been travelling for almost a month. Surrounded by wildebeest morning, noon and night. And now, after all this time, you've finally come to the earth-shattering conclusion that wildebeest are *a bit odd*!"

"Yeah! So what?" replies Bisckits, clearly failing to grasp Jaspa's point.

"Oh, Bi-zzee!" chuckles Portia affectionately.

"I still don't see... Good Grief!" Bisckits interrupts himself with a sudden, frightened yell.

"What?" shout Jaspa and Portia, startled by Bisckits' unexpected exclamation.

"Shhhh!" Bisckits replies quickly but quietly. He puts his left index finger to his lips and points into the tree above them with his right. "Up there!" he hisses.

***

It takes Jaspa a few moments to spot what has alarmed Bisckits. Finally, though, he sees it. "A leopard!" he whispers in surprise.

The big cat is perched in a fork between two branches, almost directly above them. It appears to be sleeping. At least, it has its eyes closed! With its head resting on its crossed front paws, it lies completely still, except for the tip of its tail, which twitches continuously.

Stockier and slower than a cheetah, but smaller and less powerful than a lion, leopards nevertheless thrive in the Serengeti, especially here in the Western Corridor. There are two reasons for this. Firstly, leopards aren't fussy about what they eat. They will happily hunt whatever comes along, from deer to dung beetles, a habit that provides them with an almost endless menu. Secondly, they are agile tree climbers. Trees offer leopards protection from their enemies, particularly when they're cubs, **and** provide them with a scavenger-proof larder where they can store their hard-earned food.

Under different circumstances, Bisckits and Jaspa would probably find all this extremely interesting. But at the moment, there's only one thing about the leopard above that interests them... Its teeth!

"How do we get this thing to move, again?" whispers Bisckits, prodding at the wildebeest with his foot.

"Don't worry Bizzee," Portia assures him in a normal tone. "We're quite safe,"

Bisckits and Jaspa both look at her as if she's gone insane. "Have you gone insane?" hisses Bisckits, motioning her to be quiet. "That's a leopard up there!"

"I know," says Portia calmly, "but look at its tail."

"What about its tail?" asks Jaspa, puzzled.

"Notice the way it's twitching like that? So you can see the white underside?"

"Yeah," confirms Bisckits. "That's what I saw first."

"Exactly!" declares Portia triumphantly.

The other two Giraffeses just stare at their cousin, obviously none the wiser.

Portia sighs. "Look at its spots. Up there they provide perfect camouflage amongst the light and shade. What's the point going to all that trouble to conceal yourself from your prey, and then waving a white flag around that screams, *Here I am. Look at me. Run away!?*"

Bisckits continues to look bewildered, but a *good point!* expression crosses Jaspa's face.

"When leopards flick their tails around like that, it means, *I'm full, thanks, so everyone's safe,*" Portia informs them.

"Oh!" says Bisckits, eyes wide. "Oh! Well, er... that's good then."

But he still feels relieved when their wildebeest wanders out from under the tree!

***

Later that morning, as they continue to slowly wind their way westward, an unbearable aroma of rancid dung suddenly engulfs the three cousins.

"Eeeew!" exclaims Jaspa, his voice muffled by the hand covering his nose and mouth. "What on Earth is that smell?"

"Hippos," answers Portia, without having to think.

"Hippos?" asks Jaspa uncertainly. "Are you sure?"

"Hippos!" his cousin repeats firmly.

"But why that awful smell?" asks Bisckits, also trying filter out the stench with his hands.

"They mark out their territory using their dung. In some places they make huge dung heaps. In others they use their tails to spray it all over the trees, bushes and grass."

"Aww!" laughs Bisckits. "That's disgusting!"

"Not to a hippopotamus," says Portia, with a grin. "I'm guessing some hippos passed by here last night while they were feeding and decided to refresh their boundary markers while they were about it."

The name *Hippopotamus* comes from Greek and means *water* or *river horse*. Although hippos spend their days in the water, at night they come out onto the land to graze. Portia is spot on about the territory-marking thing, but this doesn't – are you listening Bisckits?! – make hippos dirty. In fact, many animals mark their territory using some sort of *waste product*.

"First leopards, now hippos. How come you suddenly know so much about hippos?" asks Jaspa suspiciously.

"There are just some things a girl has to know," replies Portia primly.

"No, really!" her cousin persists.

"OK, I'll come clean..."

"Unlike the hippos!" giggles Bisckits.

"...There's a hippo pool near here. Tabora showed it to me last year."

"Brilliant!" says Jaspa. "Let's go and see it!"

***

"Look at the size of that one over there!" raves Bisckits.

"Which one?" asks Jaspa. "They're **all** enormous!"

The hippopotamus is the second largest land animal, after the elephant. An adult male can weigh up to four tons.

"Yes. And they're all heavy, temperamental and dangerous." says Portia.

"Yes, Mum!" teases Bisckits.

"You can laugh all you want, Bizzee! But look what happened to me last year because I was careless." She holds up her left hand for Bisckits to inspect. "**I** don't want to be the one who has to go home and tell Uncle Cookees you got squished by an unobservant hippo!"

Bisckits looks genuinely sorry. "I was only mucking about," he says quietly.

"Don't worry about it, Bizzee." Portia ruffles his mane as she speaks. "Just be careful, alright?"

Bisckits nods shyly.

"Now... Do you want to get a little closer?"

"You bet!"

***

The two brothers follow Portia closer to the pool, past a patch of mud churned up by the comings and goings of the hippos.

"Good grief!" exclaims Jaspa. "Have you seen the size of that footprint?"

"I know!" agrees Bisckits. "It's so big I could swim in it!"

"If you could swim!" taunts Jaspa.

"I'll get around to learning sometime," replies Bisckits defensively.

***

To get a better view of the wallowing hippos, they climb up onto one of the cracked, rounded boulders that stick out of the mud at regular intervals around the pool. In reality, the pool is actually a quiet backwater of the Mbalageti River, although it's only joined to the main channel by a thin neck of water.

From atop their perch, the Giraffeses can see the whole hippo gathering. Technically, a group of hippos is called a *pod* or, even more curiously, a *bloat*. This particular pod comprises perhaps 60 animals of all ages, most of which are more-or-less completely submerged, even though the water isn't actually that deep. Being so large, hippos overheat easily and so they spend their days dozing in the relative coolness of the water whilst *rafting*: resting on the bottom with only their nostrils, eyes and ears visible above the surface.

Despite this indispensable inclination towards wallowing, there's still a steady movement of beasts in and out of the pool. As some clamber out of the muddy water to catch some rays, an activity more scientifically known as *basking*, others return to cool off again. The three friends watch as a mother waddles out of the far side of the pool to allow her calf to suckle more easily, although baby hippos can close their nostrils and ears and suckle underwater if they so choose!

At least half the bobbing hippos have birds pattering about on their exposed heads and, in a few cases, backs. A single, dark brown hammerhead stork is using one individual as a living fishing platform. Standing on the hippo's half-submerged back, the stubby-necked wading bird scans the murky waters of the pool for a potential meal.

The most numerous birds, however, are red-billed oxpeckers. Living up to their nickname, tickbirds, several of them are industriously picking parasitic insects off the hippos, grabbing a meal whilst providing an invaluable service to their hosts. Unfortunately, if a host animal has a cut or sore oxpeckers will often lick blood from it, preventing the wound from healing. The bright red of their beaks and the startling yellow rings around their eyes are made all the more striking by the oxpeckers' otherwise drab, brownish plumage.

One oxpecker gets a little too familiar inside a snoozing hippo's ear, and is sent packing with a flick of said ear. Within seconds it comes scuttling back, determined to get that tick!

The peaceful scene is abruptly shattered by a loud bellow off to the Giraffeses' left. A second roar, originating from directly in front of them, immediately answers the challenge. The culprits are a pair of adolescent males who obviously feel the need to burn off some energy. They advance on each other, bellowing and snorting, insolently shoving other animals out of their way and generally disturbing everyone.

As the hothead hippos splash forward, they open their mouths in wide, aggressive *yawns*, which have nothing to do with tiredness and everything to do with intimidation, as they display their lethal-looking tusks.

The opponents clash head on. Literally! Combat is mouth-to-mouth and tusk-to-tusk. The hippopotamus equivalent of arm wrestling. With massive necks and jaws the two upstarts seek to overpower each other, but they're too evenly matched.

Then, as quickly as the uproar began, it's over. Teenage pride is apparently satisfied. And calm is restored to the pool once more.

"OK. That's enough excitement for one day," decides Portia. "I think it's time we were getting back to the herd."

"Right with you!" agrees Jaspa.

***

20. White water

The seven wildebeest herds have amassed once more. During their trek through the Western Corridor they became dispersed, as the various elements foraged independently for food. But in the last few days they have come together again, recombining in preparation for what is perhaps the most dangerous part of the whole Great Migration...

The crossing of the Grumeti River.

***

Four days ago Tabora's *Nomads*, together with the three young Giraffeses in their care, had forded the Mbalageti River without real incident. A pride of lions had killed two wildebeest as they clambered out of the river, but that sort of thing is an occupational hazard for a wildebeest. All in all, from the herd's perspective, it could have been much worse. Although, try telling that to the two animals that ended up as a lion's dinner!

The night before last they had camped at the northern edge of the Dutwa Plain. Then yesterday at first light, they'd left the plain and made their way northwards, passing between Nyambugo Hill and the eastern flanks of the Simiti Hills. By mid afternoon they'd reached the lush, riverine forest that grows along the banks of the Grumeti River and turned west once again, heading towards an uncertain date with danger.

As they marched, Jaspa had been surprised to see clouds building ominously in the skies above. True, they had enjoyed two wonderful, refreshing rain showers since they entered the Western Corridor, but the brewing storm looked far more serious. Sure enough, as evening approached the tempest had struck, throwing everything it could at the moisture-starved earth.

Thunder and lightning had clashed overhead, while wind and water ripped through the defenceless trees and rain hammered at the parched, dusty ground. The *Ses* had sought whatever protection they could find from the maelstrom. Jaspa, Bisckits and Portia had sheltered beneath a rocky overhang. But most of the wildebeest had found no such refuge and had been forced to simply endure everything the storm hit them with out in the open.

Yet in nature there's always balance. And so it was in this case. The animals withstood the storm, and next morning came their reward... Grass! Within a few hours of the downpour the first new shoots had already begun to emerge. By the next morning – this morning – a delicate, vibrant, emerald carpet had been pushing its way up through the old desiccated stems to create wildebeest heaven: a feast of fresh, lush, delicious, green grass.

But even this couldn't detain the herds too long. They had places to be and things to do, and all on the opposite side of the Grumeti River. After all, you know what they say about the grass on the other side... And following yesterday's rainstorm the grass on **this** side is pretty bloomin' exceptional, so just think of what awaits them on the far bank!

As the day had progressed, the strip of land between the Simiti Hills and the Grumeti River had become increasingly congested, as more and more animals squeezed into it. Their westward march had slowed to a walk. And then a crawl.

When the leading wildebeest had collided head on with another part of the Great Herd, coming the other way, the march finally stalled. This second mass of animals had skirted around the western side of the Simiti Hills, and had been making their way eastwards along the river, looking for a suitable place to cross.

Unable to continue forward and incapable of going back, Tabora Talekeeper had called a halt. "*Nomads* cross here!" he'd declared decisively. "But not 'til morning. Tonight *Nomads* camp and rest!"

***

There's a busy atmosphere in the camp tonight. A sense of urgency. A feeling of something that wasn't quite dread, but is somewhere close.

The older Gnuses ready themselves, physically and mentally, for the trials they'll face in the morning. Tabora, meanwhile, goes around and speaks to all the younger *Nomads* in turn. Calming their fears, boosting their confidence, reassuring them. Last of all, he comes to the three *Journeyers*.

"Not many Giraffeses challenge Mighty Grumeti two times," says the Gnuses, his voice thick with emotion. "Tabora proud to say he with Friend Portia for both!"

"Thank you, Tabora," replies Portia, tears in her eyes and voice. "Thank you for everything." She suddenly rushes forward and hugs the *Ses* who has become like a second father to her.

"Friend Jaspa. Friend Bisckits," says Tabora, clasping arms with each of them. "This Giraffeses must know... Crossing Grumeti very serious. Tabora not lie. If not careful can be **very** dangerous. Or even worse..."

He leaves the implications of his words hanging there for a few moments, allowing their importance to sink in, before going on. "But Tabora not here to frighten young Giraffeses. Tabora has beaten Grumeti many times. If Friend Jaspa and Friend Bisckits do as told tomorrow, they stay safe. Tabora promise this! Watch Friend Portia. Do what she do and everything go well. Understand?"

Unsure whether they feel more comforted or terrified by Tabora's speech, the brothers nevertheless nod their understanding.

"Good!" says Tabora. "Now, *Nomad* tradition say tonight *Tale* must be told." He gestures with his hand for them to join him. "Come. Please. Join *Nomads* in *Tale*. Together Gnuses and Giraffeses celebrate past, and prepare for future.

"Prepare for tomorrow!"

***

Jaspa doesn't sleep well. This morning his eyes feel raw and gritty, like he has half a sandbank in them. Judging from Bisckits' bleary expression, be didn't have a particularly restful night either. Portia, on the other hand, whilst not exactly sprightly, at least looks like she got **some** sleep.

"Aren't you even a little scared?" asks Jaspa.

"Of course," she replies, "though it's the wildebeest I feel sorry for. A lot of them are going to die today. But I know that Tabora won't let **us** cross until it's as safe as possible. We'll be fine, you'll see."

The sensible voice in Jaspa's head knows she's right. The only problem is, he can hardly hear what it's saying because the more emotional voice is shouting his fears over the top of it! He's so nervous it's making him feel a little queasy.

* * *

They break camp about an hour after sunrise, and head down to the river. For safety, the Giraffeses have been split up today. They ride on three different wildebeest, each accompanied by their own Gnuses guide.

Pushing their way through the crush of animals, it takes them almost an hour to reach the river. Finally, however, Jaspa gets his first view of the infamous Grumeti.

What strikes him immediately is that the channel is nowhere near as wide as he'd expected. Along this particular stretch, it's only about 200 feet, perhaps a touch more, from bank to dusty bank, and at this time of year the river itself fills little more than three-quarters of the channel's total width.

Their approach to the Grumeti has been through some fairly dense riverine forest. Indeed, looking first upstream, then downstream, Jaspa notices that large sections of the riverbank are overgrown with trees and bushes, on both sides of the channel. Fortunately, the actual crossing point is more-or-less free from vegetation, apart from an ancient sausage tree growing near the top of the far bank directly opposite them. The tree is approaching 30 feet tall and almost twice as wide. Sausage trees get their name from their strange, sausage-shaped fruits, reaching up to 20 inches in length, which dangle beneath them on long vine-like stalks.

The surface of the river itself is roughly 20 feet below the level of the surrounding land. In many places, the Grumeti seems anxious to deal with this difference as quickly as possible, and steep rivercliffs tackle it in a single sheer-sided, vertical step. In several spots, however, particularly on this side of the river, the change in height is handled in a more leisurely, considered manner, with gently sloping banks that begin further back from the channel, avoiding the need for such flashy, dramatic drops.

All in all, Jaspa feels as though a huge weight has been lifted off his shoulders. 200 feet between banks, with only 150, maybe 160, feet of water to cross along the way. A good length of more-or-less vegetation-free bank on either side. And, although a lot of the bank is admittedly quite steep, if you pick your path carefully there are several gentler slopes into, and out of, the channel...

How hard can it be? reasons Jaspa.

Judging by how worried everyone had been last night, Jaspa is certain that they must normally ford the Grumeti somewhere else. Somewhere much more difficult.

Tabora's going to be thrilled when he sees such an easy crossing point, he thinks.

***

Curiously, the wildebeest don't seem to share Jaspa's optimism. With every passing minute, more and more of them arrive, yet they all seem strangely afraid of the river. The entire mass of animals is extraordinarily agitated, as if drawn by the promises of water and the fresh grass, but at the same time repelled by them. Wildebeest stalk backwards and forwards along the top of the near bank. They stare longingly at what they want but, for reasons Jaspa can't understand, they seem unprepared to seize it. The noise of their collective, unhappy *gnu*-ing is deafening.

As more and more wildebeest join the back of the restless mob, those at the front are shoved and jostled by the increasing press of bodies. Something has to give...

...And finally it does!

A single male wildebeest loses his footing and tumbles over the face of one of the taller cliffs, to land on the steep, sandy slope that has accumulated below it. He scrambles this way and that, franticly searching for a way back up. But the harder he struggles to climb the treacherously loose material, the further down he slips, and the closer he gets to the water's edge.

It's a pitiful sight. And one that Jaspa still doesn't understand. The wildebeest must be thirsty, so why doesn't he just take a drink? Why is he so frightened of the water?

Abruptly, a different section of bank gives way under the weight of the animals jostling about on top of it. Suddenly finding themselves standing on thin air, six more wildebeest half slide, half fall down the bank and onto the dry strip of riverbed between it and the water. Even though cool, life-giving water flows past only two or three strides away, they mill around as if unsure of what to do.

Mistaking the unfortunate plight of these half dozen animals for some sort of signal, the remaining wildebeest finally begin to pour down the slopes and onto the riverbed. Eventually, a lone female nervously darts up to the river's edge, takes a quick sip of water, and scurries back to the comfort of the crowd.

This seems to be taken as another signal... *It's safe to drink!*

Suddenly, dozens of wildebeest are scrambling forward, fighting for a place next to the flowing water where, 20 seconds earlier, none had dared to stand. And all the while, more and more animals gather all along the top of the bank, before heading down onto the increasingly crowded riverbed. They spread upstream and downstream, some stooping for a drink, others pacing to and fro, all gazing longingly at the far bank. But none of the wildebeest seem ready to cross.

***

Still confused, Jaspa looks at his guide, Nagare. "What are they afraid of?" he asks.

"That!" she replies bluntly, pointing towards the river.

Jaspa follows the *Nomad's* finger. Nagare seems to be indicating a bulky, knobbly, old log, drifting slowly upstream, perhaps ten feet out from the noses of the drinking wildebeest. It's just one of several dozen large logs Jaspa can see crammed into this stretch of the river. Until now he'd not paid them any notice.

"I don't get it!" he admits.

"Look closer, Friend Jaspa," instructs Nagare. "Which way river flowing?" she adds, meaningfully.

And then it hits him. Logs don't float **upstream**! Nothing can move upstream unless it's being pushed.

Looking more carefully, he spots the unblinking eye. Then the tooth-lined crack of the mouth. Finally he spies the subtle movement of the tail, as it slowly propels its owner forwards, against the current.

***

The calm water gently flowing past the mouths of the thirsty wildebeest erupts without warning, as if a gigantic rock has just been dropped into the river from a great height. Except the massive fountain of water hasn't been caused by something falling **into** the river. It's being made by something coming out! A fearsome, armour-clad, killing-machine – little changed since the time of the dinosaurs – is launching itself out of the water, straight at the faces of the defenceless, drinking wildebeest.

Jaspa cries out in horror and alarm. But the 15 foot monster cares not at all for the unimportant concerns of a tiny, insignificant Giraffeses. It's been waiting all year for this one moment. And, at last, the time has come... The time to feast!

With a mighty flick of its tail, the Nile crocodile charges the unprotected drinkers. Reaching up to 21 feet in length and weighing as much as 2,400 pounds, Nile crocodiles are the biggest of the four African species. Individuals occasionally live past their one hundredth birthday... So it's possible that the brute currently rearing up out of the water may have been alive when Stuart Edward White first *discovered* the Serengeti!

Although the wildebeest have been keeping half an eye on the ruthless predators drifting innocently up and down the river in front of them, the speed and ferocity of the crocodile's attack still catches them by surprise. Its powerful jaws clamp around the snout of its chosen prey and, with frightening finality, it drags the thrashing wildebeest back into the river. The animal struggles heroically, but is no match for the amphibious demon that has hold of it.

The Grumeti Crossing has claimed its first victim.

***

Panic rages! Chaos reigns!

The severity of the attack strikes terror into the hearts of the wildebeest clustered along the shrunken river. They react the only way they know how...

They flee!

But there's nowhere to go. They're trapped between the croc-infested water in front and the packed, unclimbable banks behind.

In their desperate attempts to evade the first attack, several of the terrified wildebeest jump straight into the river itself. One lands right on the head of a waiting crocodile. Temporarily stunned, the floating tank provides the poor animal with an unexpected foothold from which to make a second leap... Straight into the open jaws of another crocodile.

***

As confusion spreads, more and more wildebeest swarm down the Grumeti's bank and onto the riverbed, inadvertently heading **towards** the danger. Eventually, the press of bodies becomes just too great, and wildebeest are forced into the water. Once there, instinct takes over and they swim for the opposite bank. And their lives!

As if by magic, the river is instantly choked with wildebeest. And the crocodiles gorge themselves!

Even so, there's limit to the number of animals even they can kill. And in truth, compared to the number of wildebeest streaming over the bank and through the churning waters, there are relatively few of these prehistoric gangsters. Within a few short minutes, most of them have already secured their next meal and are retiring with it. The successful reptilian assassins drag their prizes into safer waters, away from the thrashing, kicking mass of wildebeest legs and hooves. Even crocodiles aren't immune to the effects of a violent, if accidental, kick in the head.

The wildebeest, meanwhile, have lost all sense of self-control. Unaware that the main crocodile threat has passed, they continue to struggle for the far bank.

Being a wildebeest is all about the herd. The herd gives them life. The herd protects them from the Serengeti's hunters. There's safety in numbers.

But not today.

Today, terror takes over. It's every wildebeest for itself. Fear pushes each one on. Fear of crushing jaws packed with razor-sharp teeth. Those animals reaching a gently-sloping section of the far bank, like the one around the old sausage tree, scramble up and out of the channel to safety. But these are the lucky few.

Most of the wildebeest that survive the carnage of the river are immediately confronted by a new crisis: the 20 foot high wall of the far bank, blocking their escape route. Unable to go right or left, they desperately try to jump or climb their way up the vertical cliff face. All thoughts of the herd are banished from their minds. Now it's all about survival. Their own, personal survival. Unable to think of anything except getting up that bank, they trample each other in their frenzied attempts to scale it.

The damage the crocodiles did to the herds is absolutely nothing compared to what they are now doing to themselves.

***

Jaspa is appalled by what he's witnessing. He looks over at an ashen-faced Bisckits, who looks like he might have been sick. Just beyond his brother, Portia is staring purposefully straight ahead, clearly unwilling to watch the horror occurring below them. Jaspa silently scolds himself for being so innocent. For thinking that **this** crossing would be so much easier than all those that had come before.

"Is it always like this?" Jaspa asks his companion.

Nagare bows her head. "Sometimes worse," she admits. "With crossing Grumeti always come panic. With panic always come death. Same when crossing Mara."

The Mara River forms a second natural boundary between the Serengeti and the Maasai Mara. Crossing the Grumeti and Mara Rivers are the greatest challenges the herds face during the Great Migration.

The Gnuses sighs sadly. "Most difficult part of being *Nomad*, Friend Jaspa, is knowing we cannot prevent these terrors. Gnuses can guide wildebeest, but not control whole herd."

Jaspa looks at the river and shivers. "When do we cross?" he asks hesitantly.

"If Gnuses not cross river safely, no one left to lead wildebeest. So *Nomads* must wait for worst panic to pass." Nagare looks down at the river and then across at Tabora before adding, "But not long now."

"Oh good," mumbles Jaspa.

***

Sure enough, only a couple of minutes later Tabora gives the *Nomads* the signal to begin crossing the Grumeti. Still feeling ill,

Bisckits finds himself thinking of home. For a second he wishes he was back there. But he immediately feels guilty and pushes the thought aside as unworthy of him. Although he might be scared, he's still a Giraffeses of the *Herd* and no coward.

The *Nomads* travel in single file. Jaspa's wildebeest is directly in front of his, whilst Portia's is right behind. They ride determinedly down the slope towards the river. Despite the odd shove from the surrounding animals, they reach the water's edge without any real trouble. A few feet ahead, Jaspa's wildebeest forces its way into the river, the surface of which is whipped white by hundreds of terrified animals. The Gnuses sitting next to Bisckits encourages their wildebeest to follow.

Once they're in the water the riverbed drops away sharply, so that within a few short strides their wildebeest is up to its neck. With a lurch, the animal's feet and the bed of the river part company. Before he can stop himself, Bisckits lets out a small cry and automatically clutches at the *Nomad* beside him... But suddenly the animal beneath them is swimming.

***

At first, everything goes smoothly.

Then, out of the blue, there's a disturbance in the river up ahead. A whoosh of water shoots high into the air... And wildebeest are once again panicking, urgently attempting to flee from whatever it is that caused that ominous splash. With rising dread, Bisckits realises it's another crocodile. Seemingly, not all of them have had breakfast yet, after all.

The scaly titan pounces at the wildebeest next to Jaspa's... And misses!

Undeterred, the crocodile switches target, locking its mighty jaws onto the first thing they come in contact with... The left foreleg of the very wildebeest Jaspa is riding! The petrified creature struggles desperately against the croc, which is now trying to drag it under the water. The seconds tick by, and Bisckits watches in horror, powerless to help, as his brother's wildebeest battles vainly for its life.

Bisckits looks up involuntarily, startled by a loud, harsh call directly above him. Blurred wings swoop past his face, less than two feet away, and head towards the stricken wildebeest. Bisckits twists, just in time to see two great sets of talons grab Jaspa and Nagare and lift them off their exhausted, dying animal. With ponderous effort, the vulture slowly flaps its vast wings, straining to gain height, its prey gripped tightly in its savage claws.

"No!" rages Bisckits at the disappearing bird. "Noooooo!"

In his grief, Bisckits releases his hold on the wildebeest he is riding. So when a wave, created by the struggle between the crocodile and Jaspa's former mount, rocks the animal beneath him he's taken completely by surprise. He flails his arms, fighting to remain upright. But his balance is already lost, and gravity claims him as its trophy.

The last thing Bisckits hears as he tumbles off the wildebeest and into the Grumeti River is the sound of Portia shrieking in dismay. Then, as he sinks beneath the surface, a stray wildebeest hoof catches him sharply just behind his right ear and everything, mercifully, goes black.

***

21. Nippee

The vulture squeezes its vicious talons ever tighter, ruthlessly crushing the little Giraffeses trapped between them.

"Bisckits!" begs Jaspa. "Help me! Pleeeease!"

Bisckits is rooted to the spot. Unable to move. Powerless to help.

"Jaspa!" he shouts. "Jaspa!"

"Bisckits!" cries Jaspa desperately. "Why won't you help me?"

***

The vulture looks at Bisckits down the length of its cruel, half-open beak. Its eyes sparkle, overflowing with hateful mirth. It's mocking him.

"Bisckits!" begs Jaspa. "Help me! Pleeeease!"

"He's mine now!" the vulture croaks at Bisckits. Its voice is harsh and grating. Full of callous, spiteful glee.

Standing upright inside the vile creature's beak, Jaspa tries to prise the two halves apart. But all his efforts are in vain. On his own, he simply doesn't have the strength.

Bisckits watches Jaspa struggle. But when he attempts to go to his brother's aid, he finds his limbs won't obey him. Try as he might, his legs just won't move.

"Jaspa!" he shouts. "Jaspa!"

"Bisckits!" cries Jaspa desperately. "Why won't you help me?"

***

The vulture glides effortlessly between the towering rock walls of the gorge, the Giraffeses gripped firmly in its wicked claws. Jaspa struggles to free himself, pushing at the brute's talons, but all his efforts are useless.

Standing on thin air, Bisckits watches the scene from above, powerless to interfere.

"Bisckits!" begs Jaspa. "Help me! Pleeeease!"

Abruptly, Bisckits finds himself on a narrow rock ledge next to a large, messy nest. An ugly chick caws hungrily from within the nest. A vulture chick. Its parent descends, the tiny figure clutched in its talons. Suddenly, to the delight of the chick, the adult vulture drops its package into the nest.

Once again, Bisckits is unable to move. He can only watch in horror as Jaspa tumbles through the air.

"Jaspa!" he shouts. "Jaspa!"

Jaspa bounces twice, before rolling to a halt beneath the chick's drool-covered beak. The wicked-looking hatchling cackles senselessly, "Food! Tear! Rip! Shred! Eat!"

"Bisckits!" cries Jaspa desperately. "Why won't you help me?"

***

Groggily, Bisckits opens his eyes...

And finds himself staring straight into a gaping set of jaws lined with needle-sharp teeth.

"Arrrrgh!" he screams in shock, bringing his hands up to cover his face. As if that's really going to help against that set of meat-grinders!

"Hey! Hey!" says a surprisingly friendly sounding voice. "Keep calm! Everything ith going to be fine! You're thafe now."

Slowly lowering his arms, a puzzled Bisckits asks, "Thafe?"

The voice sighs, "Not thafe... *thafe!*"

Bisckits still doesn't understand, and his continuing bemusement shows on his face. Beginning to sound slightly grouchy, the speaker tries again, "Look! You try thaying *eth* with jawth like thethe!"

Finally, the penny drops. "Oh!" says Bisckits, "you can't say *s*."

"Ecthactly!" says the voice, brightening up again. "At latht! I thought we were going to have to carry on like that all day!"

"Sorry," apologises Bisckits, "I don't feel quite myself."

"Thath alright!" says the speaker, kindly. "I'm not thurprithed, after all you've been through."

The talking dentures take a step back to reveal their owner. Even so, the outsized teeth and jaws remain the most prominent feature of the *Ses* standing beside Bisckits.

Behind its monstrous muzzle the figure is actually fairly small. About the same size as Bisckits, in fact. Its whole body is covered in a scaly, green hide and its shortish limbs end in stubby paws adorned with ferocious-looking claws.

"Hi!" says the Crocodileses cheerfully.[1] "I'm Nippee."

"Er...Bisckits," says Bisckits. "Um... where am I? What happened?"

* * *

Nippee explains how he'd found Bisckits' apparently lifeless body at the bottom of the Grumeti River. At first he'd thought the Giraffeses had drowned, but Nippee had nonetheless pulled him out of the water and up onto the bank. Once there, the Crocodileses had slapped the senseless Bisckits on the back until, coughing and spluttering, he had given up the muddy river water he was jealously holding in his lungs and exchanged it for deep, life-giving gulps of air.

Once he was breathing again, Nippee had dragged the unconscious Giraffeses further up the bank, between the panicked, stamping feet of the terrified wildebeest. Amazingly they'd reached the safety of the overhanging roots, where they now sheltered, without either of them being accidentally squashed by an ill-placed wildebeest hoof.

"That wath about three hourth ago," concludes Nippee. "Thinthe then you've been athleep."

"Wow!" says Bisckits, feeling slightly stunned. "I guess I owe you my life. How can I ever thank you?"

"Oh! It'th nothing," says the Crocodileses, brushing Bisckits gratitude aside. "I couldn't jutht leave you there, could I?" In an undertone he adds to himself, "Dethpite what the Gnutheth might think of uth."

---

[1] Given that crocodiles were already around when dinosaurs ruled the Earth, it shouldn't come as any great surprise to learn that Crocodileses are probably the most ancient of all the *Ses*.

"Sorry?" asks Bisckits, puzzled once more.

"Oh, nothing," says Nippee. Eager to change the subject, he asks, "Who'th Jathpa? You kept calling hith name in your thleep. I gueth you were dreaming about him"

***

This seemingly innocent question rocks the very foundations of Bisckits' world. The events of the river come flooding back. The wildebeest. The crocodile.

The Vulture!

That flying fiend took his brother!

If only Jaspa had fallen into the water, Nippee might have saved them both. But instead, that heartless scavenger had snatched him away. And borne him off to a certain, horrible death.

Oh, Jaspa!

***

It takes Nippee over a quarter of an hour to calm the hysterical Bisckits down, and another ten minutes to coax a coherent account of what happened from him.

"Well," says the Crocodileses, when he's finally heard the whole sorry story. "It'th obviouth that we need to get you back to your couthin Portha ath quickly ath pothible."

"How?" asks Bisckits hopelessly. "Portia and the *Nomads* will be long gone by now."

"I don't think tho," Nippee gently contradicts him. "After the trauma of the crothing, the Gnutheth uthually make camp early, at a plathe not far from here."

"Really?" asks Bisckits, hardly daring to believe it might be true.

"Really," confirms his new friend. "I can thow you the way."

***

An hour or so later, Nippee comes to a halt and points. "There!" he says simply.

Bisckits looks at where the Crocodileses is pointing. "What?" he asks. "By that fever tree?"

"Yep! That'th it." Nippee stares down at his feet. He takes a deep breath, as if trying to find his courage, before looking back at

Bisckits. "You'll be OK from here. Jutht be careful of any wildebeetht hoovth," he says with forced cheerfulness.

"What do you mean?" asks Bisckits, sorrow again rising within him. "Aren't you coming with me?"

"No," says Nippee, trying to smile. "It'th better if I don't." He holds out his arms, offering them to Bisckits, but the grief-ridden little Giraffeses just sinks to the ground instead.

"Please don't leave me," he begs, on the verge of tears once more. "Please Nippee. I couldn't stand being alone right now. Not even for a moment."

For a second the Crocodileses stands firm. But the sorrowful sight of Bisckits, collapsed on the ground, pleading for him to stay, wrings his heart. Still unconvinced that he's doing the right thing, Nippee agrees to accompany the Giraffeses back to his friends. "But I thould warn you," he says seriously, "Gnutheth don't like Crocodiletheth."

"Nonsense!" sniffs Bisckits, getting back to his feet. "Why would the Gnuses have anything against you?"

"Bithckit'th... you've theen a river crothing for yourthelf. And they're all the thame. The fact of the matter ith, Gnutheth can't forgive uth for what **our** crocodileth do to **their** wildebeetht."

"But that's crazy!" exclaims Bisckits. "The *Nomads* don't hate Lionses or Hyenases, even though I'm sure lions and hyenas kill lots more wildebeest than crocodiles do. Anyway, everyone knows that no *Ses* is responsible for how their animal counterparts behave."

"That'th all true," agrees Nippee. "And I think that, deep down, the *Nomadth* know that, too. But they find the river crothingth tho horrifying, they need thomeone to blame. They feel they can't blame the crocodileth, becauthe they're jutht animalth. Tho they blame uth, inthtead." He sighs sadly.

"That's terrible!" says Bisckits. "But I'm sure Tabora doesn't think like that. You'll see!"

***

"Oh, Bisckits!" cries Portia, tears of joy streaming down her face. "We thought you were dead!"

"I would have been," says Bisckits, hugging her tightly, "if it hadn't been for Nippee. I was underwater and unconscious when he found me, but he pulled me out of the river. He saved my life!"

Portia lets go of Bisckits and turns to the Crocodileses. She reaches out to him and they clasp arms. "It's an honour to meet you, Nippee. I don't know how to thank you," she says warmly.

Nippee looks slightly embarrassed by all the praise. "It'th nothing," he says bashfully. "Any *Theth* would have done the thame."

"Tabora also thanks Friend Nippee," says the Gnuses, although with a faintly **unfriendly** tone.

Nippee bows stiffly in acknowledgement of Tabora's tainted gratitude.

Unaware of the frostiness in this exchange, Bisckits turns to the *Nomad*. "Nippee thinks that Gnuses don't like Crocodileses because of what happens at the crossings." he says naïvely. "But I told him that that wasn't true. That *Nomads* aren't like that. Isn't that right, Tabora."

The Gnuses suddenly looks very uncomfortable, but doesn't reply.

"Tabora?" asks Bisckits confused. "Tell me it isn't true. No... it can't be!"

Several long moments pass before the *Nomad* responds. Curiously, when he does answer Bisckits' question, Tabora is actually looking at Nippee.

"Friend Bisckits shame us by speaking truth. Tabora sad to say Friend Nippee right. Gnuses **have** always blamed Crocodileses for horror of crossings. Many *Nomads* know this unfair, but... subject very emotional.

"But Friend Nippee has shown today that Crocodileses just like Gnuses. Brave and honourable!" The Nomad leader holds out his arms to his former *enemy*.

"Friend Nippee," he says humbly, "Tabora cannot take back unfair way Gnuses have treated Crocodileses in past. But as Taleteller and Talekeeper he can spread truth of Crocodileses in future. Tabora ask Friend Nippee tell Crocodileses, *Nomads* ask their forgiveness."

The shocked look on the Crocodileses' face makes it clear that, whatever he'd expected when he walked into the *Nomad's* camp, this wasn't it. He slowly reaches forwards and clasps arms with Tabora.

"Thoundth good to me!" Nippee says. And, unable to contain his pleasure at this unforeseen turn of events, he grins as only a Crocodileses can!

***

22. The truth will out

The celebrations are brought to an unexpected and abrupt halt by a sudden, horrified shout from Bisckits. Portia looks at her cousin in shock, and finds his features have gone white as a ghost's. He stares, ashen-faced, over her shoulder, pointing mutely at the source of his dismay.

As one, all eyes turn to search for the source of Bisckits' alarm.

As it happens, the reason for Bisckits' horror is hard to miss. For strutting towards them through the milling wildebeest, like it owns the place, is an immense vulture.

"What on Earth's that evil thing doing here?" Bisckits screams, almost incoherent with rage.

A small figure steps out from behind its much bigger, feathered companion. "Actually... He's with me," says Jaspa.

***

Bisckits' anger evaporates in the blink of an eye. "Jaspa?" he asks in disbelief. "Jaspa? Is that really you?"

His legs don't wait for an answer, but start running of their own accord. "Oh! Jaspa!" Bisckits wails. "I thought you were dead."

Reaching his big brother, the little Giraffeses collapses into his arms, crying his bursting heart out. Much to Jaspa's bewilderment, between sobs Bisckits keeps repeating, "I did try to help you. I **did** try to help you."

***

Exhausted by the physical and mental stresses of the last few never-ending hours, Bisckits at last falls asleep in his brother's arms. Only then does Jaspa discover what has happened to Bisckits since the vulture plucked himself and Nagare off the back of their stricken wildebeest.

With tears in his eyes, Jaspa strokes Bisckits' short mane as he listens in appalled silence to Nippee's account of how he saved Bisckits from the Grumeti. Of course, being so modest, Nippee phrases it somewhat differently, but Jaspa's not fooled and knows that's essentially what happened. When the Crocodileses is finished, Jaspa gently lays his little brother down and clasps arms with Nippee. Then, overcome by emotion, he hugs the near-stranger tightly, declaring his family for generations to come in Nippee's debt.

But when Portia asks him to tell them his account of what happened at the river, Jaspa looks down at his sleeping brother and says, "I think it's best if that waits until Bisckits can hear it too."

***

Bisckits is so worn out by the day's events that he doesn't wake up until well after dark. Jaspa, who has come to check on him, suggests that his own story wait until the morning, since it's already quite late. But now that he's awake, Bisckits won't hear of it.

"Very well," agrees Jaspa reluctantly. "But there's someone you need to meet first."

"Who?" asks Bisckits suspiciously.

"I was afraid you'd be like that," sighs Jaspa. "Oh, well. There's no helping it. Come on, she's sitting by the fire with Portia and the others."

Brimming with curiosity over who this mysterious *she* could be, Bisckits follows his brother over to the campfire.

As they approach their friends, Bisckits is pleased to see Tabora and Nippee talking together. In fact, judging by Tabora's sudden roar of laughter, the two seem to be getting on famously.

Bisckits can't see the face of the *Ses* talking to Portia, since she is facing away from him, but it's undoubtedly Jaspa's fascinating new friend. Even though she's sitting down, Bisckits can already see that she's quite tall, probably half as tall again as Portia. And she seems to have a thick, shaggy coat, except on her head, which is almost bald.

Then, slowly at first, a queasy feeling begins to grow inside Bisckits' stomach. As they get closer, he sees that Jaspa's friend doesn't have a *shaggy coat* at all. She's actually covered in feathers.

No, thinks Bisckits, the sick sensation rapidly getting worse. *Please no!*

They're just a few steps away from the fire, when Portia looks up and smiles. "Ngorika," says Jaspa, with brittle cheerfulness, "I'd like to meet my brother, Bisckits. Bisckits, this is my good friend, Ngorika."

The face that turns to greet him fills Bisckits' soul with ice. "I'm so pleased to meet you at last, Bisckits," Ngorika says warmly. "I've heard so much about you."

But Bisckits makes no reply. Because Bisckits hasn't even heard what she said. Bisckits is only aware that the words are coming out of a brutal-looking, hooked beak...

Ngorika is a Vultureses.

***

Surprisingly, Nippee is the first to react. He grabs the open-mouthed, staring Bisckits by the arm and leads him a short distance away, calling over his shoulder, "Ecthcuthe uth one moment."

Once they're out of earshot of the group by the fire, he turns Bisckits to face him. "What are you doing?"

Bisckits shakes his head, as if waking from a trance. "What am **I** doing?" he cries. "*What's Jaspa doing?* don't you mean?"

"Jaspa isn't the one being incurably rude!" counters the Crocodileses.

"But she's a Vultureses!" Bisckits exclaims, confused and appalled.

"Well, hooray!" Nippee declares. "At leatht your eyeth are working even though your brain clearly ithn't!"

"What are you talking about?" asks Bisckits, unable to understand why Nippee is being so mean to him.

"I don't believe you!" the Crocodileses confesses. "Jathpa warned me about your problem with vultureth. To begin with I didn't believe him, even though we don't really know each other that well. After all, you were the one who made Tabora realithe how wrong the *Nomadth* have been for hating the Crocodiletheth all thith time.

"But then I thought...Well, nobody'th perfect! And maybe Bithckit'th **doethn't** like vultureth. Big deal! Becauth I **know** he won't hold that againtht Vulturetheth. He knowth better than that!

"Yet here you are, only a few hourth later, making me feel like a right idiot!"

During Nippee's speech Bisckits' mouth has opened wider and wider, whilst his face has become redder and redder. Unsure of whether to defend himself or apologise, for a while he does neither. Finally he settles for, "I'm sorry, all right! I just don't like vultures."

"Fine!" Nippee almost shouts. "Whatever! We're all entitled to our own little ecthentrithitieth.[1] But Ngorika ith a **Vulturetheth**, not a **vulture**!"

The gentle little Crocodileses lets out a long, frustrated breath. When he continues, it's in a much quieter, calmer tone. "You know, I talked with Ngorika quite a bit while you were athleep. And, not that it thould matter, I really like her. Yet here you are, treating her like thome kind of fiend. Even though you've never even met her!"

Bisckits doesn't respond.

"Don't you get it?" Nippee demands, his voice filled with sadness. "Ngorika thaved your brother'th life. Jutht like I thaved yourth! How would you feel if Jathpa treated me the way you're treating her? Like a monthter! Think about it..."

***

When Nippee and Bisckits return to the group by the fire, the young Giraffeses mumbles an apology to Ngorika, which she graciously dismisses as unnecessary. Clearly feeling his duty is done, Bisckits sits down and turns expectantly to his elder brother.

Jaspa sighs, but lets his younger brother's barely acceptable behaviour pass without comment, for now at least. Instead, conscious of all eyes being upon him, Jaspa begins his story.

"Well, I guess it all started a little over a year ago. Just after Portia left on her *Journey*, in fact.

"I was out walking one day, just east of the Shifting Sands, when I stumbled upon a Vultureses... Ngorika. Actually, *stumbled* is the right word, because I wasn't really paying attention to where

[1] Er... If you haven't worked it out, that would be *eccentricities!*

I was going and she was lying unconscious in the middle of the dry streambed I was wandering along.

"It was immediately obvious that her wing was hurt quite badly. I discovered later that she'd got too close to a pair of squabbling jackals and one of them had snapped at her wing.

"Anyway, as carefully as I could, I dragged Ngorika into the shade of the stream bank. That's when Hook first arrived.

"I was really scared at first, I can tell you! Back then I didn't know that Vultureses often travel together with a vulture companion."

This is true of many 'bird *Ses*'. If the bird is significantly larger than the *Ses*, as is generally the case with vultures and Vultureses, the *Ses* may even sometimes ride on the bird's back, especially on long journeys.

"What I did know was that there was an enormous, frightening-looking bird, with uncertain intentions, standing over me, watching my every move! Yet, the strangest thing was that he seemed to be just as suspicious of me as I was of him. Eventually he realised I was trying to help Ngorika and so left me in peace, though over the next couple of months Hook often returned to check on his friend.

"Ngorika remained unconscious for two full days, and I was beginning to get really worried. But when I returned on the third day... Oh, I should say that I had to leave her at night and return home, so that nobody would come looking for me and find her instead."

For the first time since he started his tale, Jaspa looks directly at his brother. "I'm sorry, Bisckits. I wanted to tell you, really I did. But at first I didn't know how, knowing your feelings about vultures and all... After that it just got harder because, on top of everything else, I'd have to try and explain why I'd not told you before."

He sighs, and then continues. "Anyway, on the third day I found Ngorika had woken up. She told me that her wing was broken and that she needed my help to straighten and splint it. At her suggestion, I went back home and scraped together a few pieces of wood and some twine.

"Splinting Ngorika's wing was probably the most difficult thing I've ever done. To begin with, she was able to talk me through what to do, but as I pulled her wing straight there was an awful grating sensation and Ngorika passed out with the pain. I was almost sick.

Finally, though, I managed to secure her wing with the wood and string.

"Over the next seven or eight weeks I visited Ngorika almost everyday, sometimes more than once a day... whenever I could, really... and we became really good friends. She gradually got better, until one day she decided it was time for the splint to come off. The wing had healed really well and, although it still wasn't strong enough for her to fly, without the splint she was able to ride on Hook's back and return to her family.

"I was really sad when she left and we didn't see each other for a couple of months. In fact, I was beginning to think she'd forgotten me." Jaspa and Ngorika both laugh at his little joke.

"Then, one day, completely unexpectedly, she came back to visit me. Since then we've met fairly regularly, including once whilst Bisckits and I were on our *Schooling* in Ngorongoro. And when our *Journey* took us up to the Hidden Valley, I was even able to go and visit Ngorika's home in the Olkarien Gorge, with Tabora's help." He nods to the Gnuses, who grins in reply.

"And that brings us up to this morning, more-or-less. Actually, there's not that much to tell about what happened at the river.

"Luckily for Nagare and me, Ngorika had decided to spring a surprise visit. Travelling with Hook, she'd followed the herds to the crossing point. With the benefit of her amazing eyesight, she spotted us just as we arrived at the river. She circled overhead with Hook, planning to see me safely across the Grumeti, then go and get lunch and return to see me this evening.

"From her superior vantage point she saw the crocodile heading towards us long before I did. Unable to do anything else, she sent Hook speeding down to rescue us. He managed to grab Nagare and me just as our poor wildebeest was pulled beneath the water.

"There's absolutely no doubt in my mind that Ngorika's quick thinking, and Hook's even faster reactions, saved both our lives."

***

Part 3

Detours

23. An unexpected guest

"I can't believe you have to leave already," says Nippee.

"Yeah," agrees Bisckits, "But Tabora says he can't wait any longer."

Yesterday, the day after the crossing, Tabora had suggested the *Nomads* and their various guests could probably do with an extra day's rest. Thanks to the rainstorm two days previously, the wildebeest had enough fresh grass to keep them happy, so the *Ses* had remained in their camp beneath the fever tree.

But their departure can't be delayed forever, and today they must move on.

The young Crocodileses sighs, "I'd love to come with you. Jutht for a while. I've alwayth wanted to thee a little of what'th beyond the bankth of the Grumeti! But..."

"So, why **don't** you come with us?" interrupts Ngorika, unexpectedly appearing behind them.

Bisckits flinches slightly. After listening to Jaspa's story (and Nippee's little lecture!) the night before last, he's been trying to treat Ngorika with the respect she undoubtedly deserves. She did save his brother's life, after all. But Bisckits is still having trouble seeing past the fact that, although Ngorika is a *Ses*, she's also distantly related to vultures.

"How can he?" Bisckits asks, with slightly exaggerated politeness, "Tabora says we have to leave this morning, and if Nippee goes too far from the river, he won't be able to find his way back."

Ngorika addresses her next question to the Crocodileses, "So, you don't really mind how far you get from the river? It's getting back that's the issue?"

"I gueth," replies Nippee, spreading his arms and shrugging. "But in the end, it'th the thame thing."

"Not necessarily," says the Vultureses, with a smile in her eyes. Having a beak, rather than lips, it's difficult for Ngorika to smile in the conventional way. "If I offered you the chance to stay with us for a few more days, whilst still being able to return to the Grumeti within an hour or two, would you be interested?

"Abtholutely," says the likeable Crocodileses, "but..."

"You've got a plan, haven't you?" interrupts Bisckits excitedly.

"Perhaps..." she replies, teasing them.

"Well, what ith it?" enquires Nippee eagerly.

The Vultureses keeps them guessing a few seconds more before giving them her simple, concise answer. "Hook!" she says.

"Hook?" asks Nippee.

Bisckits' face has fallen and he says nothing. If he's still finding it awkward to deal with Ngorika, it's nothing compared to the trouble he is having with Hook. Even though it was actually Hook who saved Jaspa, Bisckits is having real difficulties overcoming his old, if irrational, hatred of vultures.

Ngorika tactfully acts like she hasn't noticed the sudden change in Bisckits' mood. "Yes. Hook. Whenever you decide to go home, I can ask him to fly you there."

Nippee looks slightly startled. "Er... well... You know, it'th not that I'm not grateful," he stammers. "I'm jutht not thure I'd like all that dangling from talonth and thtuff."

"Oh, it's perfectly safe," the Vultureses assures him. "And anyway, Hook only grabbed Jaspa and Nagare with his feet..." A grimace passes across Bisckits' face and he winces noticeably. "...because there was no alternative. Normally, he lets me ride up between his shoulders."

Despite his reaction only seconds earlier, it's Bisckits who speaks next. "Everybody knows I've always had a problem with vultures," he says honestly. "I don't really know why. But I'm trying to get over it, really I am." This last appeal he makes to Ngorika.

The little Giraffeses then turns to Nippee and continues, "So if Ngorika is willing to do this, I for one hope you'll accept her offer. And, if it makes any difference..." He pauses, draws in a deep breath, then lets it out before concluding in a rush, as if afraid that if he doesn't say it quickly, he won't be able to say it at all, "... I'll fly with you, so you don't have to do it alone!"

The generosity of the unexpected gesture isn't wasted on the other two *Ses.* For a few seconds they both stand there, stunned, before Nippee finally responds. "Well, in that cathe... It would be rude of me to thay no!"

"Brilliant!" cries Bisckits, jumping up and punching the air.

Ngorika takes a step towards Bisckits and, bowing formally, declares, "I am proud to know you, Bisckits of the *Herd*."

"So am I!" agrees Jaspa, who's overheard the last part of the conversation as he approached. He walks up to his little brother and gives him a big Bearses hug, adding in a voice only Bisckits can hear, "And Mum would have been proud of you, too."

***

They set out less than an hour later, heading northwest towards the distant Maasai Mara. Tabora estimates there's probably 60 miles or more between the point where they crossed the Grumeti and those lush pastures.

At the end of a long day, they make camp in a patch of open acacia woodland just to the north of the Kitunge Hills. Their *Nomad* guide seems fairly happy with the day's progress. Nippee, on the other hand, is somewhat less than pleased.

"Awww! My poor aching bottom!" he complains. "I don't know if I would have agreed to come along if I'd known it would be like thith. Why didn't you warn me wildebeetht are tho uncomfortable?" he asks Bisckits accusingly.

"Oh! You get used to it after a while, "replies Bisckits airily. "Anyway, with your armour-plated behind, it's the wildebeest I feel sorry for!"

"Nithe!" retorts the Crocodileses, unsuccessfully pretending to be insulted.

"Actually," says Tabora seriously, "wildebeest that Friend Nippee ride today, ask if he carry her tomorrow. Just to be fair!"

The whole group of friends burst out laughing.

"What did Tabora say?" asks the Gnuses innocently.

"Hey!" complains Nippee, flashing his trademark grin. "Be fair! I'm the one in pain here."

"Yeah. I bet you're looking forward to riding with Hook's nice, soft feathers as padding now, aren't you?" jokes Portia.

Everybody laughs again... including Bisckits, Jaspa is pleased to note.

***

Later that evening they sit relaxing around the campfire, some of them dozing, some of them talking quietly. Bisckits is chatting with Nippee and, much to everyone's surprise, Ngorika.

Suddenly an unfamiliar voice drifts out of the darkness, from amongst the trees. "Hallo! Is there anyone there?"

They all look at each other, with the same question written on their faces: who could be wandering around the woods at this time of night?

"Over here, Friend. By fire," calls Tabora, taking control.

They all stare in the direction that the voice came from, although for a minute or two their curiosity is met only by the shuffling sound of someone making their way through dry undergrowth. The figure that finally steps out of the bush and into the circle of light provided by their campfire is unlike any *Ses* any of them have ever seen.

It's about the same height and build as Jaspa, but its long, shaggy coat prevents them from glimpsing too many of its other features. The coat itself, which appears to be a dirty grey colour, is filthy and matted, and probably the source of the unpleasant odour that accompanies the figure as it walks up to the fire.

"Hallo," says the newcomer again, the tone of its voice strongly suggesting *it* is actually a *him*. His accent is peculiar, but his manner appears friendly enough.

"I'm sorry tae disturb yers all," he continues politely, "But could I trouble ye tae assist me in a wee matter o' life an' death?"

***

It takes them a few moments to react to this extraordinary request, even after they've managed to *translate* the stranger's curious accent. In the end, Ngorika is the first to respond.

"Life and death?" she asks.

The grubby *Ses* turns to face her. "Aye, lassie, that's reit! Life an' death!"

"Are you ill, then?" the Vultureses perseveres.

"Nae, lassie, though it's reit kind o' ye tae ask." Through the figure's tangled fur Ngorika can just about see him smile. "Nae, it's the wee tall bairn that's in need o' help."

"Tall bairn?" asks Jaspa, not understanding at all.

"Aye!" says the newcomer, swinging round to look at Jaspa. "A baby, ye ken... But a greit tall thin', mebbe eight feet tall, wi' lanky legs an' a greit lang neck. Och! An' a braw wee coat like yerself."

"A Giraffe?" shout Jaspa, Bisckits and Portia in unison.

"Aye!... Mebbe," says the stranger uncertainly. "It's ower in yonder wood."

Newborn giraffe calves are approximately six feet tall. Adult females, known as cows, are about 16 feet tall on average, whilst full-grown males, called bulls, can occasionally reach 19 feet in height. Consequently, it's immediately clear to the three Giraffeses that the animal in need of help isn't very old.

"What's wrong with it?" asks Bisckits.

"It's got its wee back leg stuck in some sort o' wire hoop," explains the *Ses*. "I tried tae free it, but on mah own I'm nae strong enough tae open the loop, especially wi' the poor wee bairn kickin' so."

"It sounds like a poacher's snare," guesses Jaspa.

A snare is a type of trap, in this case a simple wire loop that catches around the animal's leg. It's particularly cruel and painful, since the more the animal struggles, the tighter the snare gets and the deeper it cuts.

Portia turns pale. "P-please... Can you show us the way?" she begs.

"Och! O' coorse, lassie. Isnae that why I'm here?"

***

As he'd promised, the peculiar *Ses* leads the six friends to where the giraffe calf is trapped. It takes them less than ten minutes to reach the spot, and even before they can see the calf they hear its heartbreaking cries echoing through the trees.

They find the distressed youngster – a male – standing in a moonlit clearing beside a wait-a-bit thorn bush, his right hind leg sticking out at an awkward angle behind him. It's obvious that, as Jaspa had grimly predicted, the leg is caught in a poacher's snare. Portia fears the worst and silent tears stream down her face.

Unaware that the *Ses* are there to help him, the calf continues his mournful bleating. Far from being silent like you might expect, young giraffes regularly make bleating, sheep-like sounds and mewing, cat-like noises. Every so often the stricken giraffe gives his trapped leg an unwise and painful tug. But there's little else he can do for himself.

Tabora bends down to look at the animal's injured leg and, with a sigh of relief, he declares that the initial news is surprisingly good. "Cut shallow. Only skin damaged. If we free him, he probably live."

The Gnuses diagnosis is greeted by fresh waves of tears from Portia.

***

24. Strangers in the night

A crashing noise from the trees off to the west announces the fact that the *Ses* aren't the only ones out in the woods tonight.

"I think the calf'th crying ith attracting thome attention," says Nippee.

"Aye," replies the newcomer. "It's probably mammy an' daddy come back tae find their wee bairn. Either that, or its somethin' wi' even mair teeth than ye've got, pal..." he winks at the Crocodileses, to show he's joking, "...lookin' for an easy meal."

"Yeah, well, even if it is someone friendly, we better get him out of this before they arrive," says Jaspa. "If he gets excited and starts tugging at this leg he could do himself some real damage."

"And make our job a lot harder, too," adds Bisckits.

"OK," says Tabora, taking charge again. "This need everyone work together, OK?"

Everyone accepts his authority unquestioningly, including the latest addition to the group. "OK!" they all repeat.

"Portia, Ngorika and Bisckits, over there. Watch for company," orders the Gnuses, pointing in the direction of the crashing sounds.

The fact that Tabora drops his usual *Friend* from each of their names is an obvious sign of the situation's urgency, which isn't lost on the others.

Even so, Bisckits starts to object, but Tabora cuts him off. "No time to argue, Bisckits!" he says decisively. "Can't all pull on wire. Yours important job, too!"

Without waiting for Bisckits' response, the Gnuses turns back to the remaining *Ses*. "We each take corner. Pull together on three."

"Thoundth like a plan!"

"Reit ye are, laddie."

"Got it!"

The calf must feel them as they take hold of the wire. Before Tabora can even start the count, he jerks his leg wildly, sending Nippee flying into the air. Tucking himself into a ball, the Crocodileses soars through the night sky with all the grace of a... of a... well, of something that isn't very graceful. After a flight of about ten feet, he crash lands smack-bang in the middle of a thorn bush amidst the crack of breaking twigs and an outpouring of moderately bad language!

***

Helped by Jaspa, and with the occasional groan and *ow!*, Nippee eventually manages to disentangle himself from the prickly shrub. "All thethe thcaleth come in handy now and then," he says, rapping on his armoured skin with his knuckles. "No harm done."

"Do you think it would help if one of us tried to keep the calf calm?" enquires Portia. "You know, talk gently to him or something?"

"Probably," agrees Jaspa. "But how do we get up near his ear without making him worse? If we try to climb up his neck and he panics he could really hurt himself!"

"And uth!" adds Nippee.

"I might have an idea." Everyone turns to stare at Ngorika, to find **she** is looking at Bisckits. "But it would mean that you'd have to really, **really** trust me, Bisckits."

All eyes shift from the Vultureses to the little Giraffeses.

"I do!" he replies in a firm voice, without the slightest hint of hesitation.

"Good," says Ngorika.

"So what's your plan," Bisckits asks.

"Just this... As long as I can lift your weight, I think I can fly you up to that branch there. The one next to the calf's head. From there you should be able to try and keep him calm."

"Why Bisckits?" demands Jaspa, feeling suddenly protective. "I'll do it!"

Ngorika begins to explain, but Bisckits interrupts her. "No Jaspa!" he says calmly. "This is my job. I'm the lightest, so Ngorika has the best chance of lifting me. Besides, Tabora needs you on the wire."

They all look at him with an increased feeling of admiration.

Jaspa puffs out a shallow breath. "Fine!" he says. "You're right. But hurry up, before I change my mind!"

"Aye, laddie," says the stranger jovially. "Be quick aboot it, afore oor uninvited guests arrive!"

Ngorika walks over to stand directly in front of Bisckits. "Now... stand up straight and lift your arms above your head," she instructs.

Bisckits does as he is told without further questions, even though this is an unusual posture for him, as he normally prefers to have all four limbs touching the ground.

"Right," Ngorika continues, "I'm going to fly above you and grip your wrists in my talons. You, in turn, should try and grip my ankles with your hands. Understand?"

"Got it!"

"You'll be hanging from your arms, so your shoulders might start to ache a bit... but I'll be as quick as I can. For both our sakes." She looks Bisckits in the eyes and slowly adds, "**I will not drop you!** OK?"

Bisckits just nods. Once.

Ngorika unfurls her wings and, with a single downward sweep, leaps into the air. She quickly and efficiently positions herself above Bisckits and grips his wrists with her feet. Just as instructed, Bisckits takes hold of her ankles.

"Ready?" she calls.

"Ready," replies the nervous, but determined-looking Giraffeses.

Ngorika begins to beat her long and graceful wings. Unfortunately, they're not really built for this kind of flying. They're designed for soaring – for the lazy freedom of riding the thermals – not flapping. And especially not whilst trying to carry another more-or-less adult *Ses*. Yet she ignores the pain and concentrates on the task at hand... Or more accurately, in her talons.

The strain also shows in Bisckits' face, though, like the Vultureses, he bears it without complaint.

Gradually, the powerful strokes of Ngorika's wings lift them higher into the air. When they're about three feet off the ground, Bisckits closes his eyes tight shut. Then he seems to change his mind and opens them again, facing his fear.

To save frightening the calf, and to make their approach to the branch a little easier, the Vultureses takes them slightly higher than their final destination. She then glides them in towards the tree, altering their course with subtle movements of the feathers at her wingtips.

As they approach their goal, she calls to Bisckits, "When I tell you, grab the branch...

"Now! Grab it!"

Bisckits lands with his back legs on one side of the branch and his front legs[1] on the other. He scrambles to get a hold on the limb to a chorus of gasps from below. But a few seconds later he's sitting safely on his perch, with Ngorika floating down to land beside him. Bisckits beams from ear to ear.

"That was great!" he calls jubilantly.

"Look at him," says Nippee in fake disgust. "That'th a bigger thmile than even I can manage!"

Jaspa gives his brother a wave. "What's the view like from up there?" he asks.

"Awesome!" grins Bisckits.

"Well done, both of you!" says Tabora, "But lots more to do yet. And not much time..."

At that instant, as if to underline Tabora's request for haste, they catch the strangest sound filtering through the trees. It's like an insane cackling laugh. Several cackling laughs, in fact. Each rising and falling, accompanied by the kind of growls that leaves the listener in no doubt that the things producing them have big, sharp, nasty – and above all, hungry – teeth!

"That dinnae sound like mammy an' daddy!"

"Right!" shouts Jaspa. "Lets get a *shift* on! Come on, everyone, you know what to do!"

[1] Or arms... Take your pick!

***

In the end, they manage to free the giraffe without further incident. Bisckits whispers gently in his ear, the soothing sound of the Giraffeses' voice keeping the calf calm. Meanwhile Tabora, Nippee, Jaspa and the stranger pull the wire snare off the subdued animal's leg. In less than a minute the calf is free. It hobbles about the clearing, testing his weight on his injured limb.

That's when the real trouble begins!

***

"Watch out!" yells Portia. "Hyenas!"

The hyena's strange appearance, chilling, human-like calls, and willingness to eat absolutely anything, have all contributed to its unfair reputation as a foul, scavenging villain. The Maasai believe that witches and sprits ride on hyenas, casting their evil spells. Of course hyenas **will** scavenge whenever they get the chance, but then so will lions. Yet surprisingly, hyenas kill most of what they eat themselves and are actually **the** most successful **hunters** in the Serengeti.

That all being said, on this moonlit night, the *Ses* grouped around the injured calf see only the menacing silhouettes of three vicious killers advancing through the trees.

"We've got to do something!" cries Portia.

"Nothing more *Ses* can do, Friend Portia. Cannot fight hyenas."

"Tabora's right," agrees Jaspa hopelessly, in answer to Portia's look of horror and disbelief. "We've done all we can. It's up to him now."

Three spotted hyenas, the biggest and most common of the three species of hyena found in the Serengeti, enter the clearing and strut towards the limping giraffe. Sadly, lions and hyenas kill between half and three-quarters of all giraffe calves.

The slavering monsters begin to circle their prey, whooping and chattering dementedly. Their meal assured, they seem in no hurry to get things over with. The calf mews like an abandoned kitten, perhaps sensing the hopelessness of his situation.

"I can hear something else coming!" Bisckits calls down from his perch. "Over that way." He points towards the trees to the north.

"That's why our three friendth here are in no hurry," realises Nippee. "They're waiting for reinforthementth to arrive."

"I don't think so!" cries Bisckits, suddenly glimpsing a head and long neck between the trees. "They're giraffes!"

Within moments two adult female giraffes come galloping out of the forest. Usually, giraffes will move at one of two speeds: walk and gallop. They can gallop for long distances at 30 miles an hour, but when necessary – like now – they can sprint for short distances at speeds of over 35 miles an hour.

Heads swinging up and down to keep their balance as they run, the females charge into the clearing. One of them goes immediately to stand protectively over the injured youngster.

"Looks like mammy's back, after all!" says the stranger gleefully.

The other giraffe advances on the three hunters who back off reluctantly, unwilling to chance a potentially fatal kick from an adult giraffe. Finally, having blown their chance of a late supper, the hyenas retreat back into the trees.

***

Portia rushes over to the messy-looking stranger and, much to his surprise, envelopes him in a hug. "Oh! Thank you!" she says, clearly on the verge of crying again. "If it wasn't for you he'd probably have been killed."

"Och!... Aye... Well... Mebbe..." he replies, sounding very embarrassed.

Jaspa walks over and clasps the newcomer's arms. "Portia's right. There's no question that you saved him... er..."

Jaspa suddenly realises he doesn't know what to call the kind-hearted, if somewhat grubby, stranger. In the rush to reach the snared giraffe, there'd been no time for introductions. "I'm sorry we don't even know your name..."

"Och! Well, that's easily fixed. Th' name's Gravee. An' I'm reit pleased tae meet yers all."

***

25. Gravee

Buzzing with excitement after their successful rescue mission, the group return to camp. Bisckits chatters tirelessly with Nippee and Ngorika, reliving his daring aerial exploits.

"It was sooo cool," he says for at least the tenth time. "Did you see me, Nippee? I was flying. Actually **flying!**..."

***

Tabora and Gravee stroll along a few steps behind them.

"Ye ken, it's a braw thin' the wee laddie cannae grow wings," Gravee speculates. "Otherwise he'd be whizzin' roond oor lugs!

By taking the words he does understand, and replacing the ones he doesn't with others that are, hopefully, relevant to the subject being discussed, Tabora finds he can just about figure out what Gravee is saying. Based on this principle, the Gnuses replies, "Friend Bisckits on ground bad enough. Friend Bisckits in air... not good, Tabora thinks!"

The two *Ses* chuckle companionably.

"Them hyenee-whotsits are a wee bit frightenin', though, eh?"

***

Bringing up the rear are Jaspa and Portia.

"When you and Tabora said we couldn't help the calf, I thought I'd die," says Portia, still a little jittery from their encounter with the giraffes and hyenas.

"I know," sympathises Jaspa. "I wasn't very happy about it myself. But at least it all turned out alright."

"Oh yes! Thanks largely to Gravee."

"No doubt," agrees her cousin. "He's a bit... odd though, isn't he?"

"Just a little," giggles Portia. "Do you get the feeling he's not from round here?"

***

Everyone's exhausted by the time they get back to the camp and, curious as they are about Gravee, they decide their questions can keep until the morning.

***

Given all the time they've lost since the crossing of the Grumeti River, Tabora is a little concerned about delaying their journey any further. Consequently, the next morning finds them all crowded onto a single male wildebeest to hear Gravee's tale as they travel. The wildebeest wanders along, grazing continually whilst still making sure he keeps pace with the rest of the herd, blissfully unaware of the, as it will turn out, historic meeting being held on his back.

"So, Gravee... er... I was wondering... What kind of *Ses* are you, exactly?" asks Jaspa, in what he hopes is a tone of polite interest.

Gravee looks a little surprised at such a peculiar question. "Why, I'm a Dogses, o' coorse!"

"Really?" asks Jaspa, before he can stop himself.

"Well, what else would I be?" asks Gravee, feeling slightly put out. "Alright, I'm nae normally so scruffy, or grey, as this... there's nae doot I could dae wi' a wash an' a bit o' a trim... but surely it's still plain tae see I'm a West Highland Dogses. An' proud o' it, I might add!"

"Oh. I see," replies Jaspa, not seeing at all. The only dogs he's ever come across are the ferocious wild dogs that roam the Serengeti in terrifying packs. Those dogs, also known as African hunting dogs or Hyena dogs, have distinctive short, blotchy black and brown coats, stubby, tooth-filled muzzles and large ears.

Gravee doesn't look **anything** like they do. Although *Ses* aren't just tiny duplicates of their larger relatives, they nonetheless retain an impression of them. And there's **nothing** about Gravee that says wild, fierce, black and brown hunter!

Picking up on something else Gravee has just said, Portia enquires, "So, do you come from the Crater Highlands then?"

"Och! Nae, lassie. The Highlands o' mah birth are in bonnie Scotland, ye ken," answers Gravee, feeling uncharacteristically self-conscious at being the centre of attention.

"Scotland? I've never heard of it," admits Portia.

"Aye, well, it's a lang ways north o' here..." he says wistfully. "But it's the bonniest land ye ever did see!"

"So how did you get here, then?" asks Ngorika.

"On one of them there aeroplane contraptions."

"Hairyplanes are those things humans use to fly around in," Bisckits, the aviation guru, informs them.

"Aye," confirms Gravee. "But I'm nae talkin' aboot th' wee ones ye see roond here, mind. I mean th' stonkin' greit ones, big enough for hundreds o' humans at a time."

"That'th not pothible!" says Nippee sceptically.

"Oh, it is!" confirms the Vultureses. "I've seen them. Enormous silver birds. You know those really straight, high clouds?... Those are their tracks."

"Wow!" gasps Bisckits the aviator, impressed.

"I think we're getting away from the point here," suggests Jaspa. "So you came by aeroplane, Gravee. But **what** are you doing here?"

"Och, reit! Well, I came here wi' a couple o' pals. They oft visit different places roond th' world, an' sometimes I tag along. So when they told me they were goin' tae Africa, I decided tae come an' see it for meself."

"Where Africa, Friend Gravee?"

"Yer **in** Africa, Tabora. This is Africa. Here."

"Tabora not argue, but here Serengeti, not this *Africa*."

"Nae, ye dinnae ken. Yer in both. Th' Serengeti an' Africa! Ye see, th' Serengeti is a wee part o' Africa."

Most of the group look suspicious of this latest revelation. Jaspa, however, not wanting to get side-tracked even further, tries to drag the conversation back to where it started.

"Sorry, Gravee, but how did you get from visiting here on an aeroplane with some friends, to wandering into our camp on your own last night?"

"Aye. Sorry. I'll get tae th' point. Mah pals were visitin' here for a couple o' weeks wi' their family. We went all ower th' place, tae see th' animals an' that. An' then, one day when we were drivin' aroond, I wisnae payin' enough attention an' I fell oot o' th' Land Rover.

"That was aboot two months ago, near as I can tell. Since then, I've been wanderin' roond tryin' tae figure oot how tae get back hame."

"But what happened to your friendth? Didn't they notithe you'd fallen out. Or come looking for you afterwardth?" asks Nippee sympathetically.

"I'm sure they wanted tae, but they were here wi' their mum an' dad, ye see. Even if they'd told their folks they were missin' their wee *Ses* pal, I doot their parents would have believed them."

During the last couple of minutes, a faint trembling sensation has lodged itself in Jaspa's stomach. Up until now it's felt just like a butterfly does when cupped in a gently closed hand – its fluttering wings brush lightly against the fingers, though it can't fly away. But Gravee's last statement has unleashed a whirlwind inside his belly.

"Gravee?" Jaspa begins nervously, hardly daring to hope, "Your friends... They weren't *Ses*, were they?"

"Nae, they wisnae... Arenae, I mean." replies Gravee, correcting himself. "They're bairns. Human bairns."

"But that would make them..." begins Portia, speaking slowly as if she can't quite believe what she's saying.

"*Seers!*" says Jaspa triumphantly.

***

"But *Theerth* are just a children'th myth!" exclaims Nippee.

"That's right," says Bisckits. "Little Giraffeses are told stories about *Seers*, but when we get older we learn they were only make-believe. Just like the *Tooth Ses.* "

Nippee nods in agreement, but Gravee's temper flares.

"I. Am. Nae. Liar!" he growls. "And it's nae very polite tae treat me like one. Yers asked me how I got here. Well, I told yers. Whether yers choose tae believe me or nae... well, that's up tae yers!"

Nippee looks shocked. "I'm really thorry Gravee. I didn't mean to offend you!"

"No! Me neither!" says Bisckits hastily.

"Tabora never met *Seer*, but he seen many other strange things. If Friend Gravee say he know *Seers*, Tabora believe him."

"Thanks, Tabora," mumbles Gravee, calming down. "But I never said that I ken '*Seers*'. Only one of mah pals is actually a *Seer*."

"I believe you, too," says Jaspa. "In fact..." He hesitates, unsure of whether to go on. Then he decides this is too important to ignore. "In fact, I think I saw him. It is a young boy, isn't it?"

All attention is suddenly focussed on Jaspa. "What are you talking about?" demands Bisckits.

"Do you remember when we were on our *Schooling*? There was a lioness, which we thought was stalking that truck full of tourists, but was actually after a gazelle?"

"Of course," answers Bisckits, failing to see the significance of Jaspa's unexpected and apparently irrelevant trip down Memory Lane. "What of it?"

"Well, at the time I was sure that one of the humans in the truck was looking at me. Not just towards me... **At** me! Like they could see me, even though I was *blending*!"

"Why didn't you tell me?" asks Bisckits, feeling sceptical on the one hand, and hurt that Jaspa hasn't told him before on the other.

"I'm not sure," admits Jaspa. "I guess, I was worried that you'd think I'd gone mental or something."

"But I've known that for ages!" grins Bisckits, trying not to make an issue of Jaspa's secrecy this time.

"Gravee... This *Seer* of yours," says Jaspa, ignoring his brother's wisecrack. "Does he have shortish, dark hair and a freckly face that looks sort of kind and thoughtful, but also a bit... um...?"

"Mischievous!" exclaims Gravee, excitedly supplying the word Jaspa is searching for. "Aye, laddie! That's him!" shouts the newcomer, jumping up and spinning Jaspa round by his arms in celebration. "That's mah *Seer*! That's Ben!"

* * *

Unfortunately, Gravee's jubilation is short-lived.

Reality comes washing back over him like a tidal wave of misery. OK, so it's exciting that Jaspa may have seen Ben, but in the end does it really make that much difference? No matter how you look at it, that was still over two months ago, Ben and Sam are still long gone, and he's still stuck here in this awful place. So what if Jaspa saw Ben? That doesn't help him with any of his present problems, does it? It certainly doesn't help him get home!

And, oh, how he wants to go home.

"Look," says Gravee, a hint of despair creeping into his voice. "I ken yers all probably think I'm some sort o' bampot. An' I ken I look awful an' probably reek worse. But I'm nae normally like this. I huvnae had a bath in weeks an' I desperately need a haircut. But what I really need, mair than anythin' in th' world, is tae just go hame tae Scotland. So I beg yers all, is there any way yers can help me?"

Gravee's heart-wrenching plea is met by a stunned silence. Of course they want to help him, but in reality what can they actually do? None of them have ever even heard of this *Scotland*. For that matter, none of them have even heard of *Africa* even though they apparently live there!

It turns out, however, that at least one of the seven *Ses* riding on that wildebeest's back **isn't** thinking this. And a single, quiet voice fills up the silence with the *bonniest* words Gravee has ever heard.

"We might be able to get you as far as the place where the big aeroplanes land and take-off," suggests Ngorika hesitantly. "Would that help?"

***

The response to the Vultureses' unexpected announcement is predictably loud, surprised and confused...

"We can?" asks Portia.

"Are you serious?" exclaims Jaspa.

"You're joking!" croaks Nippee.

"That would be reit fantastic!" sighs Gravee in disbelief.

"We're going to see the Hairyplanes?" says Bisckits dreamily, eyes wide.

In fact, the only person not to blurt out the first thing that comes into his or her head, other than Ngorika of course, is Tabora. He patiently waits for the initial hubbub to die down, before quietly stating, "Friend Ngorika already prove cleverness many times in last days. If she say she **might** have plan, Tabora bets she **does** have plan. And plan we can trust!"

"Tabora's right," agrees Jaspa quickly. "Sorry Ngorika, I didn't mean to doubt you. So tell us, how are we going to help Gravee get home?"

***

Ngorika begins by informing them that the bigger aeroplanes use a long, straight road for taking off and landing. Bisckits, air travel expert, informs them this is called the *Hairyplane Road*. By unspoken agreement the others modify this to Aeroplane Road, which has the advantage of being a lot easier and quicker to say than the *long, straight road where the big aeroplanes land and take-off*.

With that sorted out, the Vultureses explains her plan.

In contrast to the effect of her previous announcement, her words are this time met by stunned silence. A silence so intense, you can almost hear the sound of the manic grin spreading across Bisckits' face.

Eventually, Gravee says, "Dae ye want run that by me one mair time?"

So she does.

***

26. Journey's end...?

"Did Ngorika say how long she'd be gone?" Portia enquires of Jaspa, scanning the sky.

"Not really." he replies. "She did say she'd probably have to go back home to make the arrangements, so I'm guessing another day or two, at least."

It's been two days since they all made a pact to help Gravee get home. Yesterday morning, after a good night's rest, Ngorika and Hook had set out to return to the Olkarien Gorge, to seek the assistance of her Wake. The collective term for vultures is a *wake*, hence Vultureses clans are called Wakes, in the same way Jaspa's tribe is called the *Herd*.

The group as a whole has mixed feelings about the plan. Some think it's unrealistic. Some think it's dangerous. Some privately think it's more than a little reckless!

Bisckits thinks it's the most brilliant and exciting plan in the whole history of plans... And can't **wait** to be a part of it.

And Gravee... Well, Gravee's so desperate, he's willing to try just about anything that gives him even the remotest hint of a possibility of getting back home.

Personally, Jaspa thinks the plan is probably workable, if a little scary. Make that a **lot** scary! More importantly, he's got some difficult decisions to make before his Vultureses friend returns. The biggest is whether to accompany Gravee to the Aeroplane Road or whether to leave that responsibility to Ngorika. Not that he's completely happy with either option.

As if reading his mind, Portia asks, "So, have you decided whether you're going or not?"

"Not really," admits Jaspa. "I'm torn, you know? I feel like I'd be abandoning my *Journey* if I went, but it seems a bit unfair to put all the responsibility on Ngorika."

"You know Bizzee really wants to go, don't you?"

Jaspa nods but doesn't comment.

"And Nippee will go if he does," Portia persists. "But if it's really the *Journey* you're worried about, then you shouldn't. Nippee has to come back this way, more-or-less, so we can always rejoin Tabora in a few days, if we want. We'll be away for a week at most.

"You know, the *Journey* is really all about experiencing new things, " she continues. "And I can guarantee you, no *Herder* has **ever** done what we're contemplating!"

"I know," her cousin sighs at last. "It's just..." Suddenly Jaspa stops short. "Wait a second. Did you say *we*?"

"Of course, I did!" laughs Portia. "I am your *Rubani*, after all. If you decide to participate in this harebrained[1] scheme, you don't think I'm going to let you and Bizzee do it without proper adult supervision, do you?"

"Well, I didn't want to assume..." flounders Jaspa, though he feels relieved. "So, you think we should go then?"

"I'm not sure... Although I think that's mostly the fear talking," Portia admits. "I **do** know one thing for certain. Bizzee is going to be **really** disappointed if we don't go!"

***

Ngorika returns late the following afternoon, together with a wake of vultures. Six to be precise, including her lifelong companion, Hook.

Although it's a little earlier than the *Nomads* would normally make camp, Tabora calls a halt nonetheless. It's either that or spend the next few hours with a group of determined-looking vultures spiralling intently overhead. And whilst vultures are a common

---

[1] Although fairly often spelt hairbrained, this odd term most probably refers to the crazy behaviour of hares during the mating season.

sight in the Serengeti, for some reason the herds tend to get a little nervous at the sight of them continually circling over the same group of animals.

Perhaps it makes them feel like the vultures know something they don't!

***

Although those taking their leave of the *Nomads* won't depart until dawn, the scene around the campfire this evening is particularly, and predictably, emotional. The air is charged with a sizable dose of excitement combined with a fair serving of nervousness, both of which are seasoned by a good dash of sadness. Even though most of those leaving will hopefully return in a matter of days, more than a few tears are shed at the thought of saying goodbye to Tabora and the *Nomads* in the morning.

Nevertheless, one by one, the band of friends drift off to sleep, until only Jaspa and Gravee are left, talking softly next to the dying embers of the fire.

"So once you get to the Aeroplane Road, you'll be able to figure out how to get the rest of the way home?" ask Jaspa quietly.

"Och! Nae bother," replies Gravee. "Ower th' last wee while I've got quite used tae human transportation an' th' like."

The Dogses leans closer to Jaspa and whispers, "Oh, an' th' place where *Hairyplanes* take-off from is actually called an airport, by th' way. But dinnae tell Bisckits I told ye!" He sits back, grinning, and gives Jaspa a wink.

Jaspa returns the smile. "You must be looking forward to getting home."

"Jaspa, ye have nae idea!" replies the Gravee sincerely. "I mean, I ken Africa's a wonderful place, an' all. An' the Serengeti's smashin' for a visit. But I dinnae belong here, ye ken? I miss Scotland. I miss Edinburgh!"

"And Ben?" enquires Jaspa, finally approaching the subject that's been on his mind ever since he discovered that Gravee probably knows the very same *Seer* he himself had seen all those months ago.

"Aye." A faraway look comes into the Dogses' eye, almost as if part of him is already home. "An' his wee sister, Sam. They're braw wee bairns, th' pair o' them."

"I wish I'd met them," sighs Jaspa regretfully.

"Och! Ye'd love them," says Gravee enthusiastically. "They're both so full o' life, ye ken. Ben's always thinkin' about things. Never stops. Always has a heid full o' plans for what tae get up tae next. An' ye should hear th' stories Sam comes up wi'! Sometimes I huv nae idea what she's going on about, but she makes me laugh!"

"They sound great."

"Aye. I cannae tell ye how happy I am tae be goin' back!" Gravee stretches sleepily. "Well, tomorrow's goin' tae be a lang day, so we'd best get some sleep. Goodnight then, Jaspa!"

"Goodnight, Gravee," the Giraffeses replies. For some strange reason he suddenly feels very lonely. "Sleep well."

***

This morning, the nerves and excitement mean everyone is up early. Nonetheless, breakfast is a leisurely affair, since the Aeroplane Road expedition can't set off until a couple of hours after sunrise. It takes that long for the day's thermals to start building. You see, the expedition is taking a most unusual route to the Aeroplane Road...

They're travelling by vulture!

In the cold light of the Serengeti dawn, Nippee still isn't convinced the plan is a good one. But a promise is a promise. He swore that if Bisckits went, he'd accompany him, and when they were all gathered around the fire last night, Jaspa had announced that the three Giraffeses would be taking part in the expedition.

Bisckits is buzzing. His longstanding loathing of vultures has been set aside, replaced by a passion more powerful than his hatred. A passion for flying! In fact, these days he talks of little else. From the moment Ngorika revealed her plan to take Gravee to the airport astride vultures, Bisckits **begged** Jaspa and Portia to let him go too. When Jaspa finally gave in, Bisckits gave a whoop of delight so loud they probably heard it all the way back at the Shifting Sands!

***

It's with heavy hearts that they all say goodbye to Tabora. His responsibilities to the *Nomads* and their wildebeest mean he isn't joining them on their intrepid adventure. The Gnuses clasps arms and hugs each of them in turn, coming to Jaspa last of all.

"Friend Jaspa grown much since he and Tabora first meet," says the *Nomad* as they clasp arms. "Tabora proud to call him *Friend*. But paths of Tabora and Friend Jaspa now different. Safe *Journey*, Friend Jaspa."

Jaspa can't help feeling there's more significance in Tabora's words than there initially seems, but everyone is waiting for him, so there's no time to ask. Instead he says, "I'll see you in a few days... A week at most!"

The Gnuses just nods, knowingly. Does he realise the tiny longing growing in Jaspa's heart? The one Jaspa doesn't dare admit, not even to himself? No. How could he? But still...

***

Each *Ses* will ride their own, personal vulture to save tiring the birds unnecessarily. Hook will lead the way, guided by Ngorika, and the remaining birds will follow. All Jaspa and the others will have to do is hold on!

His head swimming with questions and nerves, Jaspa steps over to the Ruppell's griffon vulture that's to be his steed. It squats on the ground with its legs folded beneath it, awaiting its passenger. Jaspa climbs onto its tail feathers and then hauls himself up its back, as Ngorika had shown them all.

Before he's even finished settling himself between the bird's powerful shoulders, it stands up. The world lurches horrifyingly and, not for the last time, Jaspa wonders whether he's making a terrible mistake. Yet there's no time to reconsider, for Ngorika is already nudging Hook forwards.

Jaspa gives Tabora a final, fleeting wave goodbye, before hurriedly grasping the feathers in front of him. He needs both hands just to hang on as the vulture sets off jerkily after Hook.

With great, long, lumbering strides, the bird laboriously picks up speed. It bounds along the dry, dusty ground, flapping its wings in the most graceless fashion, as if it's not really sure what to do with them.

Jaspa's thrown around like a rag doll. He starts to wonder whether he'll be shaken to bits before they manage to get airborne. All in all, he feels the *flight* isn't going very well... And the flying part hasn't even started yet!

At that very moment, the vulture gives one final flap and leap and they're aloft...

...For about two seconds.

The bird's feet hit the ground once more with a thump, and it's again running hard. As they strike the Earth, Jaspa's face is squashed firmly into the feathers in front of him.

Then everything goes suddenly still. The jerking, juddering, jolting, headlong dash across the grass is over. All that remains is this slightly unsettled feeling in Jaspa's stomach.

It must have given up, he thinks, his face still embedded in the bird's feathers. *Thank goodness!* Clearly the vulture has finally accepted that it's never going to get off the ground.

But when Jaspa lifts his head, the rush of wind in his face tells him otherwise.

It tells him that, the first time in his life, Jaspa the Giraffeses is flying!

***

27. Flying high

Wings flapping lethargically, Jaspa's vulture climbs slowly into the air and, following Hook's lead, heads for a nearby rocky outcrop. The birds instinctively know that the bare rock will warm up faster than the surrounding land, and that a thermal will then form above it.

They're approaching the exposed rock when Jaspa is struck by a sudden panic, overcome by the sickening sensation of his vulture dropping out from beneath him. Fortunately, the feeling of falling is fleeting. **Un**fortunately, it's replaced almost immediately by another equally-frightening feeling, one of extreme heaviness. Seconds crawl past like days, before the rising air of the thermal catches the wings of his feathered mount and they accelerate upwards.

As they begin to climb, Jaspa experiences the strangest combination of feelings. For a moment it's as if he's being pushed down into the vulture's feathers, then the pressure is released and he suddenly feels like he **is** a feather, weighing nothing at all as he rockets skywards.

For a couple of seconds the vulture continues straight ahead, then it dips its left wing sharply downward, banking them in a tight left-handed circle. About halfway around, the intense heaviness Jaspa had felt a few moments ago returns without warning, but this time it stays. It's like the air and land are both pulling against them, dragging them back down towards the ground.

Obviously, you can't have a big hole in the atmosphere. So the warm, upward-moving air of the thermal must be replaced somehow. The sinking sensation Jaspa experiences is caused by a doughnut of colder air rushing in and down to fill the gap left around the rising tower of the thermal. Fortunately, the feeling persists for only a few seconds. Then, as quickly as it appeared, it's gone and they're climbing once again, shooting up into the bright blue sky.

The raptor immediately straightens up, waits another couple of seconds, before once more turning tightly to the left. They do one full circle, then a second, without the clinging, heavy sensation returning. The vulture has centred itself, and Jaspa, within the thermal. Now all it has to do is to continue spiralling anticlockwise and their own personal, invisible, insubstantial elevator will take them to the top.

***

After what seems like an age of circling, Hook levels his immense wings and dives out of the thermal, heading southeast, with the other vultures in tow. Hurtling through the air they go. Trading height for speed. Zipping over the land. Eventually, Hook decides they're getting too low and, with practised ease, locates another thermal... And they're climbing again.

And so they travel... Find a thermal. Circle tight within its confines. Let it do the work. Let it launch you higher and higher into the sky. And then, when it's taken you as high as it can... Race for the next one, losing height all the way... But that's OK, because when you catch that next rising pillar of air, up and up you go once more.

***

"Lo....er..the....!" Bisckits shouts, his words sliced up and dragged away by the wind. Jaspa has no idea what he said, or who he's talking to for that matter. Of course, it doesn't help that Jaspa has his eyes and ears buried deep in the vulture's feathers.

He lifts up his head and looks around for his brother's ride, eventually finding it almost directly below him. His stomach lurches! Bisckits is looking up at him, grinning broadly. Evidently his brother's words had been meant for him.

"Sorry?!" Jaspa calls, putting on an exaggerated expression of puzzlement and **very** briefly pointing to his ear with his left hand, before resuming his double-fisted, white-knuckled grip on the feathers in front of him.

"Loo...over..ther...!" repeats Bisckits, pointing down and to the south.

Loo over there? wonders Jaspa. It seems like such a strange thing to say. Although a toilet break might not be so bad after who knows how many hours clinging desperately to this flying duvet. But Jaspa doubts Bisckits can see an appropriate spot from this height.

Nonetheless, Jaspa dutifully gazes off in the direction his younger sibling is indicating, feeling slightly queasy as he does so. From this high up – and he's trying to avoid thinking about exactly **how** high up they are – there's a lot of **south** to cover but he eventually spots what his little brother is pointing at.

Oh! Jaspa thinks, *he must have said* look *not* loo.

For clearly, the target of Bisckits' attention is a herd of giraffes, striding majestically across the plain. From up here, they look like the figures Bisckits sometimes makes out of sticks, the patchwork of their coats shrunken to resemble the spots of a leopard.

Jaspa isn't the first to have made this comparison. The giraffe's scientific (Latin) name is *Giraffa camelopardalis*. The second part comes from the fact that the Romans thought they were a type of camel with leopard-like spots!

As Jaspa watches, one of the giraffes breaks into a gallop. The others follow suit and soon they're all loping along, their heads swinging back and forth like pendulums. He looks over at Bisckits and they exchange grins.

***

So far, Jaspa has devoted most of his attention and energy to simply staying on the back of the vulture beneath him. But at last he realises that, so long as he stays reasonably still, he's not **really** in that much danger. In fact, the way the vulture rides the thermals, its wings held rigid and still except for tiny movements of the tips to change course, actually makes it surprisingly stable.

Feeling safer than he has done since they left the ground, Jaspa finally takes the opportunity to look about a bit. He's unsure where they are, since he's never visited the land over which they're soaring. Even if he had, he's not certain he could have recognised any landmarks from this lofty viewpoint in any case.

To the north, the landscape is one of scrub and woodland, broken up by open grassy spaces, and frequently scored by river channels, most of which are dry at this time of year. Beneath them and to the south is a very different scene, with endless grasslands stretching to the horizon, the flat monotony interrupted only by an occasional cluster of kopjes or a dirt road. If Jaspa **had** to take a stab at where they are, he'd guess it was at the boundary of the central Long Grass Plains and the Northern Woodland, somewhere east of Seronera. And he'd be correct.

On the Eastern horizon, the Crater Highlands straddle their flight path like a vast wall, attempting to bar their way to Kilimanjaro and its Aeroplane Road. As they continue on their saw-toothed route towards those peaks, up within thermals and down in the gaps between them, they fly over a smaller range of hills, which Jaspa concludes are probably the Gol Hills. If that's true, then Ngorika's home in the Olkarien Gorge is down there on their far side.

Before they set off this morning, the Vultureses had told them that she would initially head for the gorge, with the aim of spending the night there. If they made good time, however, she would carry on past her home, in the interest of saving them time tomorrow. With no indication that they're descending, it seems clear to Jaspa that the Vultureses has opted for plan B... Assuming those really are the Gol Hills down there, of course!

***

In the end, Jaspa is proved right. They pass over the Olkarien Gorge with several hours of daylight still in hand and so Ngorika presses on. Continuing to head roughly southeast, they fly across the isolated Salei Plain and then over the top of the Empakaai Crater, with its jade green soda lake glistening in the light of the sinking sun.

Eventually, Ngorika guides them down, in lazy descending spirals, to land on the eastern side of the Crater Highlands, right at the very edge of the Rift Valley escarpment. Here they make camp for the night.

***

Next morning, the expedition takes to the wing as soon as the land begins to warm and the thermals start to build. Jaspa finds the take-off a lot less bone-shaking than yesterday's, although **much** more frightening... Something he wouldn't have believed possible 24 hours ago!

Making good use of the escarpment's natural shape, the vultures dispense with all that running and flapping. Instead, they simply stick out their wings and...

Drop gracelessly off the edge of the World.

The freefall probably lasts no more than a couple of seconds before the vultures' wings scoop up the air beneath them and the birds and their passengers glide out over the African Rift Valley, away from the 1600 foot high cliff off which they just flopped. Jaspa, Portia and Nippee all think it's probably the most terrifying two seconds of their entire lives. Bisckits' howl of delight as his vulture hops off the precipice and plummets towards the Rift Valley floor below makes it quite clear he disagrees with them on this one.

Their journey takes the same format as yesterday's: slow, time-consuming spirals up into the heavens riding the unseen pillars of the thermals, followed by long shallow dives that eat up the distance between them and their goal.

The vultures' wings bear them ever onward, out over the Rift Valley and across the Engaruka Basin. They soar over grassland and scrub, woodland and swamp. And all the while, two towering volcanoes, rising up from the flat floor of the rift, dominate the horizon before them. The closest is Mount Meru, the *Black Mountain*, the second highest mountain on the continent, its summit standing almost 10,000 feet above the plain below and 14,980 feet above sea level. Beyond it is the grandfather itself, the snow-capped roof of Africa... Kilimanjaro.

Gliding over the first of these mighty mountains, they look down upon its shattered, semi-circular summit. The view offers mute evidence of Mount Meru's violent history. The entire eastern side of the volcano's crater is missing, blasted apart thousands of years ago in a colossal, explosive, sideways fountain of lava, rock and ash.

Despite being almost destroyed in this tumultuous explosion, Mount Meru remains erratically active to this day, its last eruption having taken place in 1910. In fact, within the horseshoe walls of the ruined peak a new ash cone is steadily growing, little by little. A volcanic offspring that may one day rival the crippled mountain that has given birth to it.

Jaspa, however, hardly notices the rock-strewn battlements of the disfigured, crescent-shaped crater. Nor does he really take in Mount Meru's lower, forest-covered slopes. Not even the still distant, white-topped peak of majestic Kilimanjaro can hold his gaze. Amidst this incredible, breath-taking display of nature's power and beauty, the thing that captures Jaspa's attention is something nature has had very little say in... The enormous changes wrought by humans in the area south of Mount Meru.

The first things Jaspa sees as they approach the mountain are the fields. There is no agriculture in the Serengeti and Jaspa has never seen fields before. To him they look like great, straight-sided, rectangular expanses of sameness, contrasting strikingly with the curves and subtlety of the natural landscape into which they've been dropped.

Then he spies one of the cities Uncle Mackee told him and Bisckits about, nestled amongst the alien-looking fields. From his vantage point far above the ground, Jaspa looks down on the countless streets and buildings of the town of Arusha with a mixture of awe and horror. Arusha, with a population of about one and a half million people, is the heart of the Tanzanian safari industry.

But this is no sightseeing tour, and the expedition sails onwards, unseen and unaffected by the multitudes of people going about their business in the town slipping by beneath them.

***

The *Ses* continue to head southeast, Mount Meru shrinking behind them, Kilimanjaro looming large on the horizon ahead and to their left. Staring forwards over the vulture's head, Jaspa spots a greenish-brown smudge in the distance, to the southwest of Kilimanjaro. Even from this far away, it seems much too regular to be natural and he's suddenly certain that their destination is finally in sight. They draw ever nearer, and the enormous smudge becomes an immense expanse of sun-bleached, cropped grass, which dwarfs even the mightiest of the fields Jaspa's seen so far.

As Ngorika guides them even closer, the Aeroplane Road itself slowly appears out of the heat haze. Jaspa can hardly believe what he's seeing. A gigantic straight line. A single black stripe, incredibly wide and impossibly long. An enormous road to nowhere, running east-west across the plain. Even amid the strangeness and wonder of the artificial landscape unrolling below him, the Aeroplane Road stands out like a beacon. A symbol of the humans' power to change and mould the world to suit their needs and desires.

Hook begins a long, gentle dive towards the airport and the other vultures follow his lead. As they get closer, Jaspa is able to make out a series of buildings to the north of the Aeroplane Road, most noticeable of which is a colossal, shiny, white cube. This immense structure also seems to catch Ngorika's eye because, slowly but surely, she guides them down towards it.

Within a few short minutes they reach the ground, landing near the vast white construction. It turns out to be an enormous metal box, large enough to hold a forest of mature acacias. Jaspa slides down his vulture's back towards the ground and breaths a deep sigh of relief as his feet touch the solid, if slightly wobbly, earth.

After two days in the air, they've finally arrived... At the Hairyplane Road.

***

28. The hangar

As soon as all the *Ses* are safely down from their mounts, Ngorika bids farewell to Hook. She watches as her companion leads the other vultures northwards towards Kilimanjaro, away from the dangers of the airport.

The members of the expedition find themselves standing on an immense expanse of grey-brown concrete that, from their viewpoint, seems to stretch to the horizon in all directions. Behind them, about 150 feet away, the great, white aircraft hangar gleams blindingly in the sunlight, radiating heat. Off to their left, to the east, is a cluster of other buildings that form the hub of the airport. The most conspicuous of these is the air traffic control tower, a white, multi-storey building crowned with a structure that resembles a giant, angular goldfish bowl.

And in front of the *Ses*, although presently hidden from them by the grass in between, is the Aeroplane Road itself.

"Look!" cries Bisckits, pointing to the west.

They all stare in the direction Bisckits is indicating, but none of them can see what's got the young Giraffeses so excited. The flat plain stretches away south from the brooding mass of Mount Meru. Somewhere in the distance lies the town of Arusha, although it's invisible from here. In the same direction, a star hangs low in the sky, twinkling brightly in the afternoon sunshine just above the horizon.

That's odd, thinks Jaspa, *stars shouldn't be visible at this time of day.*

Even more peculiar is that the light in the sky appears to be moving. It descends steadily as they continue to watch, like a slow-motion shooting star, getting brighter all the while.

A dark disk gradually becomes visible directly above the light, but the heat haze blurs its outlines, making it vague and indistinct. Slowly, two smaller black shapes emerge from the haze on either side of the brightening light, a short distance away from it.

"What could it be?" whispers Nippee.

"A Hairyplane!" answers Bisckits in wonder.

***

As the mysterious objects get nearer, they become increasingly recognisable. Two long, thin, roughly horizontal lines flicker into view, connecting the base of the larger circular shape to the tops of the two smaller ones, and extending out beyond them. Finally, a shorter fuzzy line sprouts vertically from the top of the central blob.

Little by little, the objects' outlines solidify as they creep ever closer. The larger circle resolves into the nose of an aircraft's fuselage, the main body of an aircraft where all the people sit. The long, horizontal lines become wings, each with an engine slung underneath. The shorter vertical line becomes the upright fin of the plane's tail section. The intense light, which was originally all they could see of the aeroplane, seems to shrink as the aircraft appears, almost magically, out of the hazy air.

As the group stands gaping at the approaching marvel, they gradually become aware of the high-pitched whining of its engines. The noise grows rapidly as the plane gets nearer, until it seems to fill the whole sky with its deafening roar.

The runway is perhaps a third of a mile south of the tiny onlookers, but Bisckits' whoops of delight are nonetheless drowned out by the scream of the aircraft's engines as it makes its final descent towards the ground. With squeals and clouds of smoke from its protesting tyres, the aeroplane touches down almost directly ahead of them. At practically the same moment, although Jaspa would not have thought it possible, the noise from the plane's engines increases, as the pilot slams them into reverse.

The aircraft races down the Aeroplane Road, engines roaring as they strive, together with the brakes, to slow the vehicle's headlong charge. Gradually the speed drops off until, having successfully brought the plane to a virtual stop before running out of runway, the pilot throttles back the engines and their noise abruptly dies away.

"Wow!" shouts Bisckits, "Did you see that!?" He runs around in circles with his arms stuck out like wings. "That was awesome! I wish I could fly a Hairyplane!"

***

The excitement of the aircraft landing having passed, Ngorika turns to Gravee. "Well," she says, "I've done my part. I said I could get you to the Aeroplane Road, and here we are. The rest is up to you."

Gravee looks a little hesitant at this.

"You do know what to do now, don't you?" asks Portia, sounding concerned.

"Aye! O' coorse!" replies Gravee, although he sounds far from sure. "At least, in theory..." he adds less certainly.

"In theory?" repeats Nippee, mirroring Portia's worry.

"Well, I've never had tae **actually** find th' aeroplane meself before. I've always been in Ben's pocket, ye ken?" he admits sheepishly. "But humans dae it all th' time, so it cannae be too hard, can it? I just huv tae find th' aeroplane that goes tae Edinburgh."

"You mean we've brought you all this way," says Ngorika, feeling slightly annoyed, "And now you tell us you don't really know..."

"Where's Bisckits?" interrupts Jaspa.

***

Alarmed, the remaining *Ses* scan the area for their missing accomplice.

It's Nippee who spots him first. "Over there!" he calls. "Heading towardth that building."

Sure enough, Jaspa spots his brother *shifting* towards the partially open doors of the enormous hangar. "Bisckits!!" he shouts, but to no avail. "Bisckits! Come back!" But either Bisckits can't hear Jaspa, or he's ignoring him.

"Where's he going?" Jaspa mutters under his breath, as he sets off in pursuit of his wayward brother, the others following a little way behind.

***

By the time Jaspa catches up with Bisckits, the younger Giraffeses has already entered the hangar, but at least he's no longer *shifting*. In fact, he wanders forwards almost in a trance, turning around slowly, his head craned back, mesmerised by the aircraft looming directly overhead.

As he drifts along his feet perform an intricate dance, each step part of an unconscious yet precise ballet of which the rest of his body seems unaware. It moves him and twirls him, unhurriedly changing his position and perspective, so his eyes can lap up every detail of the silver underside of the immense flying machine.

From high above comes the sound of voices. Human voices. And the intermittent ring of metal on metal. Clearly someone is up there, working on the plane. The noises echo strangely in the confined space of the hangar, making their source seem much closer than it really is.

"What do you think you're playing at?" demands Jaspa furiously.

"Isn't it beautiful?" says Bisckits distantly, apparently unaware his brother has even spoken. He continues to stare upwards, awestruck, his head still tilted back and to one side as he strains to see the aeroplane.

Jaspa grabs Bisckits roughly by the arm, breaking the plane's spell on his brother and bringing the smaller Giraffeses' attention back to the here and now. "What were you thinking of, running off like that?"

Bisckits looks confused. "I saw the Hairyplane and wanted a closer look," he replies, as though this should be obvious.

Jaspa sighs noisily, in frustration born from worry. "Don't you realise how dangerous it is here?" he demands. "You might have got yourself killed!"

Bisckits can't understand why Jaspa's being so unreasonable. He only wanted to see the Hairyplane, after all. He opens his mouth to argue with his brother, but before he can utter a single word in his defence there comes a loud yell of annoyance from high above.

***

Tagging along behind, the other *Ses* have only just entered the hangar when the shout echoes around the enormous building. Portia,

Gravee and Ngorika ignore it. OK, so it doesn't sound too happy, but then humans rarely do! Besides, it's nothing to do with them...

All of which makes Nippee's unexpected reaction to the yell even more surprising. Within half a heartbeat the little Crocodileses is *shifting* away from the others, like a sprinter released by a starting pistol.

"What th'...!" exclaims Gravee, as Portia and Ngorika exchange a look of utter bewilderment.

***

At the shout from above, Nippee instinctively looks up... Just in time to see a smallish silvery object slip off the back of the aeroplane's enormous wing and begin its long but nonetheless unstoppable descent to the ground...

The very patch of ground currently occupied by Bisckits and Jaspa!

In the blink of an eye, the Crocodileses realises it's useless trying to alert the brothers. By the time he gets their attention and makes them understand the danger, it will already be too late. Instead, he chooses the only other option available to him. He runs!

Or, more accurately, he *shifts*.

Nippee charges at Jaspa and Bisckits as fast as his stubby green legs will carry him. He doesn't waste time shouting. What would be the point? And anyway, he doesn't have the breath to spare. *Shifting* really takes it out of you!

As he *shifts*, Nippee sees the falling object out of the corner of his eye, catching the light as it gently spins. He's no idea what it is, but that doesn't matter. The only thing that matters is that it could well kill Bisckits and his brother if it reaches them before he does!

I'm not going to make it! thinks Nippee anxiously.

But instead of panicking, the selfless Crocodileses digs deeper. Calling on an inner strength he didn't even know he had. Ignoring the agonising protests of his near-bursting lungs, he actually manages to accelerate!

***

Gravee, Ngorika and Portia stand rooted to the spot just inside the hangar doors, surprised into motionlessness by Nippee's sudden and unexplained departure. Then Ngorika spots a brief sparkle in the air directly above Jaspa and Bisckits. She points it out to the other pair, as everything becomes instantly, unbearably clear.

The unidentified falling object looks a little like an angular, metal bone. It tumbles lazily as it drops, slowly turning end over end. The three friends stare at it, hypnotised and horrified. Powerless to intervene themselves, they watch the unfolding drama helplessly, willing Nippee onwards.

For their part, Jaspa and Bisckits seem to be completely unaware of the lethal missile plummeting straight at them through the air, light flickering off its smooth, shiny surfaces as it falls.

***

The mechanic's yell reverberates around the hangar like the ringing of a bell. To Jaspa, the voice seems to echo – literally – his current feelings of exasperation and irritation at his little brother's recklessness. But before he can pursue this line of thought too far, it's violently driven from his mind, as is the breath from his body, by the shattering force of something slamming into him.

***

Nippee dives!

He tackles Jaspa in midair, crashing into his back with a bone-jarring thud. But Nippee's momentum carries them both onwards, smashing them into Bisckits. At almost the same instant, the spanner strikes the ground in the exact spot where the younger Giraffeses had so recently been standing. Its impact chisels a large chunk out of the concrete's surface, producing a brief spark in the process.

Nippee feels a wild joy flow through him! He did it! *Un-be-bloomin'-lievable!*

But a moment later, before he's even stopped rolling, Nippee feels another crack, this time on the side of his face. Except this blow feels different, somehow. Fiercer. Harder. Sharper. And his joy is instantly replaced by blinding pain.

In a cruel twist of fate, the spanner's impact with the ground has launched it straight at the little Crocodileses. Spinning much faster than before, it comes at him like a demented and spiteful Catherine wheel, intent on revenge for him having stolen its original victims.

The spanner hits Nippee's jaw with a sickening crack, snapping his head around and smacking it into the solid concrete floor, before stealing his consciousness.

***

29. The Aeroplane Road

Ngorika, Portia and Gravee skid to a halt beside their companions. Jaspa and Bisckits are already sitting up, albeit a little unsteadily... Slightly winded, but otherwise unhurt.

Nippee, on the other hand, hasn't moved. He lies as if frozen, breathing shallowly, a trickle of blood seeping from the right corner of his mouth.

***

A minute passes.

Then another.

By now, the brothers are almost fully recovered. Yet Nippee still shows no signs of stirring. This time, Portia isn't the only one with tears in her eyes. For Bisckits is intent on blaming himself for his friend's present condition.

"Wake up, Nippee," the dismayed young Giraffeses pleads. "I'm sorry! Please wake up!"

But Nippee doesn't respond. And none of the others have any idea how to help him or what to do.

***

Just when it seems matters can't get any worse, the sound of approaching footsteps, large and heavy, intrudes on their combined misery. "Someone's coming!" warns Ngorika.

"Aye!" agrees Gravee. "Prob'ly th' same greit galoot who dropped his tool on puir Nippee's heid."

"Well, they could do him a lot more harm if we don't get him to safety," says Jaspa. Even though humans can't usually see *Ses*, a misplaced foot, however unintentional, can still prove fatal.

Jaspa and Gravee each grab one of Nippee's arms and begin dragging him, as quickly but gently as they can, towards the relative shelter of the starboard[1] leg of the aeroplane's undercarriage.

"Stop!" The voice is deep and commanding and Jaspa and Gravee find themselves obeying it automatically, even though it doesn't belong to any of their party.

"What are you doing?" demands Portia, close to panic. "That's the human! It's not talking to you. Now, get a *shift* on!!"

Realising their error, Gravee and Jaspa resume pulling Nippee's unconscious body towards the protection offered by the landing gear.

"Stop!" barks the voice again.

The *Ses* aren't about to make the same mistake twice, and so they ignore its cries. They've got more important things to worry about than the irrelevant rantings of a human. For starters, the effort of hauling Nippee's limp form is slowing down their flight, since Jaspa and Gravee find themselves unable to *shift*. The stocky Crocodileses is simply too heavy. What's more, the troubled human is heading straight towards them. And the way their luck is going, it's bound to accidentally squash one or more of them on its way past.

"Please! Wait!" shouts the human again.

Finally, Ngorika grasps the impossible. "You know..." she says quietly, coming to a stop and twisting around to face the approaching human, "...I think it **is** calling to us!"

***

The others look at the Vultureses with a mixture of shock and outright disbelief. But as the human draws closer, they begin to realise she might be right, after all. Incredible as it seems, the human **does** appear to be calling to them.

Gradually, the group's flight grinds to a halt, as one by one they turn to confront this totally unforeseen situation. As they do so, the human slows to a walk. Finally, when it's only a couple of paces away, it also stops, sinking down to its knees directly in front of them.

[1] On a ship or aircraft, right is referred to as starboard, whereas left is called port.

"Hello there, little ones," the man greets them.

"You c-can s-see us?" asks Portia nervously.

"It would seem so, wouldn't it?" replies the man, with a slight smile.

"An' just what are ye gonnae dae aboot it, then?" enquires Gravee, puffing out his chest.

"Do?" asks the human, looking puzzled. "If you mean *what am I going to do to you?*, then the answer is nothing. If you mean *what am I going to do for you...* well, I will do all I can to assist you."

"Excuse me," says Bisckits in a small voice. "But my friend's hurt."

"So I see," replies the man seriously. "An airport is a dangerous place, but regrettably you've already found that out for yourselves."

"Can you help him?" begs the distressed Giraffeses.

The man sighs. "Sadly, the first thing you ask of me is something for which I am poorly equipped to help. I'm afraid I am no doctor." Then, seeing the misery in Bisckits' bloodshot eyes, he adds kindly, "Though we shall see what we can do.

"But perhaps we should first go somewhere more private. I'm sure my colleague is already on his way down to reclaim his lost spanner. It'll be best if we're gone by the time he arrives. Otherwise he'll think old Moringe has started talking to himself!"

This last remark reminds Jaspa that, although humans aren't supposed to be able to see *Ses* when they're *blending*, this old man clearly can. "Um..." he begins uncertainly. "...Are you a *Seer*?"

"What else, little one?" the human answers with a slight chuckle. "What else?"

***

Nippee stirs slightly as the *Seer* gently picks him up. Cradling the injured Crocodileses in his left hand, the man leads the other *Ses* across the hangar to a normal-sized door located just inside the monumental main hangar doors. Through it they enter a smallish, brightly lit room, which has a shabby wooden table and four mismatched chairs arranged at its centre. Of course, to the *Ses* the door, room, table and chairs all appear gigantic!

The man sits down on one of the rickety metal chairs and places Nippee on the table before him. Gravee, who's used to talking to

Seers,[1] immediately clambers up one of the table's legs and onto its notched and dented top. After a moment's hesitation, the others follow, and soon all five of them are standing next to Nippee, staring expectantly up at the human. From this close, Jaspa can see that the dark skin of the man's face is lined by age, although his eyes still sparkle like a child's.

"His breathing appears to be improving," observes the old man. "That's a good sign."

Sure enough, Nippee's breaths are now deeper and steadier than before.

The human stands up again and goes over to a sink in the corner of the room. He turns on a tap, introducing himself over his shoulder as he does so. "My name is Moringe Babu." He takes a piece of cloth and holds it briefly under the water. "And, as you have already guessed, I am what you would call a *Seer*."

Returning to the table with the damp cloth, he begins cleaning the blood away from Nippee's mouth. Almost immediately his patient groans and lifts his right arm to protect his injured face, pushing the cloth away.

"Nippee?" Bisckits almost wails, making Portia jump. "Can you hear me?"

Nippee replies with another groan. Then his eyes flutter open.

"Oww!" he says. "What hit me?"

"I thought you were dead!" whispers Bisckits in relief.

"Not yet!" grins the Crocodileses, making himself wince. He gingerly touches the right side of his jaw with tips of his fingers, whilst at the same time exploring the inside of his mouth with his tongue. Nippee grimaces, before adding, "But I don't think my thmile will ever be quite the thame again. I theem to be mithing a couple of teeth."

"I'm sorry!" blurts out Bisckits. "It's all my fault!"

"Don't be daft! It'th not you fault," says Nippee, shaking his head and then wishing he hadn't as a jolt of pain stabs into his jawbone. "It wath an acthident..."

"But if I hadn't..."

"It. Wath. An. Acthident!" repeats Nippee firmly. "Anyway,

[1]Well, one *Seer* to be precise.

there'th no real harm done. OK, tho I've got a couple leth teeth than before. Big Deal! There'th thtill plenty more where they came from!"

As if to prove it, he flashes his guilt-ridden friend a toothy smile. All Bisckits sees, however, is the black gap left by the missing teeth.

"I have to admit, though, I've got a killer headache!" Nippee confesses. He sits up and notices Moringe for the first time. "And I appear to be halluthinating!"

***

The others fill Nippee in on the frantic and fantastic events of the last five or ten minutes.

When they've finished, Nippee still looks perplexed. "But I thought *Theerth* were all children," he says to Moringe, still probing his broken teeth with a finger.

"And what did you think happened to them when they grew up, little one?" asks the old man, reasonably. "...That they simply forgot all about the *Ses*?"

Unable to think of a rational answer, Nippee simply shrugs and makes an *I hadn't thought of that* kind of face.

"In truth, though," Moringe continues, "I haven't seen a single *Ses* in years, let alone a ragtag group like you. So I'm guessing you've got quite a story to tell." He grins. "Care to share it with an old *Seer*, little ones?"

***

To begin with, the *Ses* are understandably wary. Yet Jaspa and the others can't help feeling they've stumbled across another unexpected friend. So it is that they find themselves telling Moringe Babu their story, albeit cautiously at first.

The tale takes a long time to tell, for the *Ses* frequently interrupt each other, or get sidetracked, or stop to answer one of Moringe's many questions. But gradually the old man learns all about how they met and why they've travelled to the Aeroplane Road.

"But noo we're here," concludes Gravee, "I realise I dinnae ken how tae find oot which aeroplane I need, let alone how tae get on it!"

"And where are you trying to get to, little one?" asks Moringe.

"Edinburgh. In Scotland, ye ken?" says Gravee, a sudden spark of hope kindling inside him. "Can ye help me, mebbe?"

The old man thinks for a moment, before pursing his lips and shaking his head slowly and uncertainly from side to side. "Perhaps... Although I don't believe there are any flights from here to Edinburgh."

Gravee looks crestfallen and his whole body sags. "I could huv sworn this was th' place." He sighs and looks guiltily at Ngorika, before miserably adding, "I'm reit sorry, but it looks like I've wasted all yers time."

Understanding in her eyes, the Vultureses places a sympathetic wing on Gravee's arm.

"Not necessarily," Moringe says. "Did you have to stop between Edinburgh and here? To change planes?"

"Aye, mebbe," answers Gravee uncertainly. "Tae be honest, I dinnae really remember. It were so lang ago an' so much has happened since..." His voice trails off.

"Well, don't give up hope just yet, little one. I might still be able to help," the old man says, getting to his feet. "Wait here until I get back."

And without another word of explanation, he's gone.

***

Moringe seems to take forever to return. But, just as they are about to give up on him, the door opens and he steps back into the room. He appears slightly breathless as all the *Ses* stare at him impatiently. Then a smile crosses his wrinkled face and he utters the most magical words Gravee has ever heard...

"I've found a way for you to get home."

***

Gravee sits down heavily, utterly speechless at Moringe's revelation.

Seeing his friend unable to talk, Jaspa speaks for him. "So there **is** an aeroplane here that goes to Edinburgh, after all?"

"No, little one. But there is one to Amsterdam..." the *Seer* corrects him, "...and from there Gravee can get a connecting flight to Edinburgh."

"I see," says Jaspa, not seeing at all. He's never heard of *Amsterdam* and has no idea what a *connecting flight* is.

Sensing the Giraffeses' confusion, the human explains further. "Amsterdam is a city between here and Edinburgh. It has a really big airport, with lots more flights than we get here. There aren't any flights that go straight from here to Edinburgh, but there are flights from here to Amsterdam, and other flights between there and Edinburgh."

"So, Gravee can get an aeroplane that goes from here to Amsterdam and then on to Edinburgh?" asks Jaspa.

"Almost, little one" smiles Moringe, "Except that at he'll have to change planes at Amsterdam. That's what a *connecting flight* means."

"He gets to go on **two** Hairyplanes?!" exclaims Bisckits, half impressed, half jealous. "I wish I was going!"

"Shhh!" hisses Portia, who's standing next to her cousin. "Have you already forgotten the trouble your obsession with aeroplanes has got us into today?"

Bisckits is devastated by Portia's accusation... Especially as he believes it to be true.

Nippee, however, doesn't seem to share their harsh opinion of recent events. "That wathn't fair!" he whispers, leaning over to Portia. "I thought we'd agreed it wath an acthident. They happen. And if I don't blame Bithckit'th, then neither thould you!"

Putting his arm around Bisckits' shoulders, the kindly Crocodileses leads his friend over to the opposite side of the table. Behind them they leave Portia looking slightly stunned, trying to work out how **she** ended up the baddie in all that!

***

Gravee, who hasn't heard any of the whispered conversation between Portia, Bisckits and Nippee, now looks far from happy. "I huv tae swap aeroplanes at Amsterdam, ye say? Which is much bigger than here?"

"That's right..."

"But on mah own, I wudnae even huv bin able to cope wi' **this** little airport," interrupts Gravee mournfully. "How am I supposed tae deal wi'...?".

Moringe holds up his left index finger, cutting short the unhappy Dogses' question. "I can put you on the flight from here to Amsterdam..."

"But how..."

The old man raises his finger once more and Gravee lapses back into silence. "As I was about to say, I also have all the information..." he waves the sheet of paper he has clutched in his right hand, "... you'll need to find the connecting flight in Amsterdam."

Gravee continues to look unsure. "It's nae that I'm ungrateful, ye ken. But I dinnae think I can dae this."

"I understand your concern, little one" replies Moringe kindly. "Really I do. But I'm afraid you don't have much of a choice. Unless you decide to stay here, of course... Forever."

The bluntness and honesty of Moringe's declaration takes Gravee completely by surprise and his eyes grow wide in realisation. He looks down at his feet, clearly contemplating his dilemma. A minute or more passes. Finally, he takes a deep breath...

In...

...pause...

...out.

Then, clearly steeling himself for what is to follow, he looks up into the old *Seer's* face. "Aye, then," he says determinedly. "Well, in that case, ye'd best tell me everythin' ye can."

***

30. Dreams

"The flight from here to Amsterdam takes roughly twelve hours," Moringe begins. "Once there, if there are no delays, you'll have about two hours to find the plane to Edinburgh."

"But what if I miss it?" asks Gravee, once again sounding anxious.

"Don't worry, little one," replies Moringe comfortingly, "There are usually two flights a day from Amsterdam to Edinburgh. If you miss the first one, you just have to wait around for the next."

"Och, well, that's all reit then," says the Dogses, although he still sounds a bit unsure.

Moringe goes on to carefully describe exactly what Gravee has to do, and where he has to go, once he arrives in Amsterdam. "Now, the flight to Amsterdam isn't for another three hours," he concludes. "But if I don't get back to work, people will start to wonder where I am. So, I'm going to have to leave you for a couple of hours. Don't worry, though, I'll be back in plenty of time to take you out to the plane.

"In the meantime, I suggest you all get some rest. You probably need it after all your adventures!" He turns to Nippee, and with a grin adds, "Especially you, little one!"

***

Although they're all exhausted, the intoxicating mixture of excitement at having got this far and sadness at the thought of soon having to say goodbye to Gravee means none of them is able to sleep.

After only a few minutes trying, Bisckits climbs up to a small window that looks out into the hangar, and stares longingly at the Hairyplane parked there. He's joined by Nippee almost immediately, and by Ngorika a short while later.

As the minutes tick away, Jaspa again finds himself thinking about *Seers*... And in particular about Gravee's friend, Ben. Is he really the same boy Jaspa saw back in the Ngorongoro Crater? Had that boy even seen Jaspa, or was it all in his imagination? He wished he could be certain, but he supposes he'll never know for sure. But what if... No. There's no way he could do that.

***

Just as he had promised, Moringe eventually returns. He's carrying a sky-blue bag made of heavy material and stained with grease and oil. "I usually use this for tools," he explains. "But I thought it would be quicker and easier if I used it to carry you to the plane... So long as you don't object, of course."

None of them do and so, one by one, the six *Ses* climb into the bag. Once inside, they can't see much, though they feel Moringe pick up the bag and move towards the door to the hangar. A few moments later they hear a boom, as the door slams behind the old man, followed by his unnaturally loud footsteps as he makes his way across the hangar floor, swinging the bag ever so slightly.

The echoes die away as Moringe reaches the main hangar doors. As he emerges into the sunshine tiny shafts of light pierce the bag's woven sides, falling upon its unusual occupants. Dust motes, dancing in and out of the rays, cause Portia to sneeze.

"Dorry!" she sniffs.

A few minutes later, the friends feel the bag being placed on a hard surface and almost immediately hear a small engine start. The vibration of the motor makes the whole bag quiver gently.

"We must be in some sort of vehicle," whispers Ngorika.

As if to confirm this, there's a sharp knock as their transport hits a pothole or some other bump in the road. The jar makes Nippee wince and he reaches his right hand up to cradle his aching jaw.

After only a couple of minutes, the vehicle comes to a halt and the engine is switched off. The *Ses* feel the bag being lifted once more, only to be placed on another hard surface just a few seconds later.

The amount of light filtering through the sides of the bag has greatly reduced in the last few moments and Jaspa concludes they must have entered a building or something. Even so, when Moringe unzips the bag a second or two later, all six *Ses* quickly turn away from the opening. They blink furiously and attempt to shield their eyes from the bright light that streams in at them, blinding after the relative darkness inside the bag.

***

"Whoa!"

Jaspa is still shaking his head, trying to rid his eyes of the miniature firework displays going off inside them, when he hears Bisckits' gasp of astonishment. Still squinting slightly, he finally manages to open his eyes enough to take in their surroundings.

To his surprise, Jaspa finds they're not inside at all, but rather in the immense shadow of an enormous aeroplane, which looms over them like a gigantic, silver bird.

The bag is resting on the ground, near to the aircraft's port undercarriage leg. Moringe is crouching next to it, pretending to work on the wheel. "Everybody alright?" he enquires.

After they all confirmed they're unharmed, the *Seer* looks at Gravee. "Right," he says in a businesslike tone. "This is the plane to Amsterdam. They'll be bringing the passengers out soon, so you should try to be as quick as possible. There's a set of steps over there..." He indicates a white, metal stairway leading from the ground to a door in the side of the aeroplane, perhaps ten feet above them. "They'll take you into the main cabin of the aircraft. I'm sorry, but you'll have to get up there by yourself. It'll look suspicious if I go on board this close to take-off."

Tears well up in Gravee's eyes. "Thank ye, Moringe," he says sincerely. "I'll nae forget all yer help."

Moringe nods slightly, accepting Gravee's thanks. A small smile hovers around his mouth but he doesn't speak.

Gravee turns to the others and exhales sharply. "Well. Here we are then," he says. "I still cannae believe we made it. But one thin' I dae ken... Yers th' best pals any *Ses* could wish for."

The Dogses' voice chokes. Several of the tears in the corners of his eyes escape to become lost amongst his facial fur. "Och, will ye nae look at me... Greetin' like a wee bairn!" He laughs, trying to hide his embarrassment. "Without yers, I'd be wandering roond th' Serengeti forever. I'll never be able tae thank ye enough."

Gravee clasps arms with each of his friends in turn, exchanging words of farewell and best wishes. When he comes to Jaspa, however, he doesn't take the Giraffeses offered arms. Instead, Gravee takes a step back and nods over his right shoulder towards the aeroplane.

"So. Are ye comin' then?" he asks.

***

"What?..." exclaims Jaspa in shock.

"Och, dinnae tell me ye huvnae thought aboot it!" says Gravee.

"Well... I mean... maybe... but..." Jaspa stammers. "... But I can't go with you!"

The awkward silence that follows is finally broken by a quiet voice. "Why not?"

To Jaspa's astonishment, it's Portia who's spoken. He spins around to look at her, his surprise written all over his face. "What do you mean, *why not*?" he demands. "Because I can't, that's *why not*."

"Why... not...?" repeats Portia, slowly and calmly.

"Because..." Jaspa flounders, feeling increasingly cornered.

"Yes?" prompts his cousin.

"Because... Because of a thousand reasons!" he almost shouts. "Because we have to get Nippee home... Because we've got to get back to Tabora!... Because..."

"I think you know, Tabora is well aware we might not be coming back," says Portia, interrupting him. "And I'm sure Ngorika can get Nippee home safely without our help."

The Vultureses and Crocodileses both nod their agreement.

"And we can pay Tabora a visit on the way. Let him know everything went well and that you're all safe," adds Ngorika.

Inside himself, Jaspa battles with his conflicting emotions. On the one hand, he feels trapped by his sense of duty. There's no way he can just drop everything and head off around the World on a wild *Seer* chase. On the other, he feels sorely tempted to grasp this chance to discover, once and for all, whether the boy he saw all those months ago really was Gravee's young friend.

"But what about the *Journey*?" Jaspa appeals.

"A *Journey* is whatever you choose to make it, Waver," his cousin answers sincerely. "I know they normally follow the Great Migration, but even then each one is unique. I don't think anyone will criticise you for simply following a different path."

Moringe has listened silently to all Jaspa's desperate attempts to convince the other *Ses* that he shouldn't accompany Gravee, although it seems to the *Seer* that Jaspa is really trying to persuade himself. The old man smiles broadly. "Looks like you've got an important decision to make, little one," he chuckles. "But unfortunately, if you're going to catch **this** plane, you're going to have to make it now. The passengers are on their way from the terminal."

Sure enough, a stream of humans is filing out of a nearby building and heading towards the waiting aircraft.

A small part of Jaspa is beginning to wonder why he's trying so hard. He's knows he's being offered something his heart longs for. And if truth be told, guilt is the main thing holding him back. Guilt at the idea of shirking his responsibilities.

Finally he voices his true concern. The real reason preventing him simply getting on the aeroplane and flying away with Gravee. "What about Bisckits?" Jaspa asks quietly. "I can't leave Bisckits on his own!" He looks at his brother...

Who's not there!

"Er..." begins Nippee, looking and sounding a little guilty himself. "Leaving Bithckit'th behind ithn't really going to be a problem..."

"Why not?" asks Jaspa, although he has a horrible feeling he knows what's coming.

Nippee looks over at Ngorika, who answers in his stead, "Because he's already onboard the plane."

***

"He's what?" shouts Jaspa.

"Oh no!" cries Portia. "What's he thinking?"

"That'th the whole point!" replies Nippee, "He'th not thinking... He'th **doing!**"

Comprehension dawns in Jaspa's eyes. "You mean you knew?" he asks in disbelief. "You knew and you didn't try to stop him?"

"Thtop him?!" exclaims Nippee unapologetically. "We encouraged him!"

"But why would you do such a thing?" asks Portia.

"Because Bisckits has discovered something he really loves..." answers Ngorika, "Flying!"

"Weren't you jutht telling Jathpa to make hith own *Journey?*" puts in the Crocodileses, taking over from his accomplice in crime. "To follow hith own path?... Well, Bithckit'th ith doing jutht that. In fact, he'th doing more than that... He'th following hith dream!"

"But I still can't believe he left just like that," Jaspa says. "All on his own! Without even saying goodbye!"

"He didn't do it lightly," admits Ngorika. "But doesn't that just prove how important this is to him? Bisckits knows this might be the only chance he'll ever get to fly in one of his *Hairyplanes*. The truth is, he was afraid you'd be able to talk him out of it. And that he'd regret it for the rest of his life."

Lost for words, Jaspa looks as if his world has been turned upside down. He stares down at his feet, deep in thought.

"Dinnae worry, laddie," says Gravee, trying to cheer him up. "I'll keep an eye on wee Bisckits for ye!"

Jaspa takes deep breath, before lifting his head. "No need," he declares firmly. "I'm coming with you!" He looks at Portia and adds, "I have to go after him. You understand, don't you?"

She smiles, warmly. "Of course I do, Waver." she replies. "And I think I understand how Bizzee feels, too."

"I wish I didn't have to leave you like this," says Jaspa miserably.

"You don't have to," his cousin corrects him, matter-of-factly. "I'm coming too."

***

Hastened by the approach of the aeroplane's **human** passengers, Jaspa and Portia suddenly find themselves saying hurried goodbyes to their friends. Having had no time to prepare for this moment,

Jaspa finds it incredibly difficult to cope with. By the time he gets to Ngorika he's almost in tears, and is totally unable to speak. This isn't so bad, since he can't find words to express what he wants to say, anyway.

"Don't be sad, Friend Jaspa," says the Vultureses, imitating Tabora. "We **will** meet again. I'm sure of it!"

The two friends stand hugging each other, until Portia gently takes hold of Jaspa's shoulder. "Time to go, Waver," she says softly.

Jaspa sniffs. "Right," he says, pulling himself together. "Right!"

***

Gravee and the two Giraffeses scramble up the steps leading to the aeroplane's cabin, watched from the ground by Nippee, Ngorika and Moringe. At the top, they turn and look back at the friends they're leaving behind. With a heavy heart, Jaspa gives them a final wave, before following Gravee into the aircraft.

Once inside, the Dogses confidently turns left, towards the front of the aircraft. "I bet yers any money we'll find oor wee stowaway up here."

They pass through a door and enter a room at the front of the plane, although given its size *cupboard* might be a better word. Two sturdy yet comfortable-looking chairs occupy most of the floor space. A narrow row of windows, set at what would be eye level for a human sitting in either of the chairs, ring three sides of the room. Directly in front of each chair is something that can only be a steering wheel, though the strangest Jaspa has ever seen. Every other available space – in front of the chairs, between them, wrapping around the walls beneath the windows, and even spilling up onto the ceiling – is crammed with more dials, buttons, switches and levers than Jaspa can even count!

And there, in the middle of the little area of floor not filled up with chairs or gadgets, is Bisckits. He stares up at this space age scene with his head cocked to one side and wonder on his face. He appears so small against the backdrop of the flight deck. A tiny little Giraffeses, completely out-scaled and out of place. But one look at his little brother tells Jaspa that Nippee and Ngorika were right. Bisckits **did** need to see this.

All too often, thinks Jaspa, *we regard dreams as childish flights of fancy, as if they're somehow detached from the real world. We don't allow ourselves to believe dreams might come true, perhaps to save ourselves the disappointment when they don't. We play down their importance and tell ourselves we don't really need them. That we don't really care.*

But none of that's true! Dreams **are** *important. Without them we don't live, we just exist. Treading water from the day we're born to the day we die. Treating life like a spectator sport.*

That's not how it should be. To really, truly live we have make the most of our time here on Earth. We have to seize our dreams and fight to make them real. And that's just what Bisckits is doing, here on this aeroplane. You can see it in his face. Here in this tiny room Bisckits isn't just existing... He's **living***!*

Jaspa gives a little cough, startling Bisckits from his daydream. The young Giraffeses notices the three of them standing there watching him and a look of shock passes fleetingly across his face. This is quickly replaced by a more permanent expression of alarm. Clearly, Bisckits believes he's about to get a dressing-down or, even worse, that they're going to try make him leave the Hairyplane.

His look of shock returns when Jaspa instead walks forward and wordlessly enfolds him in a hug. The look is doubled, when Portia steps up and wraps her arms around the both of them.

***

"Aye, well," says Gravee, sounding slightly embarrassed at intruding on this private moment. "We best be findin' somewhere safe tae hide afore someone treads on us."

Steering Bisckits firmly away from the flight deck, Gravee leads them in the opposite direction, between rows and rows of high-backed, blue seats. The crew are already on board but the *Ses* avoid them easily, slipping between their feet as they *shift* towards the aircraft's rear.

They've no sooner reached the back of the plane, than they hear the first sounds of the paying passengers boarding... Footsteps following them up the cabin, slightly muffled by the red and beige flecked, blue carpet. The animated chattering of the humans. The thump of bags being tossed into the numerous overhead lockers. The click of seatbelts being fastened. And all the while, in the background there's the faint, electrical hum coming from the aircraft itself. From the generator that powers its necessary systems when it's on the ground.

"In here," says Gravee, ushering them behind a metal trolley in the rear galley. "We'll be safe back here."

The smell of warming food wafts down to Jaspa, reminding him that he's not eaten since first light this morning, just before they soared out over the Rift Valley. The memory makes him think of Ngorika and Nippee, yet he's surprised to find it doesn't hurt as much as he expected it to. He realises that, in many ways, saying goodbye was actually harder than being apart from them, although Ngorika's assurances that they'll meet again perhaps has something to do with this.

Jaspa is stirred from his thoughts by the engines starting. Their high-pitched whine replaces the gentle hum of the generator. Jaspa can feel a suppressed tremble running through the aircraft, as the pilot keeps the engines' raw power in check.

***

A few minutes later, the pitch of engines increases slightly and there's a small jolt. "We're moving!" whispers Bisckits, looking as though he might explode with excitement.

It takes the pilot perhaps five minutes to taxi the massive Boeing 767 aircraft out to the western end of the runway. Once there, he smoothly turns the plane around in a half-circle, until it's pointing eastwards, right down the centre of the broad tarmac strip. Then...

He brings the aircraft to a gentle halt.

***

"Why are we stopping?" Bisckits demands, obviously worried something's gone wrong and he's going to be robbed of his flight.

"Calm yerself, wee laddie," says Gravee, "Just wait a min..."

"But what...?"

The roar of the engines drowns out Bisckits' unnecessary concerns. Jaspa feels their power shake the entire aircraft as they strive to overcome its weight and push the monstrous machine forward.

The rattling increases as the plane picks up speed, as though the aircraft itself has come alive and is fighting to remain on the ground. The conflict seems to continue for an age, and all the while they hurtle down the Aeroplane Road, continuing to gather speed as they go.

Without warning, the nose of the aircraft rears up alarmingly. Jaspa tries to grip the short tufts of the carpet, certain they're about to flip over backwards. His stomach lurches and he momentarily feels much heavier than normal, and then...

...Nothing.

The violent shuddering suddenly dies away, to be replaced by a gentle, reassuring vibration.

"We're flying!!" laughs Bisckits.

Well, thinks Jaspa, *I never expected **this** the day I set out from the Shifting Sands.*

He considers all he's been through since the day of his *Exodus*. It seems like such a long time ago. And yet, sitting here, leaning against the side of the aircraft's cabin with the unseen world rapidly dropping away beneath him, Jaspa can't help feeling his *Journey* is only just beginning.

***

Epilogue

Sam looks up from the tree she's drawing and over at her brother. He, in turn, stares moodily out of the living room window at the depressing drizzle that has been slowly but persistently drenching Edinburgh all week.

Sam knows, however, it's not just the weather that's getting her brother down. Ben has rarely been himself since they returned from their safari in the Serengeti.

At first, their parents had put Ben's gloomy behaviour down to the simple disappointment of their holiday being over. Yet they've been back in Scotland for over three months now, and Ben still shows very little sign of snapping out of his miserable mood.

But it was last week, after Mum had suggested they go down to London for a few days at the end of the month, when Sam's parents started to **seriously** worry about Ben. They'd clearly hoped the anticipation of another trip would cheer Ben up, lift him out of the rut he's been in since they got back from Africa.

Understandably then, his total lack of enthusiasm for the idea came as a real blow to them. In fact, only yesterday, Sam overheard Mum and Dad talking about sending Ben to see a *trick cyclist*. Perhaps they think this will cheer him up, although Sam's not convinced.

Of course, Sam has the benefit of knowing what's really bothering her big brother.

***

Ben gazes disinterestedly through the rain-splashed windowpane at the heavy grey clouds that seem to have taken up permanent residence over Scotland's capital city. He wishes the dismal weather didn't mirror his frame of mind so well.

Ben's an intelligent boy, and he realises his bad mood is starting to worry those people close to him, especially his parents. He's also a considerate and caring youngster, which, ironically, probably lies at the heart of why he's been feeling so low. He has been trying to at least pretend he's feeling happier these days, but he's well aware he's not really fooling anyone, least of all himself.

His problem is actually very simple. Ben **really** misses Gravee. What's worse, he feels deeply responsible for the *Ses* not being here to begin with. He not only blames himself for Gravee's initial disappearance, but also for not doing more find his friend once he discovered he was missing.

Deep down, the more sensible part of Ben knows that neither of these things are truly his fault. But the distress he feels at the thought of Gravee being lost in the Serengeti, alone and friendless in the wilds of Africa, helpless and with no hope of ever returning home to his beloved Auld Reekie,[1] defies logic.

***

The rich, ringing chime of the front doorbell reverberates through the old stone house. "Get that will you, Ben, dear?" calls his mother.

With a sigh, Ben drags himself away from the window and crosses the living room, watched all the way by his little sister, who appears to be colouring her tree blue. He turns right into the hallway and makes his way to the front door.

Ben opens the heavy wooden door and is surprised to find the six stone steps leading down to the street are completely empty.

Holding tightly to the sides of the white doorframe with both hands, he leans out as far as he can, looking first left then right around the sweeping curves of the circular street that orbits Moray Place. Even in this afternoon's dreary semi-darkness, the wet cobblestones glisten. A bird chirps stubbornly somewhere in the garden that

[1] *Auld Reekie* is an old Scottish nickname for *Edinburgh*. It means Old Smokey!

occupies the centre of the Place, but otherwise there's no sign of life, and certainly no evidence of the phantom doorbell ringer.

To add insult to injury, a large drop of water drips off the decorative iron railing that surrounds the base of the first floor window above the door. With annoying accuracy, it misses Ben's hair and T-shirt, instead finding its way straight onto his neck and down his back.

Ben shivers violently, takes two steps backwards into the hall and slams the door in disgust. He turns around and begins to head back towards the living room...

And stops dead in his tracks.

***

Jaspa feels miserable. He can't remember ever being so wet and cold in all his life. In fact, he's beginning to wish he'd returned to Tabora's *Nomads*, or gone home to the *Herd* and the Shifting Sands, or done anything that didn't involve coming to this damp, depressing city.

It doesn't help that Gravee seems completely unaware of the awful weather and Jaspa's wretchedness. As they walk up the hill from Waverley Railway Station, the Dogses becomes more and more animated, pointing out all sorts of *interesting* things, that Jaspa would really rather save for another, warmer day.

They reach the crest of the hill and start down the other side. "Nae long noo!" says Gravee cheerfully. "We'll soon be there!"

Surprisingly perhaps, this simple statement lifts Jaspa's spirits and he silently scolds himself for being so thoughtless. *Gravee has been stranded away from home for months*, he tells himself. *And for most of that time he thought he'd never be able to return. So of course he feels happy at seeing all his old haunts again. Anyone would.*

Gravee's announcement also cheers Jaspa for another, more personal reason. It reminds him that he's close to meeting the boy he's travelled all this way to see. Once again Jaspa wonders whether he'll be the same one he saw back in Ngorongoro. The thought makes him shiver, partly in anticipation, but also partly in panic.

*What if it **isn't** the same boy?*

Finally, they arrive in a street that's much quieter than most of the others Gravee has led them along. It seems to form a complete circle, with tall stone buildings lining its outer side. In the centre, however, is a pretty garden, with lawns and flowers, bushes and trees, all of which are quite unfamiliar to the three Giraffeses.

They splash through the puddles that have collected between the street's cobblestones, and stop at a set of stone steps that climb up to a large, bright red door. Gravee bends down and picks up a pebble, which he hands to Bisckits.

"See that wee button next tae th' door there, laddie?" he asks. "Dae ye think ye can hit it wi' that?"

Bisckits looks up at the doorbell, weighing the pebble thoughtfully in his hand. "I think so," he replies.

The Giraffeses throws the stone a little way into the air, straight up. As it descends he catches it and, in the same fluid movement, hurls it at the button. The pebble strikes the doorbell right in the middle, and Bisckits is rewarded by a ringing sound somewhere inside the house.

"Yes!" he says to himself.

Gravee is already clambering up the stone steps. "Come on then!" he calls.

Jaspa, Bisckits and Portia have only just made it up to the door, when it opens, spilling warmth and light out into the cold, dark street. Gravee puts a finger to his lips, signalling them to follow him into the house. They *shift* between the feet of a smallish human and part way along a corridor. After a few feet, Gravee stops and turns back to face the door through which they have just entered. With a growing feeling of excitement, Jaspa does the same.

The boy who opened the door, now slams it shut, obviously unhappy about something.

"Are ye nae goin' tae say hallo tae ye long lost pal, then?" enquires Gravee, grinning broadly.

"Gravee?" asks the boy, staring down at the dirty, scruffy, almost unrecognisable Dogses. "Gravee?" he repeats in disbelief, a smile of joy spreading across his face.

"Aye, laddie!" Gravee says. "Who else? An' what's mair, I've brought some pals tae meet ye."

Ben appears to notice Gravee's three friends for the first time.

His hand comes up to his mouth in shock. Standing in his hallway is the Giraffeses he'd first seen in Africa all those months ago.

"It's you!" the boy whispers in wonder.

Jaspa gives Ben a small wave in return.

"It's me," he agrees.